"A Winter's Tale" by Ann Cleeves
Chief Inspector Ramsay drives across snowy moors
when he investigates a woman murdered on a remote
British farm . . . and digs up his own past while
hunting for the killer.

"To Wake the Dead" by John Dickson Carr
When a young couple arrive at an elegant country
house, they don't find the party they anticipated . . .
instead they meet what may be a ghost of Christmas
past or a victim of a long-ago homicide.

"The Theft of Santa's Beard" by Edward D. Hoch
Nick Velvet is drawn into the case of the Santa
Strangler when he's hired to steal a department store
Santa's beard . . . and ends up solving a baffling
multiple murder.

"Appalachian Blackmail" by Jacqueline Vivelo
When a rich aunt's valuable ruby necklace disappears
in a poor relative's living room, the spirit of
Christmas may turn to mistrust unless the reader can
spot where the jewelry is hidden, who took it . . .
and why.

**AND EIGHT OTHER CLASSIC TALES
OF DETECTION.**

D0911021

CHRISTMAS CRIMES

Stories from
Ellery Queen's Mystery Magazine
and *Alfred Hitchcock Mystery
Magazine*

Edited by
Cynthia Manson

A SIGNET BOOK

SIGNET
Published by the Penguin Group
Penguin Books USA Inc., 375 Hudson Street,
New York, New York 10014, U.S.A.
Penguin Books Ltd, 27 Wrights Lane,
London W8 5TZ, England
Penguin Books Australia Ltd, Ringwood,
Victoria, Australia
Penguin Books Canada Ltd, 10 Alcorn Avenue,
Toronto, Ontario, Canada M4V 3B2
Penguin Books (N.Z.) Ltd, 182–190 Wairau Road,
Auckland 10, New Zealand

Penguin Books Ltd, Registered Offices:
Harmondsworth, Middlesex, England

First published by Signet, an imprint of Dutton Signet,
a division of Penguin Books USA Inc.

First Printing, November, 1996
10 9 8 7 6 5 4 3 2 1

CONTENTS

INTRODUCTION

Christmas Crimes is our fourth collection in the very popular series of books presenting short stories of crime and detection which take place at Christmastime. *Christmas Crimes* includes stories from *Ellery Queen's Mystery Magazine* and *Alfred Hitchcock Mystery Magazine*. The authors are well-known mystery writers whose diversified casts of characters include ghosts of Christmas past, con artists, murderers, police inspectors and amateur sleuths, among others.

Our favorite detectives are not on holiday in this series. There are Margery Allingham's Albert Campion investigating a case of blackmail at an old English manor, Georges Simenon's Inspector Maigret using his armchair detection to solve a complex mystery and Agatha Christie's Miss Marple behaving in her usual low-key manner to solve a case based on idle gossip. Add to this stellar cast Ann Cleeves's Inspector Ramsay as he investigates a crime of passion in the country, and Edward D. Hoch's Nick Velvet, hired to steal Santa's beard to foil a potential killer.

In contrast to the wit of these clever investigators is the whimsy of James Powell's fanciful story of the disappearance of twenty-seven people and Ron Goulart's comical tale of a down-on-his-luck actor. Finally, no Christmas anthology would be complete without a classic ghost story by the "locked room" master himself, John Dickson Carr.

Christmas Crimes presents these entertaining stories gift wrapped exclusively for our mystery fans.

—Cynthia Manson

A WINTER'S TALE
by Ann Cleeves

In the hills there had been snow for five days, the first real snow of the winter. In town it had turned to rain, bitter and unrelenting, and in Otterbridge it had seemed to be dark all day. As Ramsay drove out of the coastal plain and began the climb up Cheviot the clouds broke and there was a shaft of sunshine which reflected blindingly on the snow. For days he had been depressed by the weather and the gaudy festivities of the season, but as the cloud lifted he felt suddenly more optimistic.

Hunter, sitting hunched beside him, remained gloomy. It was the Saturday before Christmas and he had better things to do. He always left his shopping until the last minute—he enjoyed being part of the crowd in Newcastle. Christmas meant getting pissed in the heaving pubs on the Big Market, sharing drinks with tipsy secretaries who seemed to spend the last week of work in a continuous office party. It meant wandering up Northumberland Street where children queued to peer in at the magic of Fenwick's window and listening to the Sally Army band playing carols at the entrance to Eldon Square. It had nothing to do with all this space and the bloody cold. Like a Roman stationed on Hadrian's Wall, Hunter thought the wilderness was barbaric.

Ramsay said nothing. The road had been cleared of snow but was slippery, and driving took concentration. Hunter was itching to get at the wheel—he had been invited to a party in a club in Blyth and it took him as long as a teenage girl to get ready for a special evening out.

Ramsay turned carefully off the road, across a cattle grid, and onto a track.

"Bloody hell!" Hunter said. "Are we going to get up there?"

"The farmer said it was passable. He's been down with a tractor."

"I'd better get the map," Hunter said miserably. "I suppose we've got a grid reference. I don't fancy getting lost out here."

"I don't think that'll be necessary," Ramsay said. "I've been to the house before."

Hunter did not ask about Ramsay's previous visit to Blackstoneburn. The inspector rarely volunteered information about his social life or friends. And apart from an occasional salacious curiosity about Ramsay's troubled marriage and divorce, Hunter did not care. Nothing about the inspector would have surprised him.

The track no longer climbed but crossed a high and empty moor. The horizon was broken by a dry stone wall and a derelict barn, but otherwise there was no sign of habitation. Hunter felt increasingly uneasy. Six geese flew from a small reservoir to circle overhead and settle back once the car had passed.

"Greylags," Ramsay said. "Wouldn't you say?"

"I don't bloody know." Hunter had not been able to identify them even as geese. And I don't bloody care, he thought.

The sun was low in the sky ahead of them. Soon it would be dark. They must have driven over an imperceptible ridge because suddenly, caught in the orange sunlight, there was a house, grey, small-windowed, a fortress of a place surrounded by byres and outbuildings.

"That's it, is it?" Hunter said, relieved. It hadn't, after all, taken so long. The party wouldn't warm up until the pubs shut. He would make it in time.

"No," Ramsay said. "That's the farm. It's another couple of miles yet."

He was surprised by the pleasure he took in Hunter's discomfort, and a little ashamed. He thought his relationship with his sergeant was improving. Yet it wouldn't do Hunter any harm, he thought, to feel anxious and out of place. On his home ground he was intolerably confident.

The track dipped to a ford. The path through the water was rocky and the burn was frozen at the edges. Ramsay accelerated carefully up the bank and as the back wheels spun he remembered his previous visit to Blackstone-burn. It had been high summer, the moor scorched with drought, the burn dried up almost to a trickle. He had thought he would never come to the house again.

As they climbed away from the ford they saw the Black Stone, surrounded by open moor. It was eight feet high, truly black with the setting sun behind it, throwing a shadow onto the snow.

Hunter stared and whistled under his breath but said nothing. He would not give his boss the satisfaction of asking for information. The information came anyway. Hunter thought Ramsay could have been one of those guides in bobble hats and walking boots who worked at weekends for the National Park.

"It's a part of a circle of prehistoric stones," the inspector said. "Even if there weren't any snow you wouldn't see the others at this distance. The bracken's grown over them." He seemed lost for a moment in memory. "The house was named after the stone, of course. There's been a dwelling on this site since the fourteenth century."

"A bloody daft place to put a house," Hunter muttered. "If you ask me. . . ."

They looked down into a valley onto an L-shaped house built around a flagged yard, surrounded by windblown trees and shrubs.

"According to the farmer," Ramsay said, "the dead woman wasn't one of the owner's family. . . ."

"So what the hell was she doing here?" Hunter demanded. The emptiness made him belligerent. "It's not the sort of place you'd stumble on by chance."

"It's a holiday cottage," Ramsay said. "Of sorts. Owned by a family from Otterbridge called Shaftoe. They don't let it out commercially but friends know that they can stay here. . . . The strange thing is that the farmer said there was no car. . . ."

The track continued up the hill and had, Hunter supposed, some obscure agricultural use. Ramsay turned off

it down a potholed drive and stopped in the yard, which
because of the way the wind had been blowing was almost
clear of snow. A dirty green Land Rover was already
parked there, and as they approached a tall, bearded man
got out and stood impassively, waiting for them to emerge
from the warmth of their car. The sun had disappeared
and the air was icy.

"Mr. Helms." The inspector held out his hand. "I'm
Ramsay. Northumbria Police."

"Aye," the man said. "Well, I'd not have expected it to
be anyone else."

"Can we go in?" Hunter demanded. "It's freezing out
here."

Without a word the farmer led them to the front of the
house. The wall was half covered with ivy and already the
leaves were beginning to be tinged with frost. The front
door led directly into a living room. In a grate the remains
of a fire smouldered, but there was little warmth. The
three men stood awkwardly just inside the room.

"Where is she?" Hunter asked.

"In the kitchen," the farmer said. "Out the back."

Hunter stamped his feet impatiently, expecting Ramsay
to lead the way. He knew the house. But Ramsay stood,
looking around him.

"Had Mr. Shaftoe asked you to keep an eye on the
place?" he asked. "Or did something attract your attention?"

"There was someone here last night," Helms said. "I
saw a light from the back."

"Was there a car?"

"Don't know. Didn't notice."

"By man, you're a lot of help," Hunter muttered. Helms
pretended not to hear.

"But you might have noticed," Ramsay persisted,
"fresh tyre tracks on the drive."

"Look," Helms said. "Shaftoe lets me use one of his
barns. I'm up and down the track every day. If someone
had driven down using my tracks how would I know?"

"Were you surprised to see a light?" Ramsay asked.

"Not really," Helms said. "They don't have to tell me when they're coming up."

"Could they have made it up the track from the road?"

"Shaftoe could. He's got one of those posh Japanese four-wheel-drive jobs."

"Is it usual for him to come up in the winter?"

"Aye." Helms was faintly contemptuous. "They have a big do on Christmas Eve. I'd thought maybe they'd come up to air the house for that. No one's been in the place for months."

"You didn't hear a vehicle go back down the track last night?"

"No. But I wouldn't have done. The father-in-law's stopping with us and he's deaf as a post. He had the telly so loud you can't hear a thing."

"What time did you see the light?"

Helms shrugged. "Seven o'clock maybe. I didn't go out after that."

"But you didn't expect them to be staying?"

"No. Like I said, I expected them to light a fire, check the calor gas, clean up a bit, and then go back."

"So what caught your attention this morning?"

"The gas light was still on," Helms said.

"In the same room?"

Helms nodded. "The kitchen. It was early, still pretty dark outside, and I thought they must have stayed and were getting their breakfasts. It was only later, when the kids got me to bring them over, that I thought it was strange."

"I don't understand," Ramsay said. "Why did your children want to come?"

"Because they're sharp little buggers. It's just before Christmas. They thought Shaftoe would have a present for them. He usually brings them something, Christmas or not."

"So you drove them down in the Land Rover? What time was that?"

"Just before dinner. Twelvish. They'd been out sledging and Chrissie, my wife, said there was more snow on her kitchen floor than out on the fell. I thought I'd earn a few brownie points by getting them out of her hair." He paused and for the first time he smiled. "I thought I'd get a drink for my trouble. Shaftoe always kept a supply of malt whisky in the place, and he was never mean with it."

"Did you park in the yard?"

"Aye. Like I always do."

"That's when you noticed the light was still on?"

Helms nodded.

"What did you do then?"

"Walked round here to the front."

"Had it been snowing?" Ramsay asked.

"There were a couple of inches in the night but it was clear by dawn."

"What about footprints on the path? You would have noticed if the snow had been disturbed."

"Aye," Helms said. "I might have done if I'd got the chance. But I let the dog and the bairns out of the Land Rover first and they chased round to the front before me."

"But your children might have noticed," Ramsay insisted.

"Aye," Helms said without much hope. "They might."

"Did they go into the house before you?"

"No. They were still on the front lawn throwing snowballs about when I joined them. That's when I saw the door was open and I started to think something was up. I told the kids to wait outside and came in on my own. I stood in here feeling a bit daft and shouted out the back to Shaftoe. When there was no reply I went on through."

"What state was the fire in?" Ramsay asked.

"Not much different from what it's like now. If you bank it up it stays like that for hours."

There was a pause. "Come on then," Ramsay said. "We'd best go through and look at her."

The kitchen was lit by two gas lamps mounted on one wall. The room was small and functional. There was a small window covered on the outside by bacterial-shaped whirls of ice, a stainless-steel sink, and a row of units. The woman, lying with one cheek against the red tiles, took up most of the available floor space. Ramsay, looking down, recognised her immediately.

"Joyce," he said. "Rebecca Joyce." He looked at Helms.

"She was a friend of the Shaftoe family. You don't recognise her?"

The farmer shook his head.

Ramsay had met Rebecca Joyce at Blackstoneburn. Diana had invited him to the house when their marriage was in its final throes and he had gone out of desperation, thinking that on her own ground, surrounded by her family and friends, she might be calmer. Diana was related to the Shaftoes by marriage. Her younger sister Isobel had married one of the Shaftoe sons and at that summer house party they were all there: old man Shaftoe, who had made his money out of scrap, Isobel, and her husband Stuart, a grey, thin-lipped man who had brought the family respectability by proposing to the daughter of one of the most established landowners in Northumberland.

Rebecca had been invited as a friend, solely, it seemed, to provide entertainment. She had been at school with Diana and Isobel and had been outrageous, apparently, even then. Looking down at the body on the cold kitchen floor, Ramsay thought that despite the battered skull he still saw a trace of the old spirit.

"I'll be off then. . . ." Helms interrupted his daydream. "If there's nothing else."

"No," Ramsay said. "I'll know where to find you."

"Aye. Well." He sloped off, relieved. They heard the Land Rover drive away up the track and then it was very quiet.

"The murder weapon was a poker," Hunter said. "Hardly original."

"Effective though." It still lay on the kitchen floor, the ornate brass knob covered with blood.

"What now?" Hunter demanded. Time was moving on. It was already six o'clock. In another hour his friends would be gathering in the pubs of Otterbridge preparing for the party.

"Nothing," Ramsay said, "until the pathologist and the scene-of-crime team arrive." He knew that Hunter wanted to be away. He could have sent him off in the car, arranged a lift for himself with the colleagues who would arrive later, earned for a while some gratitude and peace, but a perverseness kept him quiet and they sat in the freezing living room, waiting.

When Ramsay met Rebecca Joyce it had been hot, astoundingly hot for the Northumberland hills, and they had taken their drinks outside onto the lawn. Someone had slung a hammock between two Scotch pines and Diana had lain there moodily, not speaking, refusing to acknowledge his presence. They had argued in the car on the way to Blackstoneburn and he was forced to introduce himself to Tom Shaftoe, a small, squat man with silver sideburns. Priggish Isobel and anonymous Stuart he had met before. The row had been his fault. Diana had not come home the night before, and he had asked quietly, restraining his jealousy, where she had been. She had lashed out in a fury, condemning him for his Methodist morals, his dullness.

"You're just like your mother," she had said. The final insult. "All hypocrisy and thrift."

Then she had fallen stubbornly and guiltily silent and had said nothing more to him all evening.

Was it because of her taunts that he had gone with Rebecca to look at the Black Stone? Rebecca wore a red Lycra tube which left her shoulders bare and scarcely covered her buttocks. She had glossy red lipstick and black curls pinned back with combs. She had been flirting shamelessly with Stuart all evening and then suddenly to Ramsay she said:

"Have you ever seen the stone circle?"

He shook his head, surprised, confused by her sudden interest.

"Come on then," she had said. "I'll show you."

In the freezing room at Blackstoneburn, Hunter looked at his boss and thought he was a mean bastard, a kill-joy. There was no need for them both to be there. He nodded towards the kitchen door, bored by the silence, irritated because Ramsay would not share information about the dead woman.

"What did she do then?" he asked. "For a living."

Ramsay took a long time to reply and Hunter wondered if he was ill, if he was losing his grip completely.

"She would say," the inspector answered at last, "that she lived off her wits."

He had assumed that because she had been to school with Diana and Isobel her family were wealthy, but discovered later that her father had been a hopeless and irresponsible businessman. A wild scheme to develop a Roman theme park on some land close to Hadrian's Wall had led to bankruptcy, and Rebecca had left school early because the fees could not be paid. It was said that the teachers were glad of an excuse to be rid of her.

"By man," said Hunter, "what does that mean?"

"She had a few jobs," Ramsay said. "She managed a small hotel for a while, ran the office of the agricultural supply place in Otterbridge. But she couldn't stick any of them. I suppose it means she lived off men."

"She was a whore?"

"I suppose," Ramsay said, "it was something like that."

"You seem to know a lot about her. Did you know her well, like?"

The insolence was intended. Ramsay ignored it.

"No," he said. "I only met her once."

But I was interested, he thought, interested enough to find out more about her, attracted not so much by the body in the red Lycra dress, but by her kindness. It was the show, the decadent image, which put me off. If I had been braver I would have ignored it.

Her attempt to seduce him on that hot summer night had been a kindness, an offer of comfort. Away from the house she had taken his hand and they had crossed the burn by stepping stones, like children. She had shown him the round black stones hidden by bracken and then put his hand on her round, Lycra-covered breast.

He had hesitated, held back by his Methodist morals and the thought of sad Diana lying in the hammock on the lawn. Rebecca had been kind again, unoffended.

"Don't worry," she said, laughing, kissing him lightly on the cheek. "Not now. If you need me you'll be able to find out where I am."

And she had run away back to the others, leaving him to follow slowly, giving him time to compose himself.

Ramsay was so engrossed in the memory of his encounter with Rebecca Joyce that he did not hear the vehicles outside or the sound of voices. He was jolted back to the present by Hunter shouting: "There they are. About bloody time, too." And by the scene-of-crime team at the door bending to change their shoes, complaining cheerfully about the cold.

"Right then," Hunter said. "We can leave it to the reinforcements." He looked at his watch. Seven o'clock. The timing would be tight but not impossible. "I suppose someone should see the Shaftoes tonight," he said. "They're the most likely suspects. I'd volunteer for the overtime myself but I'm all tied up this evening."

"I'll talk to the Shaftoes," Ramsay said. It was the least he could do.

Outside in the dark it was colder than ever. Ramsay's car would not start immediately and Hunter swore under his breath. At last it pulled away slowly, the heater began to work, and Hunter began to relax.

"I want to call at the farm," Ramsay said. "Just to clear up a few things."

"Bloody hell!" Hunter said, convinced that Ramsay was prolonging the journey just to spite him. "What's the matter now?"

"This is a murder enquiry," Ramsay said sharply. "Not just an interruption to your social life."

"You'll not get anything from that Helms," Hunter said. "What could he know, living up there? It's enough to drive anyone crazy."

Ramsay said nothing. He thought that Helms was unhappy not mad.

"Rebecca always goes for lonely men," Diana had said cruelly on the drive back from Blackstoneburn that summer. "It's the only way she can justify screwing around."

"What's your justification?" he could have said, but Diana was unhappy too, and there had seemed little point.

They parked in the farm yard. In a shed cattle moved and made gentle noises. A small woman with fine pale hair tied back in an untidy ponytail let them into the kitchen where Helms was sitting in a high-backed chair, his stockinged feet stretched ahead of him. He was not surprised to see them. The room was warm despite the flagstone floor. A clothes horse, held together with binder twine, was propped in front of the range and children's jeans and jerseys steamed gently. The uncurtained window was misted with condensation. Against one wall was a large square table covered by a patterned oilcloth, with a pile of drawing books and a scattering of felt-tipped pens. From another room came the sound of a television and the occasional shriek of a small child.

Chrissie Helms sat by the table. She had big hands, red and chapped, which she clasped around her knees.

"I need to know," Ramsay said gently, "exactly what happened."

Hunter looked at the fat clock ticking on the mantelpiece and thought his boss was mad. Ramsay turned to the farmer.

"You were lying," he said. "It's so far-fetched, you see. Contrived. A strange and beautiful woman found miles from anywhere in the snow. Like a film. It must be simpler than that. You would have seen tracks when you took the tractor up to the road to clear a path for us. It's lonely out here. If you'd seen a light in Blackstoneburn last night you'd have gone in. Glad of the company and old Shaftoe's whisky."

Helms shook his head helplessly.

"Did he pay you to keep quiet?" Hunter demanded. Suddenly, with a reluctant witness to bully he was in his element. "Or did he threaten you?"

"No," Helms said, "it were nothing like that."

"But she was there with some man?" Hunter was jubilant.

"Oh," Helms's wife said quietly, shocking them with her interruption, "she was there with some man."

Ramsay turned to the farmer. "She was your mistress?" he said, and Hunter realised he had known all along.

Helms said nothing.

"You must have met her at the agricultural suppliers in Otterbridge. Perhaps when you went to pay your bill. Perhaps she recognised you. She often came to Blackstoneburn."

"I recognised her," Helms said.

"You'd hardly miss her," the woman said. "The way she flaunted herself."

"No." The farmer shook his head. "No, it wasn't like that."

He paused.

"You felt sorry for her . . . ?" Ramsay prompted.

"Aye!" Helms looked up, relieved to be understood at last.

"Why did you bring her here?" Ramsay asked.

"I didn't. Not here."

"But to Blackstoneburn. You had a key? Or Rebecca did?"

Helms nodded. "She was lonely," he said. "In town. Everyone thinking of Christmas. You know."

"So you brought her up to Blackstoneburn," Hunter said unpleasantly. "For a dirty weekend. Thinking you'd sneak over to spend some time with her. Thinking your wife wouldn't notice."

Helms said nothing.

"What went wrong?" Hunter demanded. "Did she get greedy? Want more money? Blackmail? Is that why you killed her?"

"You fool!" It was almost a scream, and as she spoke the woman stood up with her huge red hands laid flat on the table. "He wouldn't have harmed her. He didn't kill her. I did."

"You must tell me," Ramsay said again, "exactly what happened."

But she needed no prompting. She was desperate for their understanding. "You don't know what it's like here," she said. "Especially in the winter. Dark all day. Every year it drives me mad. . . ." She stopped, realising she was making little sense, and continued more rationally. "I knew he had a woman, guessed. Then I saw them in town and I recognised her too. She was wearing black stockings and high heels, a dress that cost a fortune. How could I compete with that?" She looked down at her shapeless jersey and jumble-sale trousers. "I thought he'd grow out of it, that if I ignored it, he'd stop. I never thought he'd bring her here." She paused.

"How did you find out?" Ramsay asked.

"Yesterday afternoon I went out for a walk. I left the boys with my dad. I'd been in the house all day and just needed to get away from them all. It was half-past three, starting to get dark. I saw the light in Blackstoneburn and Joe's Land Rover parked outside. Like you said, we're desperate here for company, so I went around to the front and knocked at the door. I thought Tom Shaftoe was giving him a drink."

"There was no car," Ramsay said.

"No," she said. "But Tom parks it sometimes in one of the sheds. I didn't suspect a thing."

"Did you go in?"

"Not then," she said calmly. "When there was no reply I looked through the window. They were lying together in front of the fire. Then I went in. . . ." She paused again. "When she saw me she got up and straightened her clothes. She laughed. I suppose she was embarrassed. She said it was an awkward situation and why didn't we all discuss it over a cup of tea. Then she turned her back on me and walked through to the kitchen." Chrissie Helms caught her breath in a sob. "She shouldn't have turned her back," she said. "I deserved more than that. . . ."

"So you hit her," Ramsay said.

"I lost control," Chrissie said. "I picked up the poker from the grate and I hit her."

"Did you mean to kill her?"

"I wasn't thinking clearly enough to mean something."

"But you didn't stop to help her?"

"No," she said. "I came home. I left it to Joe to sort out. He owed me that. He did his best, but I knew we'd not be able to carry it through." She looked at her husband. "I'll miss you and the boys," she said. "But I'll not miss this place. Prison'll not be much different from this."

Hunter walked to the window to wait for the police Land Rover. He rubbed a space in the condensation and saw that it was snowing again, heavily. He thought that he agreed with her.

TO WAKE THE DEAD
by John Dickson Carr

Although one snowflake had already sifted past the lights, the great doors of the house stood open. It seemed less a snowflake than a shadow; for a bitter wind whipped after it, and the doors creaked. Inside, Rodney and Muriel Hunter could see a dingy, narrow hall paved in dull red tiles, with a Jacobean staircase at the rear. (At that time, of course, there was no dead woman lying inside.)

To find such a place in the loneliest part of the Weald of Kent—a Seventeenth Century country house whose floors had grown humped and its beams scrubbed by the years—was what they had expected. Even to find electricity was not surprising. But Rodney Hunter thought he had seldom seen so many lights in one house, and Muriel had been wondering about it ever since their car turned the bend in the road.

"Clearlawns" lived up to its name. It stood in the midst of a slope of flat grass, now wiry white with frost, and there was no tree or shrub within twenty yards of it. Those lights contrasted with a certain inhospitable and damp air about the house, as though the owner were compelled to keep them burning.

"But why is the front door *open*?" insisted Muriel.

In the driveway the engine of their car coughed and died. The house was now a secret blackness of gables, emitting light at every chink, and silhouetting the stalks of wisteria vines which climbed it. On either side of the front door were little-paned windows whose curtains had not been drawn. Toward their left they could see into a low dining room, with table and sideboard set for a cold supper; toward their right was a darkish library moving with the reflections of a bright fire.

The sight of the fire warmed Rodney Hunter, but it made him feel guilty. They were very late. At five o'clock, without fail, he had promised Jack Bannister, they would be at "Clearlawns" to inaugurate the Christmas party.

Engine trouble in leaving London was one thing; idling at a country pub along the way, drinking hot ale and listening to the radio sing carols until a sort of Dickensian jollity stole into you, was something else. But both he and Muriel were young; they were very fond of each other and of things in general; and they had worked themselves into a glow of Christmas, which—as they stood before the creaking doors of "Clearlawns"—grew oddly cool.

There was no real reason, Rodney thought, to feel disquiet. He hoisted their luggage, including a big box of presents for Jack and Molly's children, out of the rear of the car. That his footsteps should sound loud on the gravel was only natural. He put his head into the doorway and whistled. Then he began to bang the knocker. Its sound seemed to seek out every corner of the house and then come back like a questing dog; but there was no response.

"I'll tell you something else," he said. "There's nobody in the house."

Muriel ran up the three steps to stand beside him. She had drawn her fur coat close around her, and her face was bright with cold.

"But that's impossible!" she said. "I mean, even if they're out, the servants—! Molly told me she keeps a cook and two maids. Are you sure we've got the right place?"

"Yes. The name's on the gate, and there's no other house within a mile."

With the same impulse they craned their necks to look through the windows of the dining room on the left. Cold fowl on the sideboard, a great bowl of chestnuts; and, now they could see it, another good fire, before which stood a chair with a piece of knitting put aside on it.

Rodney tried the knocker again, vigorously, but the

sound was all wrong. It was as though they were even more lonely in that core of light, with the east wind rushing across the Weald, and the door creaking again.

"I suppose we'd better go in," said Rodney. He added, with a lack of Christmas spirit, "Here, this is a devil of a trick! What do you think has happened? I'll swear that fire has been made up in the last fifteen minutes."

He stepped into the hall and set down the bags. As he was turning to close the door, Muriel put her hand on his arm.

"I say, Rod. Do you think you'd better close it?"

"Why not?"

"I—I don't know."

"The place is getting chilly enough as it is," he pointed out, unwilling to admit that the same thought had occurred to him. He closed both doors and shot their bar into place; and, at the same moment, a girl came out of the door to the library on the right.

She was such a pleasant-faced girl that they both felt a sense of relief. Why she had not answered the knocking had ceased to be a question; she filled a void. She was pretty, not more than twenty-one or -two, and had an air of primness which made Rodney Hunter vaguely associate her with a governess or a secretary, though Jack Bannister had never mentioned any such person. She was plump, but with a curiously narrow waist; and she wore brown. Her brown hair was neatly parted, and her brown eyes—long eyes, which might have given a hint of secrecy or curious smiles if they had not been so placid—looked concerned. In one hand she carried what looked like a small white bag of linen or cotton. And she spoke with a dignity which did not match her years.

"I am most terribly sorry," she told them. "I *thought* I heard someone, but I was so busy that I could not be sure. Will you forgive me?"

She smiled. Hunter's private view was that his knocking had been loud enough to wake the dead; but he murmured conventional things. As though conscious of some faint incongruity about the white bag in her hand, she held it up.

"For Blind Man's Bluff," she explained. "They do cheat so, I'm afraid, and not only the children. If one uses an ordinary handkerchief tied round the eyes, they always manage to get a corner loose. But if you take this, and you put it fully over a person's head, and you tie it round the neck"—a sudden gruesome image occurred to Rodney Hunter—"then it works so much better, don't you think?" Her eyes seemed to turn inward, and to grow absent. "But I must not keep you talking here. You are—?"

"My name is Hunter. This is my wife. I'm afraid we've arrived late, but I understood Mr. Bannister was expecting—"

"He did not tell you?" asked the girl in brown.

"Tell me what?"

"Everyone here, including the servants, is always out of the house at this hour on this particular date. It is the custom; I believe it has been the custom for more than sixty years. There is some sort of special church service."

Rodney Hunter's imagination had been devising all sorts of fantastic explanations: the first of them being that this demure lady had murdered the members of the household, and was engaged in disposing of the bodies.

What put this nonsensical notion into his head he could not tell, unless it was his own profession of detective-story writing. But he felt relieved to hear a commonplace explanation. Then the woman spoke again.

"Of course, it is a pretext, really. The rector, that dear man, invented it all those years ago to save embarrassment. What happened here had nothing to do with the murder, since the dates were so different; and I suppose most people have forgotten now why the tenants *do* prefer to stay away during seven and eight o'clock on Christmas Eve. I doubt if Mrs. Bannister even knows the real reason, though I should imagine Mr. Bannister must know it. But what happens here cannot be very pleasant, and it wouldn't do to have the children see it—would it?"

Muriel spoke with such sudden directness that her husband knew she was afraid. "Who are you?" Muriel said. "And what on earth are you talking about?"

"I am quite sane, really," their hostess assured them,

with a smile that was half cheery and half coy. "I dare say it must be all very confusing to you, poor dear. But I am forgetting my duties. Please come in and sit down before the fire, and let me offer you something to drink."

She took them into the library on the right, going ahead with a walk that was like a bounce, and looking over her shoulder out of those long eyes. The library was a long low room with beams. The windows toward the road were uncurtained; but those in the side wall, where a faded red-brick fireplace stood, were bay windows with draperies closed across them. As their hostess put them before the fire, Hunter could have sworn he saw one of the draperies move.

"You need not worry about it," she assured him, following his glance toward the bay. "Even if you looked in there, you might not see anything now. I believe some gentleman did try it once, a long time ago. He stayed in the house for a wager. But when he pulled the curtain back, he did not see anything in the bay—at least, anything quite. He felt some hair, and it moved. That is why they have so many lights nowadays."

Muriel had sat down on a sofa, and was lighting a cigarette—to the rather prim disapproval of their hostess, Hunter thought.

"May we have a hot drink?" Muriel asked crisply. "And then, if you don't mind, we might walk over and meet the Bannisters coming from church."

"Oh, please don't do that!" cried the other. She had been standing by the fireplace, her hands folded and turned outward. Now she ran across to sit down beside Muriel; and the swiftness of her movement, no less than the touch of her hand on Muriel's arm, made the latter draw back.

Hunter was now completely convinced that their hostess was out of her head. Why she held such fascination for him, though, he could not understand. In her eagerness to keep them there, the girl had come upon a new idea. On a table behind the sofa, bookends held a row of modern novels. Consciously displayed—probably due to Molly

Bannister's tact—were two of Rodney Hunter's detective stories. The girl put a finger on them.

"May I ask if you wrote these?"

He admitted it.

"Then," she said with sudden composure, "it would probably interest you to hear about the murder. It was a most perplexing business, you know; the police could make nothing of it, and no one ever has been able to solve it." An arresting eye fixed on his. "It happened out in the hall there. A poor woman was killed where there was no one to kill her, and no one could have done it. But she was murdered."

Hunter started to get up from his chair; then he changed his mind, and sat down again. "Go on," he said.

"You must forgive me if I am a little uncertain about dates," she urged. "I think it was in the early eighteen-seventies, and I am sure it was in early February—because of the snow. It was a bad winter then; the farmers' livestock all died. My people have been bred up in the district for years, and I know that. The house here was much as it is now, except that there was none of this lighting—only paraffin lamps, poor girl! And you were obliged to pump up what water you wanted; and people read the newspaper quite through, and discussed it for days.

"The people were a little different to look at, too. I am sure I do not understand why we think beards are so strange nowadays; they seem to think that men who had beards never had any emotions. But even young men wore them then, and looked handsome enough. There was a newly married couple living in this house at the time—at least, they had been married only the summer before. They were named Edward and Jane Waycross, and it was considered a good match everywhere.

"Edward Waycross did not have a beard, but he had bushy side-whiskers which he kept curled. He was not a handsome man, either, being somewhat dry and hard-favored; but he was a religious man, and a good man, and an excellent man

of business, they say—a manufacturer of agricultural imple-
ments at Hawkhurst.

"He had determined that Jane Anders would make him
a good wife, and I dare say she did. The girl had several
suitors. Although Mr. Waycross was the best match, I
know it surprised people a little when she accepted him,
because she was thought to have been fond of another
man—a more striking man, whom many of the young
girls were after.

"This was Jeremy Wilkes who came of a very good
family, but was considered wicked. He was no younger
than Mr. Waycross, but he had a great black beard, and
wore white waistcoats with gold chains, and drove a gig.
Of course, there had been gossip, but that was because
Jane Anders was considered pretty."

Their hostess had been sitting back against the sofa,
quietly folding the little white bag with one hand, and
speaking in a prim voice. Now she did something which
turned her hearers cold.

You have probably seen the same thing done many
times. She had been touching her cheek lightly with the
fingers of the other hand. In doing so, she touched the
flesh at the corner under her lower eyelid, and acciden-
tally drew down the corner of that eyelid—which should
have exposed the red part of the inner lid at the corner of
the eye. It was not red. It was of a sickly pale color.

"In the course of his business dealings," she went on,
"Mr. Waycross had often to go to London, and usually he
was obliged to remain overnight. But Jane Waycross was
not afraid to remain alone in the house. She had a good
servant, a staunch old woman, and a good dog. Even so,
Mr. Waycross commended her for her courage."

The girl smiled. "On the night I wish to tell you of, in
February, Mr. Waycross was absent. Unfortunately, too,
the old servant was absent; she had been called away as a
midwife to attend her cousin, and Jane Waycross had allowed her to go. This was known in the village, since all
such affairs are well known, and some uneasiness was
felt—this house being isolated, as you know. But Jane
was not afraid.

"It was a very cold night, with a heavy fall of snow which had stopped about nine o'clock. You must know, beyond doubt, that poor Jane Waycross was alive after it had stopped snowing. It must have been nearly half-past nine when a Mr. Moody—a very good and sober man who lived in Hawkhurst—was driving home along the road past this house. As you know, it stands in the middle of a great bare stretch of lawn; and you can see the house clearly from the road.

"Mr. Moody saw poor Jane at the window of one of the upstairs bedrooms, with a candle in her hand, closing the shutters. But he was not the only witness who saw her alive.

"On that same evening, Mr. Wilkes—the handsome gentleman I spoke to you of a moment ago—had been at a tavern in the village of Five Ashes with Dr. Sutton, the local doctor, and a racing gentleman named Pawley. At about half-past eleven they started to drive home in Mr. Wilkes's gig to Cross-in-Hand. I am afraid they had been drinking, but they were all in their sober senses.

"The landlord of the tavern remembered the time because he had stood in the doorway to watch the gig, which had fine yellow wheels, go spanking away as though there were no snow; and Mr. Wilkes was wearing one of the new round hats with a curly brim.

"There was a bright moon. 'And no danger,' Dr. Sutton always said afterwards; 'shadows of trees and fences as clear as though a silhouette cutter had made 'em for sixpence.' But when they were passing this house Mr. Wilkes pulled up sharp. There was a bright light in the window of one of the downstairs rooms—this room, in fact. They sat out there looking round the hood of the gig, and wondering.

"Mr. Wilkes spoke. 'I don't like this,' he said. 'You know, gentlemen, that Waycross is still in London; and the lady in question is in the habit of retiring early. I am going up there to find out if anything is wrong.'

"With that he jumped out of the gig, his black beard jutting out and his breath smoking. He said, 'And if it is a burglar, then, by Something, gentlemen'—I will not repeat the word he used—'by Something, gentlemen, I'll settle him.'

"He walked through the gate and up to the house—they could follow every step he made—and looked into the windows of this room here. Presently he returned looking relieved—they could see him by the light of the gig lamps—but wiping the moisture off his forehead.

" 'It is all right,' he said to them. 'Waycross has come home. But, by Something, gentlemen, he is growing thinner these days, or it is shadows.'

"Then he told them what he had seen. If you look through the front windows—there—you can look sideways and see out through the doorway into the main hall. He said he had seen Mrs. Waycross standing in the hall with her back to the staircase, wearing a blue dressing wrap over her nightgown, and her hair down round her shoulders. Standing in front of her, with his back to Mr. Wilkes, was a tallish, thin man like Mr. Waycross, with a long greatcoat and a tall hat like Mr. Waycross'.

"*She* was carrying either a candle or a lamp; and he remembered how the tall hat seemed to wag back and forth, as though the man were talking to her or putting out his hands towards her. For he said he could not see the woman's face.

"Of course, it was not Mr. Waycross; but how were they to know that?

"At about seven o'clock next morning, Mrs. Randall, the old servant, returned. A fine boy had been born to her cousin the night before. Mrs. Randall came home through the white dawn and the white snow, and found the house all locked up. She could get no answer to her knocking. Being a woman of great resolution, she eventually broke a window and got in. But when she saw what was in the front hall, she went out screaming for help.

"Poor Jane was past help. I know I should not speak of these things; but I must. She was lying on her face in the hall. From the waist down her body was much charred and—unclothed, you know, because fire had burned away most of the nightgown and the dressing wrap. The tiles of the hall were soaked with blood and paraffin oil, the oil having come from a broken lamp with a thick blue-silk shade which was lying a little distance away. Near it was a china candlestick with a candle.

"This fire had also charred a part of the paneling of the wall, and a part of the staircase. Fortunately, the floor is of brick tiles, and there had not been much paraffin left in the lamp, or the house would have been set afire.

"But she had not died from burns alone. Her throat had been cut with a deep slash from some very sharp blade. But she had been alive for a while to feel both things, for she had crawled forward on her hands while she was burning. It was a cruel death, a horrible death for a soft person like that."

There was a pause. The expression on the face of the narrator, the plump girl in the brown dress, altered slightly. So did the expression of her eyes. She was sitting beside Muriel, and moved a little closer.

"Of course, the police came. I do not understand such things, I am afraid, but they found that the house had not been robbed. They also noticed the odd thing I have mentioned—that there was both a lamp *and* a candle in a candlestick near her. The lamp came from Mr. and Mrs. Waycross' bedroom upstairs, and so did the candlestick; there were no other lamps or candles downstairs except the lamps waiting to be filled next morning in the back kitchen.

"But the police thought she would not have come downstairs carrying both the lamp *and* the candle as well.

"She must have brought the lamp, because that was broken. When the murderer took hold of her, they thought, she had dropped the lamp, and it went out; the paraffin spilled, but did not catch fire. Then this man in the tall hat, to finish his work after he had cut her throat, went upstairs, got a candle, and set fire to the spilled oil.

"I am stupid at these things; but even I should have guessed that this must mean someone familiar with the house. Also, if she came downstairs, it must have been to let someone in at the front door; and that could not have been a burglar.

"You may be sure all the gossips were like police from

the start, even when the police hemmed and hawed, because they knew Mrs. Waycross must have opened the door to a man who was not her husband. And immediately they found an indication of this, in the mess that the fire and blood had made in the hall. Some distance away from poor Jane's body there was a medicine bottle, such as chemists use. I think it had been broken in two pieces; and on one intact piece they found sticking some fragments of a letter that had not been quite burned.

"It was in a man's handwriting, not her husband's, and they made out enough of it to understand. It was full of—expressions of love, you know, and it made an appointment to meet her there on that night."

Rodney Hunter, as the girl paused, felt impelled to ask a question.

"Did they know whose handwriting it was?"

"It was Jeremy Wilkes's," replied the other simply. "Though they never proved that, never more than slightly suspected it, and the circumstances did not bear it out. In fact, a knife stained with blood was actually found in Mr. Wilkes's possession. But the police never brought it to anything; for, you see, not Mr. Wilkes—or anyone else in the world—could possibly have done the murder."

"I don't understand that," said Hunter, rather sharply.

"Forgive me if I am stupid about telling things," urged their hostess in a tone of apology. She seemed to be listening to the chimney growl under a cold sky, and listening with hard, placid eyes. "But even the village gossips could tell that. When Mrs. Randall came here to the house on that morning, both the front and the back doors were locked and securely bolted on the inside. All the windows were locked on the inside. If you will look at the fastenings in this dear place, you will know what that means.

"But, bless you, that was the least of it! I told you about the snow. The snowfall had stopped at nine o'clock in the evening, hours and hours before Mrs. Waycross was murdered. When the police came, there were only two separate sets of footprints in the great unmarked half acre of snow round the house. One set belonged to Mr. Wilkes, who had come up and looked in through the window the night before. The other belonged to Mrs. Randall. The police could follow and explain both sets of tracks; *but there were no other tracks at all, and no one was hiding in the house!*

"Of course, it was absurd to suspect Mr. Wilkes. It was not only that he told a perfectly straight story about the man in the tall hat; but both Dr. Sutton and Mr. Pawley, who drove back with him from Five Ashes, were there to swear he could not have done it. You understand, he came no closer to the house than the windows of this room. They could watch every step he made in the moonlight, and they did.

"Afterwards he drove home with Dr. Sutton, and slept there, or, I should say, they continued their terrible drinking until daylight. It is true that they found in his possession a knife with blood on it, but he explained that he had used the knife to gut a rabbit.

"It was the same with poor Mrs. Randall, who had been up all night about her midwife's duties, though naturally it was even more absurd to think of *her*. But there were no other footprints at all, either coming to or going from the house, in all that stretch of snow; and all the ways in or out were locked on the inside."

It was Muriel who spoke then, in a voice that tried to be crisp, but wavered in spite of her. "Are you telling us that all this is true?" she demanded.

"I am teasing you a little, my dear," said the other. "But, really and truly, it all did happen. Perhaps I will show you in a moment."

"I suppose it was really the husband who did it?" asked Muriel in a bored tone.

"Poor Mr. Waycross!" said their hostess tenderly. "He spent that night in a temperance hotel near Charing Cross Station, as he always did, and, of course, he never left it. When he learned about his wife's duplicity"—again Hunter thought she was going to pull down a corner of her eyelid—"it nearly drove him out of his mind. I think he gave up agricultural machinery and took to preaching, but

I am not sure. I know he left the district soon afterwards, and before he left he insisted on burning the mattress of their bed. It was a dreadful scandal."

"But in that case," insisted Hunter, "who did kill her? And if there were no footprints and all the doors were locked, how did the murderer come or go? Finally, if all this happened in February, what does it have to do with people being out of the house on Christmas Eve?"

"Ah, that is the real story. That is what I meant to tell you."

She grew very subdued.

"It must have been very interesting to watch the people alter and grow older, or find queer paths, in the years afterwards. For, of course, nothing did happen as yet. The police presently gave it all up; for decency's sake it was allowed to rest. There was a new pump built in the market square; and the news of the Prince of Wales's going to India in '75 to talk about; and presently a new family came to live at 'Clearlawns,' and began to raise their children. The trees and the rains in summer were just the same, you know. It must have been seven or eight years before anything happened, for Jane Waycross was very patient.

"Several of the people had died in the meantime. Mrs. Randall had, in a fit of quinsy; and so had Dr. Sutton, but that was a great mercy, because he fell by the way when he was going out to perform an amputation with too much of the drink in him. But Mr. Pawley had prospered—and, above all, so had Mr. Wilkes. He had become an even finer figure of a man, they tell me, as he drew near middle age. When he married he gave up all his loose habits. Yes, he married; it was the Tinsley heiress, Miss Linshaw, whom he had been courting at the time of the murder; and I have heard that poor Jane Waycross, even after *she* was married to Mr. Waycross, used to bite her pillow at night because she was so horribly jealous of Miss Linshaw.

"Mr. Wilkes had always been tall, and now he was finely stout. He always wore frock coats. Though he had lost most of his hair, his beard was full and curly; he had twinkling black eyes, and ruddy cheeks, and a bluff voice. All the children ran to him. They say he broke as many feminine hearts as before. At any wholesome entertainment he was always the first to lead the cotillion or applaud the fiddler, and I do not know what hostesses would have done without him.

"On Christmas Eve, then—remember, I am not sure of the date—the Fentons gave a Christmas party. The Fentons were the very nice family who had taken this house afterwards, you know. There was to be no dancing, but all the old games. Naturally, Mr. Wilkes was the first to be invited, and the first to accept; for everything was all smoothed away by time, like the wrinkles in last year's counterpane; and what's past *is* past, or so they say. They had decorated the house with holly and mistletoe, and guests began to arrive as early as two in the afternoon.

"I had all this from Mrs. Fenton's aunt—one of the Warwickshire Abbotts—who was actually staying here at the time. In spite of such a festal season the preparations had not been going at all well that day, though such preparations usually did. Miss Abbott complained that there was a nasty earthy smell in the house.

"It was a dark and raw day, and the chimneys did not seem to draw as well as they should. What is more, Mrs. Fenton cut her finger when she was carving the cold fowl, because she said one of the children had been hiding behind the window curtains in here, and peeping out at her; she was very angry. But Mr. Fenton, who was going about the house in his carpet slippers before the arrival of the guests, called her 'Mother' and said that it was Christmas.

"It is certainly true that they forgot all about this when the fun of the games began. Such squealings you never heard!—or so I am told. Foremost of all at bobbing for apples or nuts was Mr. Jeremy Wilkes. He stood, gravely paternal, in the midst of everything, with his ugly wife beside him, and stroked his beard. He kissed each of the ladies on the cheek under the mistletoe; there was also some scampering to kiss him; and, though he *did* remain for longer than was necessary behind the window curtains with the younger Miss Twigelow, his wife only smiled.

"There was only one unpleasant incident, soon forgotten.

Towards dusk a great gusty wind began to come up, with the chimneys smoking worse than usual. It being nearly dark, Mr. Fenton said it was time to fetch in the snapdragon bowl, and watch it flame. You know the game? It is a great bowl of lighted spirit, and you must thrust in your hand and pluck out a raisin from the bottom without scorching your fingers.

"Mr. Fenton carried it in on a tray in the half darkness; it was flickering with that blueish flame you have seen on Christmas puddings. Miss Abbott said that once, in carrying it, he started and turned round. She said that for a second she thought there was a face looking over his shoulder, and it wasn't a nice face.

"Later in the evening, when the children were sleepy and there was tissue paper scattered all over the house, the grownups began their games in earnest. Someone suggested Blind Man's Bluff. They were mostly using the hall and this room here, as having more space than the dining room. Various members of the party were blindfolded with the men's handkerchiefs; but there was a dreadful amount of cheating.

"Mr. Fenton grew quite annoyed about it, because the ladies almost always caught Mr. Wilkes when they could; Mr. Wilkes was laughing heartily, and his great cravat with the silver pin had almost come loose.

"To make it certain nobody could cheat, Mr. Fenton got a little white linen bag—like this one. It was the pillow cover off the baby's cot, really; and he said nobody could look through that if it were tied over the head.

"I should explain that they had been having some trouble with the lamp in this room. Mr. Fenton said, 'Confound it, mother, what is wrong with that lamp? Turn up the wick, will you?' It was really quite a good lamp from Spence and Minstead's, and should not have burned so dull as it did.

"In the confusion, while Mrs. Fenton was trying to make the light better, and he was looking over his shoulder at her, Mr. Fenton had been rather absently fastening the bag on the head of the last person caught. He has said since that he did not notice who it was. No one else no-

ticed, either, the light being so dim and there being such a
large number of people. It seemed to be a girl in a broad
blueish kind of dress, standing over near the door.

"Perhaps you know how people act when they have just
been blindfolded in this game. First they usually stand
very still, as though they were smelling or sensing in
which direction to go. Sometimes they make a sudden
jump, or sometimes they begin to shuffle gently forward.
Everyone noticed what an air of *purpose* there seemed to
be about this person whose face was covered; she went
forward very slowly, and seemed to crouch down a bit.

"It began to move towards Mr. Wilkes in very short but
quick little jerks, the white bag bobbing on its face. At
this time Mr. Wilkes was sitting at the end of the table,
laughing with his face pink above the beard, and a glass
of our Kentish cider in his hand. I want you to imagine
this room as being very dim, and much more cluttered,
what with all the tassels they had on the furniture then;
and the high-piled hair of the ladies, too.

"The hooded person got to the edge of the table. It began to edge along towards Mr. Wilkes's chair; and then it
jumped.

"Mr. Wilkes got up and skipped—yes, skipped—out of
its way, laughing. It waited quietly, after which it went, in
the same slow way, towards him, again. It nearly got him
again, by the edge of the potted plant. All this time it did
not say anything, you understand, although everyone was
applauding it and crying encouraging advice. It kept its
head down.

"Miss Abbott says she began to notice an unpleasant
faint smell of burned cloth or something worse, which
turned her half ill. By the time the hooded person came
stooping clear across the room, as certainly as though it
could see him, Mr. Wilkes was not laughing any longer.

"In the corner by one bookcase, he said out loud, 'I'm
tired of this silly, rotten game; go away, do you hear?'
Nobody there had ever heard him speak like that, in such
a loud, wild way, but they laughed and thought it must be
the Kentish cider.

" 'Go away!' cried Mr. Wilkes again, and began to

strike at it with his fist. All this time, Miss Abbott says, she had observed his face gradually changing. He dodged again, very pleasant and nimble for such a big man, but with the perspiration running down his face. Back across the room he went again, with it following him; and he cried out something that most naturally shocked them all inexpressibly.

"He screamed out, 'For God's sake, Fenton, take it off me!'

"And for the last time the thing jumped.

"They were over near the curtains of that bay window, which were drawn as they are now. Miss Twigelow, who was nearest, says that Mr. Wilkes could not have seen anything, because the white bag was still drawn over the woman's head. The only thing she noticed was that at the lower part of the bag, where the face must have been, there was a curious kind of discoloration, a stain of some sort which had not been there before: something seemed to be seeping through.

"Mr. Wilkes fell back between the curtains, with the hooded person after him, and he screamed again. There was a kind of thrashing noise in or behind the curtains; then they fell straight again, and everything grew quiet.

"Now, our Kentish cider is very strong, and for a moment Mr. Fenton did not know what to think. He tried to laugh at it, but the laugh did not sound well. Then he went over to the curtains, calling out gruffly to them to come out of there and not play the fool. But after he had looked inside the curtains, he turned round very sharply and asked the rector to get the ladies out of the room.

"This was done, but Miss Abbott often said that she had one quick peep inside. Though the bay windows were locked on the inside, Mr. Wilkes was now alone on the window seat. She could see his beard sticking up, and the blood. He was dead, of course. But, since he had murdered Jane Waycross, I sincerely think that he deserved to die."

For several seconds the two listeners did not move. She had all too successfully conjured up this room in the late 'seventies, whose stuffiness still seemed to pervade it.

"But look here!" protested Hunter, when he could fight down an inclination to get out of the room quickly. "You say he killed her after all? And yet you told us he had an absolute alibi. You said he never went closer to the house than the windows . . ."

"No more he did, my dear," said the other.

"He was courting the Linshaw heiress at the time," she resumed; "and Miss Linshaw was a very proper young lady who would have been horrified if she had heard about him and Jane Waycross. She would have broken off the match, naturally. But poor Jane Waycross meant her to hear. She was much in love with Mr. Wilkes, and she was going to tell the whole matter publicly; Mr. Wilkes had been trying to persuade her not to do so."

"But—"

"Oh, don't you see what happened?" cried the other in a pettish tone. "It is so dreadfully simple. I am not clever at these things, but I should have seen it in a moment: even if I did not already know. I told you everything so that you should be able to guess.

"When Mr. Wilkes and Dr. Sutton and Mr. Pawley drove past here in the gig that night, they saw a bright light burning in the windows of this room. I told you that. But the police never wondered, as anyone should, what caused that light.

"Jane Waycross never came into this room, as you know; she was out in the hall, carrying either a lamp or a candle. But that lamp in the thick blue-silk shade, held out there in the hall, would not have caused a bright light to shine through this room and illuminate it. Neither would a tiny candle; it is absurd. And I told you there were no other lamps in the house except some empty ones in the back kitchen.

"There is only one thing they could have seen. They saw the great blaze of the paraffin oil round Jane Waycross' body.

"Didn't I tell you it was dreadfully simple? Poor Jane was upstairs waiting for her lover. From the upstairs window she saw Mr. Wilkes's gig drive along the road in the moonlight, and she did not know there were other men in it; she thought he was alone. She came downstairs—

"It is an awful thing that the police did not think more about that broken medicine bottle lying in the hall, the large bottle that was broken in just two long pieces. She must have had a use for it; and, of course, she had. You knew that the oil in the lamp was almost exhausted, although there was a great blaze round the body.

"When poor Jane came downstairs, she was carrying the unlighted lamp in one hand; in the other hand she was carrying a lighted candle and an old medicine bottle containing paraffin oil. When she got downstairs, she meant to fill the lamp from the medicine bottle, and then light it with the candle.

"But she was too eager to get downstairs, I am afraid. When she was more than halfway down, hurrying, that long nightgown tripped her. She pitched forward down the stairs on her face. The medicine bottle broke on the tiles under her, and poured a lake of paraffin round her body. Of course, the lighted candle set the paraffin blazing when it fell; but that was not all.

"One intact side of that broken bottle, long and sharp and cleaner than any blade, cut into her throat when she fell on the smashed bottle. She was not quite stunned by the fall. When she felt herself burning, and the blood almost as hot, she tried to save herself. She tried to crawl forward on her hands, forward into the hall, away from the blood and oil and fire.

"That was what Mr. Wilkes really saw when he looked in through the window.

"You see, he had been unable to get rid of the two fuddled friends, who insisted on clinging to him and drinking with him. He had been obliged to drive them home. If he could not go to 'Clearlawns' now, he wondered how at least he could leave a message; and the light in the window gave him an excuse.

"He saw pretty Jane propped up on her hands in the hall, looking out at him beseechingly while the blue flame ran up and turned yellow. You might have thought he would have pitied her, for she loved him very much. Her wound was not really a deep wound. If he had broken into the house at that moment, he might have saved her life.

"But he preferred to let her die—because now she would make no public scandal and spoil his chances with the rich Miss Linshaw. That was why he returned to his friends and told a lie about a murderer in a tall hat. It is why, in heaven's truth, he murdered her himself. But when he returned to his friends, I do not wonder that they saw him mopping his forehead. You know now how Jane Waycross came back for him, presently."

The girl got to her feet, with a sort of bouncing motion which was as suggestive as it was vaguely familiar. It was as though she were about to run. She stood there, a trifle crouched, in her prim brown dress, so oddly narrow at the waist after an old-fashioned pattern; and in the play of light on her face Rodney Hunter fancied that its prettiness was only a shell.

"The same thing happened afterwards, on some Christmas Eves," she explained. "They played Blind Man's Bluff over again. That is why people who live here do not care to risk it nowadays. It happens at a quarter-past seven—"

Hunter stared at the curtains. "But it was a quarter-past seven when we got here!" he said. "It must now be—"

"Oh, yes," said the girl, and her eyes brimmed over. "You see, I told you that you had nothing to fear; it was all over then. But that is not why I thank you. I begged you to stay, and you did. You have listened to me, as no one else would. And now I have told it at last, and now I think both of us can sleep."

Not a fold stirred or altered in the dark curtains that closed the window bay; yet, as though a blurred lens had come into focus, the curtains now seemed innocent and devoid of harm.

Rodney Hunter, with Muriel following his gaze, walked across and threw back the curtains. He saw a quiet window seat covered with chintz, and the rising moon beyond the window. When he turned round, the girl in the old-fashioned dress was not there. But the front doors were

open again, for he could feel a current of air blowing
through the house.

With his arm around Muriel, who was white-faced, he
went out into the hall. They did not look long at the
scorched and beaded stains at the foot of the paneling, for
even the scars of fire seemed gentle now. Instead, they
stood in the doorway looking out, while the house threw
its great blaze of light across the frosty Weald. It was a
welcoming light.

Over the rise of a hill, black dots trudging in the frost
showed that Jack Bannister's party was returning; and
they could hear the sound of voices carrying far. They
heard one of the party carelessly singing a Christmas
carol for glory and joy, and the laughter of children coming home.

THE THEFT OF SANTA'S BEARD
by Edward D. Hoch

The New York stores had closed at nine that evening, disgorging gift-laden Christmas shoppers by the hundreds. Most were too busy shifting the weight of their parcels and shopping bags to bother digging for coins as they passed the bell-ringing Santa on the corner. He was a bit thin and scraggly compared to the overstuffed Santas who worked the department stores and bounced tiny children on their knees while asking for their Christmas lists. His job was only to ring a little hand-held bell and accept donations in a chimney-shaped container.

This Santa's name was Russell Bajon and he'd come to the city expecting better things. After working at a variety of minimum-wage jobs and landing a couple of short-lived acting roles off Broadway, he'd taken the Santa Claus job for the holidays. There was no pay, but they supplied his meals and a place to sleep at night. And there were good fringe benefits, enough to keep him going till he was back on his feet with a part in a decent play.

After another fifteen minutes the crowd from the stores had pretty well scattered. There were still people on the dark streets, as there would be for most of the night, but those remaining hurried by his chimney without even a glance. He waited a few more minutes and then decided to pack up. The truck would be coming by shortly to collect the chimney and give him a ride back to the men's dorm where he slept.

He was bending over the chimney with its collection basket when someone bumped him from behind. He straightened and tried to turn, but by that time the thin copper wire was cutting into his throat.

* * *

By the time the second Santa Claus had been strangled to death, the tabloids had the story on page one. *No Clues to Claus Killer,* one of them trumpeted, while another proclaimed, *Santa Strangler Strikes Again.* Nick Velvet glanced over the articles with passing interest, but at that point they were nothing to directly affect him.

"Where was the latest killing?" Gloria asked as she prepared breakfast.

"In the subway. An elderly Santa on his way to work."

She shook her head. "What's this world coming to when somebody starts strangling Santa Clauses?"

The next morning Nick found out. He was seated in the office of the Intercontinental Protection Service, across the desk from a man named Grady Culhane. The office was small and somewhat plain, not what Nick had expected from the pretentious name. Culhane himself was young, barely past thirty, with black hair, thick eyebrows, and an Irish smile. He spread his hands flat on the uncluttered desktop and said, "I understand you steal things of little or no value."

"That's correct," Nick replied. "My standard fee is twenty-five thousand dollars, unless it's something especially hazardous."

"This should be simple enough. I want you to steal the beard from a department store Santa Claus. It's the Santa at Kliman's main store, and it must be done tomorrow before noon. Santa's hours there are noon to four and five to eight."

"What makes it so valuable to you?"

"Nothing. It's worth no more than any other false white beard. I just need it tomorrow."

"I usually get half the money down and the other half after the job," Nick said. "Is that agreeable?"

"Sure. It'll have to be a check. I don't have that much cash on hand."

"So long as I can cash it at your bank."

He made out the check and handed it over. "Here's a sketch map I drew of Kliman's fourth floor. This is the dressing room Santa uses."

"So the beard is probably there before noon. Why don't you just walk in and steal it?" Nick wondered. "Why do you need me?"

"You ever been in Kliman's? They've got security cameras all over the store, including hidden ones in the dressing rooms. This is only Santa's room during the Christmas season. The rest of the year it's used by the public, and the camera is probably still operational. I can't afford to be seen stealing the beard or anything else."

"What about me?"

"That's your job. That's what I'm paying you for."

"Fair enough," Nick agreed, folding the check once and slipping it into his pocket. "I'll be back here tomorrow with the beard."

Nothing had been said about the two Santa Claus killings, but somehow, as Nick Velvet left the building, he had the feeling he was becoming involved in something a lot more complex than a simple robbery.

The Santa Claus killings were still big news the following morning, and Nick read the speculations about possible motives as he traveled into midtown on the subway. The second man to die, Larry Averly, was a retired plumber who'd been earning some spare cash as a holiday Santa Claus. The first victim, Bajon, had died on Monday evening, the fourteenth, while the second death came the following morning. Nick had the feeling the press was almost disappointed that another killing had not followed on Wednesday. Now it was Thursday, eight days before Christmas, and the street before Kliman's block-long department store was crowded with shoppers.

He entered the store with the first wave of customers when the doors opened at ten, making his way up the escalator to the fourth floor. After a half-hour of lingering in the furniture department, he wandered over to the dressing-room door that Grady Culhane had indicated on his map. When no one was looking, he slipped inside.

His first task was to locate the closed-circuit television camera. He found it without difficulty—a circular lens

embedded in the very center of a round wall clock. Not
wanting to blot out the view entirely and arouse the suspicion of possible observers, Nick moved a coat rack in
front of the clock, blocking most of the little room. Then
he quickly opened a pair of lockers. But there was no
Santa Claus costume, no beard, in either one. He'd been
hoping that the store's Santa changed into his costume on
the premises, but it looked as if he might come to work already dressed, like the street Santa who'd been strangled
in the subway.

If that was the case, however, Culhane wouldn't have
told him to come to this room. It was already nearly
eleven and Nick decided to wait till noon to see what
happened. He positioned himself behind the clothes rack,
but at the far end, away from the television camera. Exactly at eleven-thirty, the door opened and someone came
in. He could see a tall, fairly broad-shouldered person
carrying a large canvas tote bag. There was a flash of red
as a Santa Claus suit came into view.

Nick Velvet breathed a sigh of relief. The white beard
came out of the bag and he saw the prize within his grasp.
He stepped from his hiding place, ready to deliver a
knockout blow if necessary. "Keep quiet and give me the
beard," he said.

The figure turned and Nick froze in his tracks. Santa
was a woman.

She was probably in her late thirties, large boned but
not unattractive, with dark brown hair that was already
partly covered by the Santa Claus wig and cap. Nick's
sudden appearance seemed not to have frightened her but
only angered her as any unexpected interruption might.
"You just made the mistake of your life, mister," she told
him in a flat tone of voice.

"I don't want to hurt you. Give me that beard."

"I have a transmitter in my pocket. I've already called
for help."

He realized suddenly that she thought he was the Santa
strangler. "I'm not here to hurt you," he tried to assure
her.

But it was too late for assurances. The dressing-room door burst open and Nick faced two men with drawn revolvers. "Freeze!" the first man ordered, crouching in a shooter's stance. "Police!"

"Look, this is all a mistake."

"And you made it, mister!" The second man moved behind Nick to frisk him.

Nick decided it was time for a bit of his own electronic technology. He brought his left arm down enough to hit the small transmitter in his breast pocket. Immediately there was a sharp crack from the direction of the furniture department, and billowing smoke could be seen through the open dressing-room door. The first man turned his head and Nick kicked the gun from his hand, poking his elbow back simultaneously to catch the second detective in the ribs. As he went out the door he made a grab for the white beard the lady Santa was holding in her hand, but he missed by several inches.

"Stop or I'll shoot!" one of the detectives yelled, but Nick knew he wouldn't. The floor was crowded with shoppers, and the cloud from Nick's well-placed smoke bomb was already enveloping everyone.

Five minutes later he was out of the store and safely away, but without the beard he'd been hired to steal.

Later that afternoon Nick returned to the office of the Intercontinental Protection Service. Grady Culhane was not in a pleasant mood. "That was you at the store this morning, wasn't it?" he asked pointedly. "The radio says someone set off a smoke bomb and two shoppers were slightly injured in the panic."

"I'm sorry if anyone was hurt. You didn't tell me Santa Claus was a woman. That threw off my timing and enabled a couple of detectives to get the drop on me."

"What about the beard?"

"I didn't get it."

Culhane cursed. "That means Santa will be back in place as soon as they get the smoke cleared out and things back to normal."

Nick was beginning to see at least a portion of the

scheme. "You wanted the beard stolen so Santa couldn't appear."

"Sure. It was easier than stealing the whole costume, except that you bungled it."

"They could have found another beard quickly enough," Nick argued.

Grady Culhane shook his head. "They don't sell them in the store. I checked. The delay would have been an hour or two, and that was all I needed."

"For what?"

He eyed Nick uncertainly for a moment before deciding to yield. "All right, I'll tell you about it. But I want something in return. I want that beard tomorrow, and no slip-ups this time!"

"You'll have it, so long as you play square with me. What's this all about? Does it involve the Santa Claus killings?"

The dark-haired young man reached into a desk drawer and extracted a sheet of paper which he passed across the desk to Nick. It was a copy of a crudely printed extortion letter addressed to the president of Kliman's department store: "Tuesday, December 15—I have just come from killing my second Santa Claus of the Christmas season. The deaths of Bajon and Averly were meant as a demonstration. A third Santa Claus will die in your store, in full view of the children, unless you are prepared to pay me one million dollars in cash within forty-eight hours, by noon Thursday." There was no signature.

"Sounds like a crackpot," Nick decided, returning the letter. "He doesn't even give directions for paying the money."

"This letter was hand-delivered by a messenger service Tuesday afternoon. A second letter came yesterday, with instructions. They haven't shown me that one."

"You've been hired by Kliman's store?"

Culhane nodded. "Frankly, it's the first major client I've had. Even though the police have been called in, the store is paying me as a personal bodyguard for Santa."

"Or Mrs. Santa."

He smiled. "She's an unemployed actress named Vivian Delmos. I just met her yesterday after I talked with you. There are some female Santas around. They're good with children. If their voices are deep enough and the suit is padded enough, no one knows the difference. I didn't know the cops would be guarding her too."

"How much are they paying you?" Nick asked.

"That's proprietary information," the young man answered stiffly.

"I figure fifty thousand, at least, if you can afford to pay me twenty-five."

"I don't get a thing if the Santa strangler kills her."

"You thought he'd strike right at noon, so you needed me to keep her from going out there then. That means they decided not to pay."

"It's not just them. There are other stores involved. The killer is trying to shake down the largest stores in New York."

"The police must have a description from the messenger company that delivered this note."

Grady Culhane shook his head. "They deny any knowledge of it. One of their messengers was probably stopped in the street and paid to deliver it. Naturally he won't admit it now and risk losing his job."

"What happens after the smoke is cleared out?"

"The Delmos woman puts on her beard and goes back out there. I'll probably have to be standing next to her, and I'm too big for those elves' costumes."

"Don't worry," Nick promised. "This time I'll get the beard."

On his second visit to the store Nick Velvet wore a grey wig and a matching false moustache. He was taking no chances on coming face-to-face with one of those detectives again. In the atrium at the center of the main floor where Santa's throne was in place, a sign announced that he would not return until noon the following day due to the illness of one of his reindeer. Nick found a pay telephone and called Culhane at his office.

"You're off the hook until tomorrow," he said.

"I just heard from the store."

"Do you still want the beard?"

"Of course—unless the police come up with the extortionist by then."

Nick hung up and decided he should know more than he did about the Santa Claus killings. He went down to the subway newsstand and bought all the local papers. It wasn't the lead item anymore but the unsolved killings still filled several columns inside each paper. The first victim, Russell Bajon, was a young homeless man—a would-be actor—who'd been staying at the men's dorm maintained by a charitable organization. He'd been collecting money for the charity at one of their Christmas chimneys when he'd been strangled. One of the other Santas, a man named Chris Stover, had come by in a van a few minutes later to find a crowd gathering around the fallen man. No one admitted to having seen the actual killing.

The second victim had followed less than twelve hours later, on Tuesday morning. Larry Averly lived in a run-down hotel on the fringes of Greenwich Village, a place where Nick had grown up. His Christmas job as a Santa Claus for a local radio station's holiday promotion involved coming to work in costume that day, since they were doing a remote broadcast from the Central Park skating rink. He'd been heading for a subway exit near the park when the killer struck. This time two people saw the attack and scared him off, but not in time to save the victim. The killer was described as a white man of uncertain age wearing a bulky coat. Averly hadn't been carrying any identification in his shabby wallet and it had taken police most of the day to trace his room key to the hotel where he'd been staying. The radio station had hired him through an employment agency and didn't even know his name. They'd finally learned it just in time for the six o'clock news.

The papers, of course, carried nothing about the extortion plot. That would have been enough to get the story back on page one. Nick read them all and then tossed them aside. He had his own problem to consider. Stealing Santa's beard the following day would be next to impossible in Kliman's store, but the alternatives were equally impossible. He knew Vivian Delmos carried her costume to work in a large canvas bag, but he wasn't about to mug her on the way to work. Still . . .

Culhane had mentioned that the lady Santa Claus was an unemployed actress. Nick phoned Actors' Equity and had her address within minutes. Vivian Delmos resided on East Forty-ninth Street. He called her number and got the expected answering machine. Next he phoned Gloria to say that he wouldn't be home till late.

The address on Forty-ninth was past Third Avenue, in an apartment building across the street from the Turtle Bay block. The Delmos woman must have been successful at some stage of her career to afford the moderately high rents in the neighborhood. There was no answer to Nick's ring so he took up a position down the block on the other side of the street. Within twenty minutes he saw Vivian Delmos appear, walking briskly and carrying her canvas bag. He crossed the street to intercept her at her door, but she was a bit faster than he'd realized. She was halfway through the door by the time he reached it.

Blocking its closing with his hand, he began, "Miss Delmos—"

She turned, recognized him instantly, and acted without a word, yanking on his wrist and pulling him inside but off balance. He felt himself falling forward as she twisted his arm behind him. Then he was on the floor, his cheek pressed against the hall carpeting, while she pulled painfully on the arm. Her foot was on his neck.

"Mister, you just made your second big mistake. I hope you don't mind a broken arm."

"Wait a minute! I just want to talk!"

"How'd you find me? Did you follow me home?"

"Through Equity."

"Got a job for me?" She gave his arm a painful wrench. "I'm real good in action parts."

"I don't doubt it! Please let me up."

"Nice and slow," she warned, relaxing the pressure on his arm. "We're going upstairs while I call the police."

"All right."

She led him ahead of her up the stairs, keeping a grip on his arm. They paused outside a door at the top while she put down the canvas bag and got out her key. "Inside!"

The apartment was large but plainly furnished, as if in some sort of limbo while awaiting its permanent decor. "I'm not trying to kill you," Nick assured her. "When you saw me earlier I was only trying to steal your beard."

"My what?"

"The beard from your Santa Claus outfit."

She released his arm and gave him a shove toward the sofa. "What's your name?"

"Nick Velvet. I steal things." He decided to stay on the sofa for the moment. Facing her now, he had a chance to confirm his earlier impressions. She was into early middle age but still had a good figure. By the strength she'd shown in overpowering him, he guessed that she worked out regularly. It had been an unlucky day from the start.

"I'm Vivian Delmos, but I guess you know that. You called me by name." She walked to the phone without taking her eyes off him.

"I was hired to steal your beard," he told her. "You have nothing to fear from me."

"The people at Kliman's weren't too happy when you set off that smoke bomb."

"I only did it to escape. If I hadn't needed it I'd have returned later and removed it."

"What does all this have to do with the Santa strangler?"

"The killings are part of an extortion plot against the big department stores. My job was to keep you from being the next victim."

"By stealing my beard?" She gave a snort of disbelief. "Kliman's wanted to replace me with a cop but I wouldn't let them. I finally convinced everyone I could take care of myself, but they still made me carry that beeper. And this noon after you tried to attack me—"

"Steal your beard," Nick corrected.

"—steal my beard, they canceled Santa's appearances for the rest of the day. I lost a day's pay because of you!"

"Give me the beard and stay home tomorrow, too. I'll pay you a thousand dollars for it."

"Are you whacky or something?"

"Just a good businessman. I'm getting too old to be tossed around by a woman who works out at the gym every day."

"Three times a week," she corrected. "I'm an actress and I find it a good way to keep fit."

Nick worked his shoulder a bit, getting the kinks out. "It sure doesn't keep me fit. How about it? A thousand dollars?"

"They'll find another beard for me, or use the cop after all." She'd moved away from the phone at least, and Nick was thankful for that.

"It's the easiest money you'll ever make. Far easier than doing some off-Broadway play eight times a week."

"How'd you know I was off-Broadway?" she asked, immediately suspicious.

"I guessed. What difference does it make?"

"You didn't—" she began and then cut herself short. "Look, I'll agree to your condition if you do one thing for me."

"What's that?"

"I want you to go down to the men's dorm at the Outreach Center and pick up Russell Bajon's belongings."

"Bajon? The first victim?"

"That's right."

"Did you know him?"

"Slightly. We appeared in a play together."

Nick shook his head. "I don't understand any of this. What right do you have to his belongings?"

"As much right as anyone. The paper says he left no family."

"But why would you want his things?"

"Just to remember him by. He was a nice guy."

"Why can't you get them yourself?"

"I don't want people to see me there."

It was a weak reason, and her whole story was weak, but Nick was into it now. Unless he wanted to risk seriously injuring her, it seemed the only way to get the beard. "All right. I'll go down there now and then I'll be back for the beard."

Outside it had started to snow a little, but somehow it didn't seem much like the week before Christmas.

The Outreach Center was a sort of nondenominational mission located on the West Side near the river. Some of their operating expenses came from the city, but much of the money was from private donors. The Center gave homeless people a safe place to sleep if they were afraid of the city shelters, but certain rules applied. Drugs, alcohol, and weapons were forbidden, and guests of the Center were expected to earn their keep. In December that often meant dressing up in a Santa Claus suit and manning one of the Center's plywood chimneys with a donation bag inside.

The first person Nick saw as he entered the front door of the Outreach Center was a young man in sweater and jeans seated at an unpretentious card table. "I've come to pick up Russell Bajon's belongings," Nick told him. "The family sent me."

The young man seemed indifferent to the request. Apparently people who stayed at the men's dorm weren't expected to have anything worth stealing. "I'll get Chris."

Nick waited in the bare hallway until the young man returned with an older worker with thinning hair, wearing a faded Giants sweatshirt. "I'm Chris Stover. What can I do for you?"

"Russell Bajon's family sent me for his belongings."

The man frowned. "Didn't know he had a family. There sure wasn't much in the way of belongings. We were going to throw them out."

"Could I see them?"

Stover hesitated and then led him down the corridor to a storage room. For all its drabness, the dormitory building seemed to be well fitted for its clients, with a metal railing along the wall and smoke alarms in the ceiling. Nick stood by the door as Stover pulled out some boxes from one shelf in the storage room. "If I'd been five minutes earlier, Russ might be alive today," he said.

"I think I saw your name in the paper—"

"Sure! I placed him there and I was picking him up. When I rounded the corner I saw a crowd of people gathering. He was dead by the time I got to him."

"Nobody saw anything?"

"I guess not. Who pays attention in New York? I swear once I was driving by Radio City Music Hall about six in the morning, when they were having their Christmas show. Some guy was walking two camels around the block for their morning exercise and hardly anyone even noticed." He slit open the tape on one of the boxes and peered inside. "Nothing but clothing in here."

"I'll just take it along anyway."

When he opened the second box he frowned a bit. "Well, there are some letters in this one, and a couple of books." He looked up at Nick. "Maybe I should have some sort of authorization to release these."

"I can give you his sister's phone number." He'd worked that out with Vivian in advance. "You can check with her."

"Never heard about a sister," the man muttered. Then, "Our director is away today. I better wait till he gets back. Come back tomorrow."

"Sure thing." Nick turned to leave, his hand unobtrusively on the door's latchbolt. Stover shut the door and they walked back down the corridor together.

"See you later," the man told him and disappeared into a little office.

Immediately Nick turned and vaulted onto the handrail that ran along the wall, steadying himself with one hand against the ceiling. With his other hand he reached toward one of the smoke alarms. This model had a plastic button in the center of the unit for testing the battery, and he shoved a thin dime between the button and the casing, keeping it depressed. Immediately a loud blaring noise filled the hall. He jumped down to the floor as people began to look out of the rooms.

Some headed immediately for the exits while others stood around looking for some sign of smoke. Nick slipped into the storeroom just as Chris Stover emerged

from his office to join the others. There was little chance
of getting out with two boxes so Nick settled for the one
containing the letters and books. He peeked down the hall
and saw that Stover had gotten a ladder from somewhere
to examine the blaring alarm. Perhaps he had noticed the
edge of the dime holding the button in.

Nick went out the storeroom window as the smoke
alarm was suddenly silenced.

Vivian Delmos seemed just a bit surprised to see him
back so soon. "I thought you were going to get me Russell
Bajon's things."

"I did. They're in this box. There was another box with
a few pants and shirts, but I figured this was what you
wanted."

"I'll know soon enough."

· She opened the box and began looking through the ob-
jects, setting aside a worn pair of shoes and some socks
and handkerchiefs. When she came to the books she examined them more carefully. One was a paperback edition
of some of Shakespeare's tragedies, the others were a
small dictionary and a book on acting. But she soon
tossed these aside too, and turned only briefly to the letters, shaking the envelopes to make certain nothing small
was hidden in them.

"You got the wrong box," she grumbled.

"I'm sorry."

She seemed to relent then. "No, what I'm looking for
probably wasn't in the other box either. Somebody told
me Bajon was involved with a shoplifting ring, stealing
watches and jewelry from fancy stores during the Christmas season. I thought if he had anything in his belongings—"

"—that you'd take it?"

She flushed a bit at Nick's words. "I'm no thief. When
Russell and I were in the play together I loaned him a
few hundred dollars. I could use that money now. I figured
anything I found among his belongings would pay the
debt."

"Any jewelry or valuables he had were probably re-

moved by whoever went through his clothes." As he
spoke he was looking down at one of the envelopes that
had been in the box. It was addressed to Russell Bajon at
the Outreach Center. The return address bore only the surname of the sender: *Averly.*

It took him a few seconds to realize the significance of
the name. The Santa strangler's second victim had been
named Larry Averly. Nick slipped the letter out of the
envelope and read the few lines quickly: "Russ—I was
happy to do you the favor. No need to send me any more
money. Keep some of the pie for yourself. Merry Christmas! Larry." The note was undated, but the envelope had
been postmarked December second.

Nick returned the letter to its envelope and slipped it
into his pocket. It told him nothing, except that the two
victims might have known each other. Maybe Bajon had
replaced Averly as one of the Santas.

"Thanks for your efforts anyway," Vivian Delmos said.

"I did what I could."

When he didn't move, she asked, "Are you waiting for
something more?"

"Yes."

"What's that?"

"Your beard."

That evening Nick returned to Grady Culhane's little
office off Times Square. The young security man seemed
uneasy as soon as he walked in the door. "I was hoping
you wouldn't come here," he said.

Nick opened the paper bag he was carrying. "Why's
that? I've brought you the beard."

"The beard was yesterday. Things have moved beyond
that now. The cops are all over the place."

"What do you mean?"

"The extortion payoff. The money was left exactly as
instructed, on the upper deck of the ferry that left Staten
Island at three o'clock, before the evening rush hour. The
police had it covered from every angle, even if he'd
tossed the package overboard to a waiting boat."

"What happened?"

"Nothing. When the ferry docked in Manhattan some little old lady picked up the package and turned it in to lost and found."

"She got to it before the extortionist."

"Maybe," Culhane answered gloomily.

"What's the matter?"

"The Outreach Center reported that someone was snooping around the first victim's things this afternoon, and stole a box."

"That was me."

"I was afraid it might be. That means the cops are after you."

"How come?"

"They figure the killer was at the Outreach Center and that's why he couldn't pick up the extortion money from the three o'clock ferry."

"I certainly don't go around strangling Santas!" Nick objected. "You didn't even hire me till after the killings."

"I know, but try to tell them that! They need a fall guy, right away, or the city could lose millions in Christmas sales this final week. Who wants to bring the kids to see Santa Claus if he might be dead?"

A thought suddenly struck Nick. "You seemed nervous when I came in. Are they watching this office?"

"I had to tell them you were the one who set off the smoke bomb in the store yesterday. They were spending too much time on that angle and I tried to show them it was a dead end by admitting my part in it. Instead they got to thinking you were involved somehow."

"Just give me the rest of my money and I'm out of here."

"I don't have it right now."

Nick decided he'd overstayed his welcome. "I'll be in touch," he promised as he headed for the door.

They were waiting in the hall. A tall black man with a badge in one hand and a gun in the other barked, "Police! Up against the wall!"

His name was Sergeant Rynor and he was no more friendly within the confines of the precinct station. "You deny you were at the Outreach Center between three and four this afternoon, Mr. Velvet?"

"I told you I want a lawyer," Nick answered.

"He'll be here soon enough. And when he arrives we're going to run a lineup. Then we'll talk about the Santa Claus killings."

Ralph Aarons was a dapper Manhattan attorney whom Nick had used on rare occasions. He wasn't in the habit of getting in legal jams, especially in the New York area. Aarons made a good appearance, but he was hardly the sort to defend an accused serial Santa strangler.

"They've got a witness named Stover," the lawyer told him. "If he can place you at the Outreach Center, it may be trouble."

"We'll see," Nick said. He'd been thinking hard while he waited for Aarons to arrive.

Sergeant Rynor appeared in the doorway. "We're ready for you, Velvet. Up here on stage, please."

There were five other men, and Nick took the third position. The others were about his age and size but with different coloring and appearance. He guessed at least two of them were probably detectives. Chris Stover was brought in and escorted into a booth with a one-way glass. Over a loudspeaker, each of them was asked to step forward in turn. Then it was over. Apparently it had taken only a moment for Stover to identify him.

As Nick was being led away, Chris Stover and the other detectives came out of the booth. Nick paused ten feet from him and pointed dramatically. "That's the man!" his voice thundered like the wrath of God. "He's the one who killed the Santas and I can prove it!"

Nick couldn't prove it, and Chris Stover should have snorted and kept on walking. But he was taken off guard, startled into a foolish action. Perhaps in that unthinking instant he imagined the whole lineup had been merely a trick to unmask him. He gave one terrified glance at Nick and then tried to run, shoving two detectives out of the way in his dash for freedom.

It was Sergeant Rynor who finally grabbed him, before he even got close to the door.

* * *

"We're holding him," the black detective told Nick Velvet ten minutes later in the interrogation room, "but you'd better have a good story. Are you trying to tell us that Chris Stover is the extortionist who's been threatening the city's department stores for the past several days?"

"I don't think there was ever a real extortion plot. It was a matter of a big threat being used as a smokescreen to hide a smaller but no less deadly crime—the murders of Russell Bajon and Larry Averly."

"You'd better explain that."

Nick leaned back in the chair and collected his thoughts. "Grady Culhane told me about the extortion threats and even showed me a copy of the first letter. It was delivered to Kliman's president on Tuesday afternoon, shortly after the second strangling of a Santa Claus. Those two killings were meant to appear to be random acts against two random Santas, committed as a demonstration that the extortionist meant business. But the note mentioned the names of the two victims—Bajon and Averly. You didn't identify the second victim until later that day, and the killer had no chance to steal identification from his victim. The strangler knew the names of Bajon and Averly because these killings weren't random at all. He deliberately selected these victims, not as part of an extortion plot but for another motive altogether."

Rynor was making notes now, along with taping Nick's interrogation. Ralph Aarons, perhaps sensing things were going well for Nick, made no attempt to interrupt. "What other motive?" the detective asked.

"I learned earlier today that Bajon might have been involved in a shoplifting ring. And I also have a letter here that the second victim sent to Bajon two weeks ago. Not only did they know each other, but Averly had arranged for Bajon to take over some money-making enterprise from him. I think you'll find that Averly used to act as a Santa Claus for the Outreach Center. This year he passed the job on to Bajon, who became involved with the shop-lifting."

"You're telling me that a man dressed in a bulky and highly visible Santa Claus costume was shoplifting?"

"No, I'm telling you that Santa stood on the corner with his collection chimney and the shoplifters came out of the stores with watches, rings, and other jewelry, and dropped them in the chimney. If the man was caught, there was no evidence on him, and the store detectives never consid-ered Santa as an accessory."

"It's just wild enough to be true. But why would Stover kill them?"

"Bajon must have been skimming off the loot, or threat-ening to blackmail Stover. Once he decided to kill Bajon, he knew he had to kill Averly too, because the older man knew what was going on. When I guessed about Santa's chimney being used for shoplifting loot, Chris Stover became the most likely brains behind the operation. After all, he was the one who picked up the Santas and chimneys each night. He was the one who told them where to stand. Only Monday night he parked the van in the next block and walked up and strangled Bajon, then hurried back to the van and acted like he was just driving up."

"Maybe," Sergeant Rynor said thoughtfully. "It could have been like that. The extortion letter was just a red herring to cover the real motive. He never had any in-tention of going after that money on the Staten Island ferry."

"Can you prove all this?" Aarons asked, his legal mind in gear.

"We'll get a search warrant for Stover's office and room at the Center. If we find any shoplifted items there, I think he'll be ready to talk, and name the rest of the gang."

Nick knew he wasn't off the hook unless they found what they were looking for, but he came up lucky. The police uncovered dozens of jewelry items, along with a spool of wire that matched the wire used to kill the two Santas. After that, Chris Stover ceased his denials.

The way things turned out, Nick never did collect the balance of his fee from Grady Culhane. Some people just didn't have any Christmas spirit.

BELIEVING IN SANTA
by Ron Goulart

As it turned out, he didn't get a chance to murder anybody. He did make an impressive comeback, revitalizing his faltering career and saying goodbye to most of his financial worries. But in spite of all that, there are times when Oscar Sayler feels sad about not having been able to knock off his former wife.

Twenty-five years ago Oscar had been loved by millions of children. Well, actually, they adored his dummy, Screwy Santa, but they tolerated Oscar. For several seasons his early morning kid show was the most popular in the country, outpulling Captain Kangaroo and all the other competition. Multitudes of kids, and their parents, doted on Oscar's comic version of Santa Claus and tried to live by the show's perennial closing line—"Gang, try to act like it was Christmas every day!"

For the past decade and more, though, Oscar hadn't been doing all that well. In early December of last year, when he got the fateful phone call from the New York talent agency, he was scraping by on the $25,000 a year he earned from the one commercial voice job he'd been able to come up with lately. Oscar lived alone in a one-bedroom condo in a never-finished complex in New Beckford, Connecticut. He was fifty-five—well, fifty-seven actually—and he didn't look all that awful.

Since he'd given up drinking, his face was no longer especially puffy and it had lost that lobsterish tinge. His hair, which was nearly all his own, still had a nice luster to it. There was, really, no reason why he couldn't appear on television again.

When the agent called him at a few minutes after four

P.M. on a bleak, chill Monday afternoon, Oscar was flat on his back in his small tan living room. He'd vowed to complete two dozen situps every day.

He crawled over to the phone on the coffee table. "Hello?"

"Is your son there?"

Oscar pulled himself up onto the sofa arm, resting the phone on his knees. "Don't have a son. My daughter, however, is the noted television actress Tish Sale, who stars in the *Intensive Care* soap opera, and hasn't set foot across dear old Dad's threshold for three, possibly four—"

"Spare me," requested the youthful, nasal voice. "You must be Oscar Sayler then. You sounded so old that I mistook you for your father."

"Nope, my dad sounded like this—'How about a little nip after dinner, my boy?' Much more throaty and with a quaver. Who the hell are you, by the way?"

"Vince Mxyzptlk. I'm with Mimi Warnicker & Associates, the crackerjack talent agency."

"Oops." Oscar sat on a cushion and straightened up. "That's a powerful outfit."

"You bet your ass it is," agreed the young agent. "You're not represented at the moment, are you?"

"No, because I find I can get all the acting jobs I want without—"

"C'mon, Oscar, old buddy, you ain't exactly rolling in work right now," cut in Vince disdainfully. "In fact, your only gig is doing the voice of the infected toe in those godawful Dr. Frankel's Foot Balm radio spots." He made a scornful noise.

"I do a very convincing itching toe, Vince. Fact is, there's talk of—"

"Listen, I can get you tons of work. Talk shows, commercials, lectures, TV parts, eventually some plum movie work. But first you—"

"How exactly are—"

"But first you have got to win your way back into the hearts and minds of the public."

"Just how do I accomplish that, Vince?"

"You just have to sit there with that lamebrained dummy on your knee."

"Screwy Santa? Hell, nobody's been interested in him for years."

"Let me do the talking for a bit, okay? Here's what's under way," continued the agent. *"Have a Good Day, USA!,* which has just become the top morning talk and news show, is planning a six-minute nostalgia segment for this Friday. The theme is 'Whatever happened to our favorite kids' shows?' Something they calculate'll have a tremendous appeal for the Boomers and Busters who make up their pea-brained audience. So far they've signed that old duffer who used to be Captain Buckeroo and—"

"Kangaroo."

"Oscar, are you more interested in heckling me than in making an impressive comeback? Would you prefer to go on living in squalor in that rural crackerbox, to voice tripe for Dr. Frankel throughout the few remaining years of your shabby life?"

"Okay, but his name is Captain Kangaroo, not—"

"Attend to me, Oscar. I assured Liz, who's putting this segment together, that I'd dig you up, wipe off the cobwebs, and have you there bright and early Friday. Can you drag yourself into Manhattan and meet me at the Consolidated Broadcasting headquarters building on Fifty-third no later than six A.M.?"

"Sure, that's no problem."

"Most importantly, can you bring that dimwitted dummy?"

Without more than a fraction of a second of hesitation Oscar answered, "Of course, yeah, absolutely." It didn't seem the right time to tell Mxyzptlk that his former wife, who currently loathed him and had ousted him eleven long years ago from the mansion they once shared, had retained custody of the only existing Screwy Santa dummy in the world. "We'll both see you on Friday, Vince."

It commenced snowing at dusk, a paltry, low-budget snow that didn't look as though it was up to blanketing the condo-complex grounds and masking its raw ugliness.

Glancing at his wristwatch once more, Oscar punched out his daughter's New York City number.

After four rings there came a twanging noise. "Merry Christmas," said Tish in her sexiest voice. "I'm not able to come to the phone right now, but if you'll leave your name and number, I'll get back to you real soon."

Oscar had been working all afternoon on the voice he was going to use. A mixture of paternal warmth and serious illness. "Patricia, my dear," he began, getting the quaver just about perfect, "this is your dad. Something quite serious has come up and I'd like very much to speak to you, my only child, in the hope that—"

"Holy Jesus," observed his daughter, coming onto the line. "What was that old television show you used to tell me about when I was little? Where they gave the contestants the gong for a rotten perf—"

"*The Amateur Hour.* Now, kid, I need—"

"Consider yourself gonged, Pop."

"Okay, all right, I overdid it a mite," he admitted. "Yet I do have a serious problem."

"My time is sort of limited, Dad. I'm getting ready for a date. You should've phoned me earlier."

"I assumed you were taping *Intensive Care.*"

She sighed. "Didn't you tell me you watched my soap faithfully?"

"I do, kid. It's on my must-see list every day."

"I've been in a coma for two weeks. So I don't have to show up at—"

"Sorry to hear that. Anything serious?"

"Near-fatal car crash. We killed that asshole, Walt Truett, thank God."

"But you'll survive?"

"Sure, with only a touch of amnesia."

Oscar asked, "When are you due to come out of your stupor?"

"Next Thursday."

"I'll start watching, I swear," he promised his daughter. "Now, as to the purpose of this call."

"It's Mom, isn't it?"

"Well, not exactly, kid." He filled her in about the offer

from the talent agency and the upcoming appearance on
Have a Good Day, USA! "This will revive my career."

"You think so? A couple of early morning minutes with
a pack of over-the-hill doofers?"

"It's a shot. The only snag is—well, kid, they insist that
I bring Screwy along."

"Obviously. You guys are a team."

"And your dear mother has custody of him."

Tish said, "She's not going to loan him to you."

"She might, if you were to—"

"Nope, she won't. A few months ago, when I noticed
him up on a shelf in the mud room, I suggested that—"

"She keeps the most beloved dummy in America in the
mud room?"

"In a shoe box," she answered. "And, Dad, Screwy
Santa hasn't been beloved for a couple of decades now."

"I know, neither have I," he said ruefully. "But, damn
it, he helped pay for that mansion."

"Her romantic novels are paying for things now. Did
you notice that *Kiss Me, My Pirate* was number two on
the *Times*—"

"I extract the book section from the Sunday paper with
surgical gloves and toss it immediately into the trash un-
opened. To make certain I never see so much as a mention
of that slop she cranks out or, worse, a publicity photo of
her mottled countenance."

"Let's get back to the point. I suggested to her back
then that she return Screwy Santa to you."

"And?"

"You don't want to hear what she said," his daughter
assured him. "It had, among other things, to do with Hell
freezing over. But can't you dig up another dummy by
Friday?"

"Impossible, that's the only one extant. We lost the
backup copy during that ill-fated nostalgia tour through
the Midwest years ago."

"Couldn't you carve another, since you built the others?"

"Kid, I may've fudged the truth a bit when I used to re-
count Screwy's history to you," he said. "In reality, the

dummies were built by a prop man at the old WWAG-TV studios. And he, alas, is long in his grave."

"This is very disillusioning," Tish complained. "One of the few things I still admired about you, Dad, was your woodcarving ability."

"Listen, couldn't you call Mitzi and tell her that I'm expiring, that I want to be reunited with my dummy for one last time before I go on to glory?"

"She'd burst out laughing if I told her you were about to kick off, Dad. And probably dance a little jig."

"Okay, suppose we make a business deal with her? Offer the old shrew, say, fifteen percent of the take."

"What take? *Have a Good Day, USA!* pays scale. I know, I did one last year to plug my abortion on *Intensive Care.*"

"You looked terrific on that broadcast."

"You didn't even see it."

"Didn't I?"

"No, and you admitted as much at the time."

"Well, back to my immediate problem."

"Why don't you use one of the old Screwy Santa dolls? They look a lot like the dummy."

"Except they don't have movable mouths."

"It'd be better than nothing. I can loan you mine," she offered. "It's stuffed away in a closet."

"No, kid, I really have to have the real dummy."

"Afraid there's nothing I can do. I mean, if I so much as mention that you need Screwy Santa, Mom's liable to take an axe to him."

"Well, thanks anyway for listening to an old man's woes and—"

"Here comes the gong again," his daughter said. "Anyhow, I have to go put on some clothes. Bye."

After hanging up, he stayed on the sofa and brooded. After about ten minutes he said aloud, "I'll have to outwit Mitzi."

The snow improved the next morning, giving a Christmas-card gloss to the usually dismal view from his small living room window.

At ten A.M. he put the first phase of his latest plan into operation. He phoned his former wife's mansion over in Westport.

"Residence of Mitzi Sunsett Sayler," answered a crisp female voice.

"Yes, how are you?" inquired Oscar in a drawling, slightly British accent. "Ogden Brokenshire here."

"Yes?"

"Ogden Brokenshire of the Broadcasting Hall of Fame. Have I the honor of addressing the esteemed novelist Mitzi Sunsett Sayler herself?"

"Of course not, Mr. Brokenshire. I'm Clarissa Dempster, Mrs. Sayler's secretary."

"I see, my dear. Well, perhaps I can explain my mission to you, child, and you can explain the situation to your employer."

"That depends on—"

"We would like to enshrine Screwy Santa."

"Enshrine whom?"

"The ingenious dummy that Mrs. Sayler's one-time husband used in the days when he brought joy and gladness to the hearts of—"

"Oh, that thing," said the secretary. "My parents, wisely, never allowed me to watch that dreadful show when I was a child."

"Nonetheless, dear child, our board has voted, unanimously I might add, to place Screwy Santa on permanent display in the museum."

"Hold on a moment. I'll speak to Mrs. Sayler." The secretary went away.

In less than two minutes Mitzi started talking. "Who is this?"

"Good morning, I'm Ogden Brokenshire. As I was explaining to your able secretary, my dear Mrs. Sayler, I'm an executive with the Broadcasting Hall of—"

"You haven't improved at all, you no-talent cheesehead."

"I beg your pardon, madam?"

"Oscar, love, you never could do a believable Brit."

"I don't happen to be British, dear lady. The fact that I

was educated in Boston sometimes gives people that impression."

"Forget it, Oscar," advised his erstwhile wife. "I don't know why you want to get your clammy hands on that wooden dornick, but you'll never have him. And, dear heart, if you ever try to communicate with me again—in whatever wretched voice—I'll sic the law on you." She, rather gently, hung up on him.

"Looks like," decided Oscar, "I'm going to need a new plan."

He kept working on plans for nearly an hour, pacing his small living room, muttering, pausing now and then to gaze out at the falling snow.

Then the phone rang.

"Yeah?"

"We have hit a slight snag," announced Vince Mxyzptlk.

"Don't they want me?"

"Sure they want you, old buddy. Hell, they're prowling the lofty corridors at Consolidated crying out for you," said the youthful agent. "In fact, they can't wait until Friday."

"What do you mean—do they want me to do a separate segment on my own?"

"Not exactly. But Liz, *and* her boss, are very anxious to see you tomorrow."

Frowning, Oscar nodded. "An audition, huh?"

"Sort of, yeah," admitted the agent. "It has nothing, really, to do with you. But when one of their scouts unearthed the clunk who used to be Mr. Slimjim on that *Mr. Slimjim & Baby Gumdrop* turkey, he turned out to weigh three hundred pounds now and possess not a single tooth. So, as you can understand, Oscar, they want to see and hear all these wonderful stars of yesteryear in advance."

"Tomorrow?"

"At three P.M. Is that a problem for you?"

"Not exactly, but I—"

"I'm getting a lot of interest in you. Once you do well on Friday, the jobs will start rolling in."

"I understand, it's only—"

"I needn't remind you, Oscar, that a lot of talents in your present position would kill for this opportunity."

"You're absolutely right," he agreed. "See you tomorrow."

He had a great new plan worked out by three that afternoon. But he had to wait until after dark to get going on it.

Dressed in dark clothes, Oscar slipped quietly out of his apartment and into the lean-to that passed for a garage. As usual, none of the roads in the sparsely inhabited complex had been plowed. The snow was soft, though, and not too high, and Oscar was able to drive down to the plowed lanes and byways of New Beckford without any serious delays.

He drove over to nearby Westport and parked in the lot behind Borneo's. There were only a few spaces left and he could see that the restaurant-bar was packed with people. The food and drink at Borneo's was just passable, but it sat only a half mile over the hill from Mitzi's mansion.

As he was crossing the lot a fire engine went hooting by, headed downhill.

Borneo himself was behind the bar. "Evening, Oscar."

He managed to elbow his way up to a narrow spot at the ebony bar. "The usual."

Borneo scratched at his stomach through the fabric of his bright tropical shirt. "Refresh my memory."

"Club soda, alas."

"Coming up."

Outside in the snowy night another fire engine went roaring by, followed by what sounded like a couple of police cars.

Oscar hoped all this activity wouldn't foul up his plan. So far everything was going well. People were seeing him, he was establishing an alibi. In another ten or fifteen minutes he'd go back to the john. Then he'd slip out the side door.

Once in the open, he'd make his way down to the

mansion. Being careful, of course, that no one noticed him sneaking off.

Mitzi, being a skinflint, and in spite of her great wealth, had never bothered to put in a new alarm system. The original setup was still in place, and he knew how to disarm that.

Okay, once he got inside, after making certain that she was alone, he'd . . . well, he'd use the length of pipe he dug up in the garage this afternoon.

Once Mitzi was dead and done for, he'd gather up enough jewels and valuables to make it look like the usual burglary. Then he'd rescue Screwy Santa from the mud room and get the hell away.

Back here at the parking lot he'd stash the loot in his car, slip unobtrusively back into the place, and tell Borneo he'd had a sudden touch of stomach flu and had to stay back in the bathroom a few minutes.

It wasn't exactly foolproof, but it ought to work. He'd own Screwy again and Mitzi would be gone from his life.

He chuckled at the thought. Yeah, the idea of killing her off had come to him this afternoon and he'd taken to it immediately.

Tish might be a little suspicious about how he came by the dummy. He'd tell her something along the lines that he'd found the heirs of the old defunct prop man at the last minute and, gosh, they had a spare Screwy Santa. He'd always been a gifted liar and conning his daughter wouldn't be all that difficult.

"Don't worry about that now," he told himself.

"How's that?" inquired Borneo, setting a glass of sparkling water down in front of him.

"Nothing, I was just—"

"That must be some fire." Borneo paused to listen as yet another truck went howling by out in the night.

Oscar sipped the club soda, drumming the fingers of his free hand on the dark bar top. He'd make his move in about five minutes.

The phone behind the bar rang and Borneo caught it up. "Borneo's. Huh? Channel eight? Okay." Hanging up, he switched channels on the large television set mounted above the mirror.

And there was Mitzi, glowering out of the screen. Wearing a fuzzy bathrobe and not enough makeup, she was being interviewed by a slim black newswoman and gesturing at the mansion that was blazing behind her up across the wide night lawn.

"Good God," muttered Oscar.

"That's just downhill from us," observed Borneo.

"Yeah, I know."

The entire sprawling house was going up in flames.

"What exactly happened, Mrs. Sayler?" the reporter asked her.

"It was that goddamn cheesehead."

"Which cheesehead would that be?"

"Screwy Santa, that abominable dummy."

"I'm not certain that I quite under—"

"Aw, you're too damn young. Everybody is these days. I always knew that dornick would do me in eventually."

"You mean this was arson?"

"I mean, dear heart, that I decided to cremate that loathsome lump of wood. I took him and his shoebox, carried them into the living room, and tossed him into the fireplace."

Oscar pressed both hands to his chest. "There goes my comeback."

Mitzi continued, "Then . . . I don't know. His stupid beard seemed to explode . . . flames came shooting out of the fireplace. They hit the drapes and those caught fire . . . then the damn furniture started to go." She shook her head angrily. "Now the whole shebang is ablaze." Looking directly into the camera, she added, "If you're out there watching, Oscar . . ." She gave him the finger.

Borneo raised his shaggy eyebrows high. "Hey, is she talking to you, Oscar?"

"I'm not in the mood for conversation just now." Abandoning his club soda, he walked out into the night.

His daughter phoned a few minutes shy of midnight. "I didn't want you to worry."

"I'm way beyond worry, kid."

"When I caught the report about Mom's mansion on the news, I figured you'd assume that Screwy Santa was gone."

"Certainly I assumed that. There was Mitzi, fatter than ever, hollering for all the world to hear that my poor hapless creation was the cause of the whole blinking conflagration."

"It was a ringer, Dad."

"Eh?"

"I dropped by to visit Mom this afternoon and when she went away to yell at Clarissa, I substituted my old Screwy Santa doll for your dummy," explained Tish. "In a way, I may be responsible for that dreadful fire. The doll's a lot more flammable than—"

"No, there was some parent flap at the time, but we proved beyond a doubt that the dolls were perfectly safe if—"

"I have your dummy here in my apartment."

"You've really got Screwy?"

"Yes, he's sitting on my bed right this minute," she assured her father. "It's lucky I went out there when I did and saved him before Mom got going on her plan to destroy the little guy. Why did you go and telephone her and make it crystal clear that you were in desperate need of him? That was dippy, since it inspired her to destroy him."

"I didn't call her as myself. But somehow she penetrated my—"

"That's because, trust me, you do a terrible British voice. When do you need him?"

"Tomorrow."

"I thought you weren't doing the show until Friday."

"Well, and keep this to yourself, kid, there's a possibility they'll devote a separate seg all to me."

"That would be great."

"So can I pick him up tomorrow?"

"Sure, come by around one and I'll take you to lunch."

"Can't make lunch, because I have some people to see while I'm in the Apple. But I'll pop in, give you a paternal hug, and grab Screwy Santa," he said. "Thanks. You're a perfect daughter."

"Perfect for you, I guess. Bye."

Everything worked out well for Oscar. He did, in fact, do a segment of his own, which ran nearly four minutes, on *Have a Good Day, USA!*. And Vince Mxyzptlk was able to get him an impressive batch of other jobs. At the moment there's also the possibility of a new kid show for Oscar and Screwy Santa on cable.

Oscar was able to leave his forlorn condo for a three-bedroom colonial in Brimstone, Connecticut last month.

While he was packing, he came across the length of pipe he'd intended to use on Mitzi. He slapped it across the palm of his hand a few times, and, sighing, tossed it into a carton.

THE CASE IS ALTERED
by Margery Allingham

Mr. Albert Campion, sitting in a first-class smoking compartment, was just reflecting sadly that an atmosphere of stultifying decency could make even Christmas something of a stuffed-owl occasion, when a new hogskin suitcase of distinctive design hit him on the knees. At the same moment a golf bag bruised the shins of the shy young man opposite, an armful of assorted magazines burst over the pretty girl in the far corner, and a blast of icy air swept round the carriage. There was the familiar rattle and lurch which indicates that the train has started at last, a squawk from a receding porter, and Lance Feering arrived before him apparently by rocket.

"Caught it," said the newcomer with the air of one confidently expecting congratulations, but as the train bumped jerkily he teetered back on his heels and collapsed between the two young people on the opposite seat.

"My dear chap, so we noticed," murmured Campion, and he smiled apologetically at the girl, now disentangling herself from the shellburst of newsprint. It was his own disarming my-poor-friend-is-afflicted variety of smile that he privately considered infallible, but on this occasion it let him down.

The girl, who was in the early twenties and was slim and fair, with eyes like licked brandy-balls, as Lance Feering inelegantly put it afterward, regarded him with grave interest. She stacked the magazines into a neat bundle and placed them on the seat opposite before returning to her own book. Even Mr. Feering, who was in one of his more exuberant moods, was aware of that chilly protest. He began to apologize.

Campion had known Feering in his student days, long before he had become one of the foremost designers of stage decors in Europe, and was used to him, but now even he was impressed. Lance's apologies were easy but also abject. He collected his bag, stowed it on a clear space on the rack above the shy young man's head, thrust his golf things under the seat, positively blushed when he claimed his magazines, and regarded the girl with pathetic humility. She glanced at him when he spoke, nodded coolly with just enough graciousness not to be gauche, and turned over a page.

Campion was secretly amused. At the top of his form Lance was reputed to be irresistible. His dark face with the long mournful nose and bright eyes were unhandsome enough to be interesting, and the quick gestures of his short painter's hands made his conversation picturesque. His singular lack of success on this occasion clearly astonished him and he sat back in his corner eyeing the young woman with covert mistrust.

Campion resettled himself to the two hours' rigid silence which etiquette demands from firstclass travelers who, although they are more than probably going to be asked to dance a reel together if not to share a bathroom only a few hours hence, have not yet been introduced.

There was no way of telling if the shy young man and the girl with the brandy-ball eyes knew each other, and whether they too were en route for Underhill, Sir Philip Cookham's Norfolk place. Campion was inclined to regard the coming festivities with a certain amount of lugubrious curiosity. Cookham himself was a magnificent old boy, of course, "one of the more valuable pieces in the Cabinet," as someone had once said of him, but Florence was a different kettle of fish. Born to wealth and breeding, she had grown blasé towards both of them and now took her delight in notabilities, a dangerous affectation in Campion's experience. She was some sort of remote aunt of his.

He glanced again at the young people, caught the boy unaware, and was immediately interested.

The illustrated magazine had dropped from the young

man's hand and he was looking out of the window, his
mouth drawn down at the corners and a narrow frown
between his thick eyebrows. It was not an unattractive
face, too young for strong character but decent and open
enough in the ordinary way. At that particular moment,
however, it wore a revealing expression. There was reck-
lessness in the twist of the mouth and sullenness in the
eyes, while the hand which lay upon the inside arm rest
was clenched.

Campion was curious. Young people do not usually go
away for Christmas in this top-step-at-the-dentist's frame
of mind. The girl looked up from her book.

"How far is Underhill from the station?" she inquired.

"Five miles. They'll meet us." The shy young man
turned to her so easily and with such obvious affection
that any romantic theory Campion might have formed was
knocked on the head instantly. The youngster's troubles
evidently had nothing to do with love.

Lance had raised his head with bright-eyed interest at
the gratuitous information and now a faintly sardonic expression appeared upon his lips. Campion sighed for him.
For a man who fell in and out of love with the abandon-
ment of a seal round a pool, Lance Feering was an impossible optimist. Already he was regarding the girl with that
shy despair which so many ladies had found too piteous to
be allowed to persist. Campion washed his hands of him
and turned away just in time to notice a stranger glancing
in at them from the corridor. It was a dark and arrogant
young face and he recognized it instantly, feeling at the
same time a deep wave of sympathy for old Cookham.
Florence, he gathered, had done it again.

Young Victor Preen, son of old Preen of the Preen Aero
Company, was certainly notable, not to say notorious. He
had obtained much publicity in his short life for his sensa-
tional flights, but a great deal more for adventures less
creditable; and when angry old gentlemen in the arm-
chairs of exclusive clubs let themselves go about the
blackguardliness of the younger generation, it was very
often of Victor Preen that they were thinking.

He stood now a little to the left of the compartment

window, leaning idly against the wall, his chin up and his heavy lids drooping. At first sight he did not appear to be taking any interest in the occupants of the compartment, but when the shy young man looked up, Campion happened to see the swift glance of recognition, and of something else, which passed between them. Presently, still with the same elaborate casualness, the man in the corridor wandered away, leaving the other staring in front of him, the same sullen expression still in his eyes.

The incident passed so quickly that it was impossible to define the exact nature of that second glance, but Campion was never a man to go imagining things, which was why he was surprised when they arrived at Minstree station to hear Henry Boule, Florence's private secretary, introducing the two and to notice that they met as strangers.

It was pouring with rain as they came out of the station, and Boule, who, like all Florence's secretaries, appeared to be suffering from an advanced case of nerves, bundled them all into two big Daimlers, a smaller car, and a shooting-brake. Campion looked round him at Florence's Christmas bag with some dismay. She had surpassed herself. Besides Lance there were at least half a dozen celebrities: a brace of political highlights, an angry looking lady novelist, Madja from the ballet, a startled R. A., and Victor Preen, as well as some twelve or thirteen unfamiliar faces who looked as if they might belong to Art, Money, or even mere Relations.

Campion became separated from Lance and was looking for him anxiously when he saw him at last in one of the cars, with the novelist on one side and the girl with brandy-ball eyes on the other, Victor Preen making up the ill-assorted four.

Since Campion was an unassuming sort of person he was relegated to the brake with Boule himself, the shy young man, and the whole of the luggage. Boule introduced them awkwardly and collapsed into a seat, wiping the beads from off his forehead with a relief which was a little too blatant to be tactful.

Campion, who had learned that the shy young man's name was Peter Groome, made a tentative inquiry of him as they sat jolting shoulder to shoulder in the back of the car. He nodded.

"Yes, it's the same family," he said. "Cookham's sister married a brother of my father's. I'm some sort of relation, I suppose."

The prospect did not seem to fill him with any great enthusiasm and once again Campion's curiosity was piqued. Young Mr. Groome was certainly not in seasonable mood.

In the ordinary way Campion would have dismissed the matter from his mind, but there was something about the youngster which attracted him, something indefinable and of a despairing quality, and moreover, there had been that curious intercepted glance in the train.

They talked in a desultory fashion throughout the uncomfortable journey. Campion learned that young Groome was in his father's firm of solicitors, that he was engaged to be married to the girl with the brandy-ball eyes, who was a Miss Patricia Bullard of an old north country family, and that he thought Christmas was a waste of time.

"I hate it," he said with a sudden passionate intensity which startled even his mild inquisitor. "All this sentimental good-will-to-all-men business is false and sickening. There's no such thing as good will. The world's rotten."

He blushed as soon as he had spoken and turned away.

"I'm sorry," he murmured, "but all this bogus Dickensian stuff makes me writhe."

Campion made no direct comment. Instead he asked with affable inconsequence, "Was that young Victor Preen I saw in the other car?"

Peter Groome turned his head and regarded him with the steady stare of the willfully obtuse.

"I was introduced to someone with a name like that, I think," he said carefully. "He was a little baldish man, wasn't he?"

"No, that's Sir George." The secretary leaned over the luggage to give the information. "Preen is the tall young man, rather handsome, with the very curling hair. He's *the* Preen, you know." He sighed. "It seems very young to be a millionaire, doesn't it?"

"Obscenely so," said Mr. Peter Groome abruptly, and returned to his despairing contemplation of the landscape.

Underhill was *en fête* to receive them. As soon as Campion observed the preparations, his sympathy for young Mr. Groome increased, for to a jaundiced eye Lady Florence's display might well have proved as dispiriting as Preen's bank balance. Florence had "gone all Dickens," as she said herself at the top of her voice, linking her arm through Campion's, clutching the R. A. with her free hand, and capturing Lance with a bright birdlike eye.

The great Jacobean house was festooned with holly. An eighteen-foot tree stood in the great hall. Yule logs blazed on iron dogs in the wide hearths and already the atmosphere was thick with that curious Christmas smell which is part cigar smoke and part roasting food.

Sir Philip Cookham stood receiving his guests with pathetic bewilderment. Every now and again his features broke into a smile of genuine welcome as he saw a face he knew. He was a distinguished-looking old man with a fine head and eyes permanently worried by his country's troubles.

"My dear boy, delighted to see you. Delighted," he said, grasping Campion's hand. "I'm afraid you've been put over in the Dower House. Did Florence tell you? She said you wouldn't mind, but I insisted that Feering went over there with you and also young Peter." He sighed and brushed away the visitor's hasty reassurances. "I don't know why the dear girl never feels she has a party unless the house is so overcrowded that our best friends have to sleep in the annex," he said sadly.

The "dear girl," looking not more than fifty-five of her sixty years, was clinging to the arm of the lady novelist at that particular moment and the two women were emitting mirthless parrot cries at each other. Cookham smiled.

"She's happy, you know," he said indulgently. "She enjoys this sort of thing. Unfortunately I have a certain amount of urgent work to do this weekend, but we'll get in a chat, Campion, some time over the holiday. I want to hear your news. You're a lucky fellow. You can tell your adventures."

The lean man grimaced. "More secret sessions, sir?" he inquired.

The cabinet minister threw up his hands in a comic but expressive little gesture before he turned to greet the next guest.

As he dressed for dinner in his comfortable room in the small Georgian dower house across the park, Campion was inclined to congratulate himself on his quarters. Underhill itself was a little too much of the ancient monument for strict comfort.

He had reached the tie stage when Lance appeared. He came in very elegant indeed and highly pleased with himself. Campion diagnosed the symptoms immediately and remained irritatingly incurious.

Lance sat down before the open fire and stretched his sleek legs.

"It's not even as if I were a goodlooking blighter, you know," he observed invitingly when the silence had become irksome to him. "In fact, Campion, when I consider myself I simply can't understand it. Did I so much as speak to the girl?"

"I don't know," said Campion, concentrating on his dressing. "Did you?"

"No." Lance was passionate in his denial. "Not a word. The hard-faced female with the inky fingers and the walrus mustache was telling me her life story all the way home in the car. This dear little poppet with the eyes was nothing more than a warm bundle at my side. I give you my dying oath on that. And yet—well, it's extraordinary, isn't it?"

Campion did not turn round. He could see the artist quite well through the mirror in front of him. Lance had a sheet of notepaper in his hand and was regarding it with that mixture of feigned amusement and secret delight which was typical of his eternally youthful spirit.

"Extraordinary," he repeated, glancing at Campion's

unresponsive back. "She had nice eyes. Like licked brandy-balls."

"Exactly," agreed the lean man by the dressing table. "I thought she seemed very taken up with her fiancé, young Master Groome, though," he added tactlessly.

"Well, I noticed that, you know," Lance admitted, forgetting his professions of disinterest. "She hardly recognized my existence in the train. Still, there's absolutely no accounting for women. I've studied 'em all my life and never understood 'em yet. I mean to say, take this case in point. That kid ignored me, avoided me, looked through me. And yet look at this. I found it in my room when I came up to change just now."

Campion took the note with a certain amount of distaste. Lovely women were invariably stooping to folly, it seemed, but even so he could not accustom himself to the spectacle. The message was very brief. He read it at a glance and for the first time that day he was conscious of that old familiar flicker down the spine as his experienced nose smelled trouble. He re-read the three lines.

> "There is a sundial on a stone pavement just off the drive. We saw it from the car. I'll wait ten minutes there for you half an hour after the party breaks up tonight."

There was neither signature nor initial, and the summons broke off as baldly as it had begun.

"Amazing, isn't it?" Lance had the grace to look shamefaced.

"Astounding." Campion's tone was flat. "Staggering, old boy. Er—fishy."

"Fishy?"

"Yes, don't you think so?" Campion was turning over the single sheet thoughtfully and there was no amusement in the pale eyes behind his horn-rimmed spectacles. "How did it arrive?"

"In an unaddressed envelope. I don't suppose she caught my name. After all, there must be some people who don't know it yet." Lance was grinning impudently.

"She's batty, of course. Not safe out and all the rest of it. But I liked her eyes and she's very young."

Campion perched himself on the edge of the table. He was still very serious.

"It's disturbing, isn't it?" he said. "Not nice. Makes one wonder."

"Oh, I don't know." Lance retrieved his property and tucked it into his pocket. "She's young and foolish, and it's Christmas."

Campion did not appear to have heard him. "I wonder," he said. "I should keep the appointment, I think. It may be unwise to interfere, but yes, I rather think I should."

"You're telling me." Lance was laughing. "I may be wrong, of course," he added defensively, "but I think that's a cry for help. The poor girl evidently saw that I looked a dependable sort of chap and—er—having her back against the wall for some reason or other she turned instinctively to the stranger with the kind face. Isn't that how you read it?"

"Since you press me, no. Not exactly," said Campion, and as they walked over to the house together he remained thoughtful and irritatingly uncommunicative.

Florence Cookham excelled herself that evening. Her guests were exhorted "to be young again," with the inevitable result that Underhill contained a company of irritated and exhausted people long before midnight.

One of her ladyship's more erroneous beliefs was that she was a born organizer, and that the real secret of entertaining people lay in giving everyone something to do. Thus Lance and the R. A.—now even more startled-looking than ever—found themselves superintending the decoration of the great tree, while the girl with the brandy-ball eyes conducted a small informal dance in the drawing room, the lady novelist scowled over the bridge table, and the ballet star refused flatly to arrange amateur theatricals.

Only two people remained exempt from this tyranny. One was Sir Philip himself, who looked in every now and again, ready to plead urgent work awaiting him in his study whenever his wife pounced upon him, and the other was Mr. Campion, who had work to do on his own account and had long mastered the difficult art of self-effacement. Experience had taught him that half the secret of this maneuver was to keep discreetly on the move and he strolled from one part to another, always ready to look as if he belonged to any one of them should his hostess's eye ever come to rest upon him inquiringly.

For once his task was comparatively simple. Florence was in her element as she rushed about surrounded by breathless assistants, and at one period the very air in her vicinity seemed to have become thick with colored paper wrappings, yards of red ribbons, and a colored snowstorm of little address tickets as she directed the packing of the presents for the Tenants' Tree, a second monster which stood in the ornamental barn beyond the kitchens.

Campion left Lance to his fate, which promised to be six or seven hours' hard labor at the most moderate estimate, and continued his purposeful meandering. His lean figure drifted among the company with an apparent aimlessness which was deceptive. There was hidden urgency in his lazy movements and his pale eyes behind his spectacles were inquiring and unhappy.

He found Patricia Bullard dancing with Preen, and paused to watch them as they swung gracefully by him. The man was in a somewhat flamboyant mood, flashing his smile and his noisy witticisms about him after the fashion of his kind, but the girl was not so content. As Campion caught sight of her pale face over her partner's sleek shoulder his eyebrows rose. For an instant he almost believed in Lance's unlikely suggestion. The girl actually did look as though she had her back to the wall. She was watching the doorway nervously and her shiny eyes were afraid.

Campion looked about him for the other young man who should have been present, but Peter Groome was not in the ballroom, nor in the great hall, nor yet among the bridge tables in the drawing room, and half an hour later he had still not put in an appearance.

Campion was in the hall himself when he saw Patricia

slip into the anteroom which led to Sir Philip's private
study, that holy of holies which even Florence treated
with a wholesome awe. Campion had paused for a moment to enjoy the spectacle of Lance, wild eyed and tight
lipped, wrestling with the last of the blue glass balls and
tinsel streamers on the Guests' Tree, when he caught sight
of the flare of her silver skirt disappearing round a familiar doorway under one branch of the huge double staircase.

It was what he had been waiting for, and yet when it
came his disappointment was unexpectedly acute, for he
too had liked her smile and her brandy-ball eyes. The
door was ajar when he reached it, and he pushed it open
an inch or so farther, pausing on the threshold to consider
the scene within. Patricia was on her knees before the
paneled door which led into the inner room and was trying somewhat ineffectually to peer through the keyhole.

Campion stood looking at her regretfully, and when she
straightened herself and paused to listen, with every line
of her young body taut with the effort of concentration, he
did not move.

Sir Philip's voice amid the noisy chatter behind him
startled him, however, and he swung round to see the old
man talking to a group on the other side of the room. A
moment later the girl brushed past him and hurried away.

Campion went quietly into the anteroom. The study
door was still closed and he moved over to the enormous
period fireplace which stood beside it. This particular
fireplace, with its carved and painted front, its wrought
iron dogs and deeply recessed inglenooks, was one of the
showpieces of Underhill.

At the moment the fire had died down and the interior
of the cavern was dark, warm and inviting. Campion
stepped inside and sat down on the oak settee, where the
shadows swallowed him. He had no intention of being un-
duly officious, but his quick ears had caught a faint sound
in the inner room and Sir Philip's private sanctum was no
place for furtive movements when its master was out of
the way. He had not long to wait.

A few moments later the study door opened very quietly and someone came out. The newcomer moved across the room with a nervous, unsteady tread, and paused abruptly, his back to the quiet figure in the inglenook. Campion recognized Peter Groome and his thin mouth narrowed. He was sorry. He had liked the boy.

The youngster stood irresolute. He had his hands behind him, holding in one of them a flamboyant parcel wrapped in the colored paper and scarlet ribbon which littered the house. A sound from the hall seemed to fluster him for he spun round, thrust the parcel into the inglenook which was the first hiding place to present itself, and returned to face the new arrival. It was the girl again. She came slowly across the room, her hands outstretched and her face raised to Peter's.

In view of everything, Campion thought it best to stay where he was, nor had he time to do anything else. She was speaking urgently, passionate sincerity in her low voice.

"Peter, I've been looking for you. Darling, there's something I've got to say and if I'm making an idiotic mistake then you've got to forgive me. Look here, you wouldn't go and do anything silly, would you? Would you, Peter? Look at me."

"My dear girl." He was laughing unsteadily and not very convincingly with his arms around her. "What on earth are you talking about?"

She drew back from him and peered earnestly into his face.

"You wouldn't, would you? Not even if it meant an awful lot. Not even if for some reason or other you felt you *had* to. Would you?"

He turned from her helplessly, a great weariness in the lines of his sturdy back, but she drew him round, forcing him to face her.

"Would he what, my dear?"

Florence's arch inquiry from the doorway separated them so hurriedly that she laughed delightedly and came briskly into the room, her gray curls a trifle disheveled and her draperies flowing.

"Too divinely young, I love it!" she said devastatingly.

"I must kiss you both. Christmas is the time for love and
youth and all the other dear charming things, isn't it?
That's why I adore it. But my dears, not here. Not in this
silly poky little room. Come along and help me, both of
you, and then you can slip away and dance together later
on. But don't come in this room. This is Philip's dull part
of the house. Come along this minute. Have you seen my
precious tree? Too incredibly distinguished, my darlings,
with two great artists at work on it. You shall both tie on a
candle. Come along."

She swept them away like an avalanche. No protest was
possible. Peter shot a single horrified glance towards the
fireplace, but Florence was gripping his arm; he was
thrust out into the hall and the door closed firmly behind
him.

Campion was left in his corner with the parcel less than
a dozen feet away from him on the opposite bench. He
moved over and picked it up. It was a long flat package
wrapped in holly-printed tissue. Moreover, it was unexpectedly heavy and the ends were unbound.

He turned it over once or twice, wrestling with a strong
disinclination to interfere, but a vivid recollection of the
girl with the brandy-ball eyes, in her silver dress, her
small pale face alive with anxiety, made up his mind for
him and, sighing, he pulled the ribbon.

The typewritten folder which fell on to his knees surprised him at first, for it was not at all what he had
expected, nor was its title, "Report on Messrs. Anderson
and Coleridge, Messrs. Saunders, Duval and Berry, and
Messrs. Birmingham and Rose," immediately enlighten-
ing, and when he opened it at random a column of incom-
prehensible figures confronted him. It was a scribbled
pencil note in a precise hand at the foot of one of the
pages which gave him his first clue.

"These figures are estimated by us to be a reliable
forecast of this firm's full working capacity,"

he read, and after that he became very serious indeed.

Two hours later it was bitterly cold in the garden and a

thin white mist hung over the dark shrubbery which lined the drive when Mr. Campion, picking his way cautiously along the clipped grass verge, came quietly down to the sundial walk. Behind him the gabled roofs of Underhill were shadowy against a frosty sky. There were still a few lights in the upper windows, but below stairs the entire place was in darkness.

Campion hunched his greatcoat about him and plodded on, unwonted severity in the lines of his thin face.

He came upon the sundial walk at last and paused, straining his eyes to see through the mist. He made out the figure standing by the stone column, and heaved a sigh of relief as he recognized the jaunty shoulders of the Christmas tree decorator. Lance's incurable romanticism was going to be useful at last, he reflected with wry amusement.

He did not join his friend but withdrew into the shadows of a great clump of rhododendrons and composed himself to wait. He intensely disliked the situation in which he found himself. Apart from the extreme physical discomfort involved, he had a natural aversion towards the project on hand, but little fairhaired girls with shiny eyes can be very appealing.

It was a freezing vigil. He could hear Lance stamping about in the mist, swearing softly to himself, and even that supremely comic phenomenon had its unsatisfactory side.

They were both shivering and the mist's damp fingers seemed to have stroked their very bones when at last Campion stiffened. He had heard a rustle behind him and presently there was a movement in the wet leaves, followed by the sharp ring of feet on the stones. Lance swung round immediately, only to drop back in astonishment as a tall figure bore down.

"Where is it?"

Neither the words nor the voice came as a complete surprise to Campion, but the unfortunate Lance was taken entirely off his guard.

"Why, hello, Preen," he said involuntarily. "What the devil are you doing here?"

The newcomer had stopped in his tracks, his face a white blur in the uncertain light. For a moment he stood perfectly still and then, turning on his heel, he made off without a word.

"Ah, but I'm afraid it's not quite so simple as that, my dear chap."

Campion stepped out of his friendly shadows and as the younger man passed, slipped an arm through his and swung him round to face the startled Lance, who was coming up at the double.

"You can't clear off like this," he went on, still in the same affable, conversational tone. "You have something to give Peter Groome, haven't you? Something he rather wants?"

"Who the hell are you?" Preen jerked up his arm as he spoke and might have wrenched himself free had it not been for Lance, who had recognized Campion's voice and, although completely in the dark, was yet quick enough to grasp certain essentials.

"That's right, Preen," he said, seizing the man's other arm in a bear's hug. "Hand it over. Don't be a fool. Hand it over."

This line of attack appeared to be inspirational, since they felt the powerful youngster stiffen between them.

"Look here, how many people know about this?"

"The world—" Lance was beginning cheerfully when Campion forestalled him.

"We three and Peter Groome," he said quietly. "At the moment Sir Philip has no idea that Messr. Preen's curiosity concerning the probable placing of government orders for aircraft parts has overstepped the bounds of common sense. You're acting alone, I suppose?"

"Oh, lord, yes, of course." Preen was cracking dangerously. "If my old man gets to hear of this I—oh, well, I might as well go and crash."

"I thought so." Campion sounded content. "Your father has a reputation to consider. So has our young friend Groome. You'd better hand it over."

"What?"

"Since you force me to be vulgar, whatever it was you

were attempting to use as blackmail, my precious young friend," he said. "Whatever it may be, in fact, that you hold over young Groome and were trying to use in your attempt to force him to let you have a look at a confidential government report concerning the orders which certain aircraft firms were likely to receive in the next six months. In your position you could have made pretty good use of them, couldn't you? Frankly, I haven't the faintest idea what this incriminating document may be. When I was young, objectionably wealthy youths accepted I. O. U.'s from their poorer companions, but now that's gone out of fashion. What's the modern equivalent? An R. D. check, I suppose?"

Preen said nothing. He put his hand in an inner pocket and drew out an envelope which he handed over without a word. Campion examined the slip of pink paper within by the light of a pencil torch.

"You kept it for quite a time before trying to cash it, didn't you?" he said. "Dear me, that's rather an old trick and it was never admired. Young men who are careless with their accounts have been caught out like that before. It simply wouldn't have looked good to his legal-minded old man, I take it? You two seem to be hampered by your respective papas' integrity. Yes, well, you can go now."

Preen hesitated, opened his mouth to protest, but thought better of it. Lance looked after his retreating figure for some little time before he returned to his friend.

"Who wrote that blinking note?" he demanded.

"He did, of course," said Campion brutally. "He wanted to see the report but was making absolutely sure that young Groome took all the risks of being found with it."

"Preen wrote the note," Lance repeated blankly.

"Well, naturally," said Campion absently. "That was obvious as soon as the report appeared in the picture. He was the only man in the place with the necessary special information to make use of it."

Lance made no comment. He pulled his coat collar more closely about his throat and stuffed his hands into his pockets.

All the same the artist was not quite satisfied, for, later still, when Campion was sitting in his dressing gown writing a note at one of the little escritoires which Florence so thoughtfully provided in her guest bedrooms, he came padding in again and stood warming himself before the fire.

"Why?" he demanded suddenly. "Why did I get the invitation?"

"Oh, that was a question of luggage," Campion spoke over his shoulder. "That bothered me at first, but as soon as we fixed it onto Preen that little mystery became blindingly clear. Do you remember falling into the carriage this afternoon? Where did you put your elegant piece of gent's natty suitcasing? Over young Groome's head. Preen saw it from the corridor and assumed that the chap was sitting *under his own bag*! He sent his own man over here with the note, told him not to ask for Peter by name but to follow the nice new pigskin suitcase upstairs."

Lance nodded regretfully. "Very likely," he said sadly. "Funny thing. I was sure it was the girl."

After a while he came over to the desk. Campion put down his pen and indicated the written sheet.

"Dear Groome," it ran, "I enclose a little matter that I should burn forthwith. The package you left in the inglenook is still there, right at the back on the left-hand side, cunningly concealed under a pile of logs. It has not been seen by anyone who could possibly understand it. If you nipped over very early this morning you could return it to its appointed place without any trouble. If I may venture a word of advice, it is never worth it."

The author grimaced. "It's a bit avuncular," he admitted awkwardly, "but what else can I do? His light is still on, poor chap. I thought I'd stick it under his door."

Lance was grinning wickedly.

"That's fine," he murmured. "The old man does his stuff for reckless youth. There's just the signature now and that ought to be as obvious as everything else has been to you. I'll write it for you. 'Merry Christmas. Love from Santa Claus.' "

"You win," said Mr. Campion.

MAIGRET'S CHRISTMAS
by Georges Simenon

The routine never varied. When Maigret went to bed he must have muttered his usual, "Tomorrow morning I shall sleep late." And Mme. Maigret, who over the years should have learned to pay no attention to such casual phrases, had taken him at his word this Christmas day.

It was not quite daylight when he heard her stirring cautiously. He forced himself to breathe regularly and deeply as though he were still asleep. It was like a game. She inched toward the edge of the bed with animal stealth, pausing after each movement to make sure she had not awakened him. He waited anxiously for the inevitable finale, the moment when the bedspring, relieved of her weight, would spring back into place with a faint sigh.

She picked up her clothing from the chair and turned the knob of the bathroom door so slowly that it seemed to take an eternity. It was not until she had reached the distant fastness of the kitchen that she resumed her normal movements.

Maigret had fallen asleep again. Not deeply, nor for long. Long enough, however, for a confused and disturbing dream. Waking, he could not remember what it was, but he knew it was disturbing because he still felt vaguely uneasy.

The crack between the window drapes which never quite closed became a strip of pale, hard daylight. He waited a while longer, lying on his back with his eyes open, savoring the fragrance of fresh coffee. Then he heard the apartment door open and close, and he knew that Mme. Maigret was hurrying downstairs to buy him hot croissants from the bakery at the corner of the Rue Amelot.

He never ate in the morning. His breakfast consisted of black coffee. But his wife clung to her ritual: on Sundays and holidays he was supposed to lie in bed until mid-morning while she went out for croissants.

He got up, stepped into his slippers, put on his dressing gown, and drew the curtains. He knew he was doing wrong. His wife would be heartbroken. But while he was willing to make almost any sacrifice to please her, he simply could not stay in bed longer than he felt like it.

It was not snowing. It was nonsense, of course, for a man past fifty to be disappointed because there was no snow on Christmas morning; but then middle-aged people never have as much sense as young folks sometimes imagine.

A dirty, turbid sky hung low over the rooftops. The Boulevard Richard-Lenoir was completely deserted. The words *Fils et Cie., Bonded Warehouses* on the sign above the porte-cochère across the street stood out as black as mourning crêpe. The *F*, for some strange reason, seemed particularly dismal.

He heard his wife moving about in the kitchen again. She came into the dining room on tiptoe, as though he were still asleep instead of looking out the window. He glanced at his watch on the night table. It was only ten past eight.

The night before the Maigrets had gone to the theatre. They would have loved dropping in for a snack at some restaurant, like everyone else on Christmas Eve, but all tables were reserved for *Réveillon* supper. So they had walked home arm in arm, getting in a few minutes before midnight. Thus they hadn't long to wait before exchanging presents.

He got a pipe, as usual. Her present was an electric coffee pot, the latest model that she had wanted so much, and, not to break with tradition, a dozen finely embroidered handkerchiefs.

Still looking out the window, Maigret absently filled his new pipe. The shutters were still closed on some of the windows across the boulevard. Not many people were up. Here and there a light burned in a window, probably left by children who had leaped out of bed at the crack of dawn to rush for their presents under the Christmas tree.

In the quiet Maigret apartment the morning promised to be a lazy one for just the two of them. Maigret would loiter in his dressing gown until quite late. He would not even shave. He would dawdle in the kitchen, talking to his wife while she put the lunch on the stove. Just the two of them.

He wasn't sad exactly, but his dream—which he couldn't remember—had left him jumpy. Or perhaps it wasn't his dream. Perhaps it was Christmas. He had to be extra-careful on Christmas Day, careful of his words, the way Mme. Maigret had been careful of her movements in getting out of bed. Her nerves, too, were especially sensitive on Christmas.

Oh, well, why think of all that? He would just be careful to say nothing untoward. He would be careful not to look out of the window when the neighborhood children began to appear on the sidewalks with their Christmas toys.

All the houses in the street had children. Or almost all. The street would soon echo to the shrill blast of toy horns, the roll of toy drums, and the crack of toy pistols. The little girls were probably already cradling their new dolls.

A few years ago he had proposed more or less at random: "Why don't we take a little trip for Christmas?"

"Where?" she had replied with her infallible common sense.

Where, indeed? whom would they visit? They had no relatives except her sister who lived too far away. And why spend Christmas in some second-rate country inn, or at a hotel in some strange town?

Oh, well, he'd feel better after he had his coffee. He was never at his best until he'd drunk his first cup of coffee and lit his first pipe.

Just as he was reaching for the knob, the door opened noiselessly and Mme. Maigret appeared carrying a tray.

She looked at the empty bed, then turned her disappointed eyes upon her husband. She was on the verge of tears.

"You got up!" She looked as though she had been up for hours herself, every hair in place, a picture of neatness in her crisp, clean apron. "And I was so happy about serving your breakfast in bed."

He had tried a hundred times, as subtly as he could, to make her understand that he didn't like eating breakfast in bed. It made him uncomfortable. It made him feel like an invalid or a senile old gaffer. But for Mme. Maigret breakfast in bed was the symbol of leisure and luxury, the ideal way to start Sunday or a holiday.

"Don't you want to go back to bed?"

No, he did not. Decidedly not. He hadn't the courage.

"Then come to breakfast in the kitchen. And Merry Christmas."

"Merry Christmas!—You're not angry?"

They were in the dining room. He surveyed the silver tray on a corner of the table, the steaming cup of coffee, the golden-brown croissants. He put down his pipe and ate a croissant to please his wife, but he remained standing, looking out the window.

"It's snowing."

It wasn't real snow. It was a fine white dust sifting down from the sky, but it reminded Maigret that when he was a small boy he used to stick out his tongue to lick up a few of the tiny flakes.

His gaze focused on the entrance to the building across the street, next door to the warehouse. Two women had just come out, both bareheaded. One of them, a blonde of about thirty, had thrown a coat over her shoulders without stopping to slip her arms into the sleeves. The other, a brunette, older and thinner, was hugging a shawl.

The blonde seemed to hesitate, ready to turn back. Her slim little companion was insistent and Maigret had the impression that she was pointing up toward his window. The appearance of the concierge in the doorway behind them seemed to tip the scales in favor of the little brunette. The blonde looked back apprehensively, then crossed the street.

"What are you looking at?"

"Nothing. Two women."

"What are they doing?"

"I think they're coming here."

The two women had stopped in the middle of the street and were looking up in the direction of the Maigret apartment.

"I hope they're not coming here to bother you on Christmas Day. My housework's not even done." Nobody would have guessed it. There wasn't a speck of dust on any of the polished furniture. "Are you sure they're coming here?"

"We'll soon find out."

To be on the safe side, he went to comb his hair, brush his teeth, and splash a little water on his face. He was still in his room, relighting his pipe, when he heard the doorbell. Mme. Maigret was evidently putting up a strong hedgehog defense, for it was some time before she came to him.

"They insist on speaking to you," she whispered. "They claim it's very important and they need advice. I know one of them."

"Which one?"

"The skinny little one, Mlle. Doncoeur. She lives across the street on the same floor as ours. She's a very nice person and she does embroidery for a firm in the Faubourg Saint-Honoré. I sometimes wonder if she isn't in love with you."

"Why?"

"Because she works near the window, and when you leave the house in the morning she sometimes gets up to watch you go down the street."

"How old is she?"

"Forty-five to fifty. Aren't you getting dressed?"

Doesn't a man have the right to lounge in his dressing gown, even if people come to bother him at 8:30 on Christmas morning? Well, he'd compromise. He'd put his trousers on underneath the robe.

The two women were standing when he walked into the dining room.

"Excuse me, mesdames—"

Perhaps Mme. Maigret was right. Mlle. Doncoeur did not blush; she paled, smiled, lost her smile, smiled again. She opened her mouth to speak but said nothing.

The blonde, on the other hand, was perfectly composed. She said with a touch of humor: "Coming here wasn't my idea."

"Would you sit down, please?"

Maigret noticed that the blonde was wearing a house-dress under her coat and that her legs were bare. Mlle. Doncoeur was dressed as though for church.

"You perhaps wonder at our boldness in coming to you like this," Mlle. Doncoeur said finally, choosing her words carefully. "Like everyone in the neighborhood, we are honored to have such a distinguished neighbor—" She paused, blushed, and stared at the tray. "We're keeping you from your breakfast."

"I've finished, I'm at your service."

"Something happened in our building last night, or rather this morning, which was so unusual that I felt it was our duty to speak to you about it immediately. Madame Martin did not want to disturb you, but I told her—"

"You also live across the street, Madame Martin?"

"Yes, Monsieur." Madame Martin was obviously unhappy at being forced to take this step. Mlle. Doncoeur, however, was now fully wound up.

"We live on the same floor, just across from your windows." She blushed again, as if she were making a confession. "Monsieur Martin is often out of town, which is natural enough since he is a traveling salesman. For the past two months their little girl has been in bed, as a result of a silly accident—"

Maigret turned politely to the blonde. "You have a daughter?"

"Well, not a daughter exactly. She's our niece. Her mother died two years ago and she's been living with us ever since. The girl broke her leg on the stairs. She should have been up and about after six weeks, but there were complications."

"Your husband is on the road at present?"

"He should be in Bergerac."

"I'm listening, Mlle. Doncoeur."

Mme. Maigret had detoured through the bathroom to regain the kitchen. The clatter of pots and pans had resumed. Maigret stared through the window at the leaden sky.

"I got up early this morning as usual," said Mlle. Doncoeur, "to go to first mass."

"And you did go to church?"

"Yes. I stayed for three masses. I got home about 7:30 and prepared my breakfast. You may have seen the light in my window."

Maigret's gesture indicated he had not been watching.

"I was in a hurry to take a few goodies to Colette. It's very sad for a child to spend Christmas in bed. Colette is Madame Martin's niece."

"How old is she?"

"Seven. Isn't that right, Madame Martin?"

"She'll be seven in January."

"So at eight o'clock I knocked at the door of their apartment—"

"I wasn't up," the blonde interrupted. "I sometimes sleep rather late."

"As I was saying, I knocked. Madame Martin kept me waiting for a moment while she slipped on her negligee. I had my arms full, and I asked if I could take my presents in to Colette."

Maigret noted that the blonde was making a mental inventory of the apartment, stopping occasionally to dart a sharp, suspicious glance in his direction.

"We opened the door to her room together—"

"The child has a room of her own?"

"Yes. There are two bedrooms in the apartment, a dressing room, a kitchen, and a dining room. But I must tell you— No, I'm getting ahead of myself. We had just opened the door and since the room was dark, Madame Martin had switched on the light—"

"Colette was awake?"

"Yes. It was easy to see she'd been awake for some

time, waiting. You know how children are on Christmas morning. If she could use her legs, she would certainly have got up long since to see what Father Christmas had brought her. Perhaps another child would have called out. But Colette is already a little lady. She's much older than her age. She thinks a lot."

Now Madame Martin was looking out the window. Maigret tried to guess which apartment was hers. It must be the last one to the right, the one with the two lighted windows.

"I wished her a Merry Christmas," Mlle. Doncoeur continued. "I said to her, and these were my exact words, 'Darling, look what Father Christmas left in my apartment for you.' "

Madame Martin was clasping and unclasping her fingers.

"And do you know what she answered me, without even looking to see what I'd brought? They were only trifles, anyhow. She said, 'I saw him.'

" 'Whom did you see?'

" 'Father Christmas.'

" 'When did you see him?' I asked. 'Where?'

" 'Right here, last night. He came to my room.'

"That's exactly what she said, isn't it, Madame Martin? With any other child, we would have smiled. But as I told you, Colette is already a little lady. She doesn't joke. I said, 'How could you see him, since it was dark?'

" 'He had a light.'

" 'You mean he turned on the electricity?'

" 'No. He had a flashlight. Look, Mama Loraine.'

"I must tell you that the little girl calls Madame Martin 'Mama,' which is natural enough, since her own mother is dead and Madame Martin has been taking her place."

The monologue had become a confused buzzing in Maigret's ears. He had not drunk his second cup of coffee and his pipe had gone out. He asked without conviction: "Did she really see someone?"

"Yes, Monsieur l'Inspector. And that's why I insisted that Madame Martin come to speak to you. Colette did see someone and she proved it to us. With a sly little smile she threw back the bedsheet and showed us a magnificent doll, a beautiful big doll she was cuddling and which I swear was not in the house yesterday."

"You didn't give your niece a doll, Madame Martin?"

"I was going to give her one, but mine was not nearly as nice. I got it yesterday afternoon at the Galeries, and I was holding it behind me this morning when we came into her room."

"In other words, someone *did* come into your apartment last night?"

"That's not all," said Mlle. Doncoeur quickly; she was not to be stopped. "Colette never tells lies. She's not a child who imagines things. And when we questioned her, she said the man was certainly Father Christmas because he wore a white beard and a bright red coat."

"At what time did she wake up?"

"She doesn't know—sometime during the night. She opened her eyes because she thought she saw a light. And there was a light, shining on the floor near the fireplace."

"I can't understand it," sighed Madame Martin. "Unless my husband has some explanation."

But Mlle. Doncoeur was not to be diverted from her story. It was obvious that she was the one who had questioned the child, just as she was the one who had thought of Maigret. She resumed:

"Colette said, 'Father Christmas was squatting on the floor, and he was bending over, as though he were working at something.' "

"She wasn't frightened?"

"No. She just watched him. This morning she told us he was busy making a hole in the floor. She thought he wanted to go through the floor to visit the people downstairs—that's the Delormes who have a little boy of three—because the chimney was too narrow. The man must have sensed she was watching him, because he got up, came over to the bed, and gave Colette the big doll. Then he put his finger to his lips."

"Did she see him leave?"

"Yes."

"Through the floor?"

"No, by the door."

"Into what room does this door open?"

"Directly into the outside hall. There is another door that opens into the apartment, but the hall door is like a private entrance because the room used to be rented separately."

"Wasn't the door locked?"

"Of course," Madame Martin intervened. "I wouldn't let the child sleep in a room that wasn't locked from the outside."

"Then the door was forced?"

"Probably. I don't know. Mlle. Doncoeur immediately suggested we come to see you."

"Did you find a hole in the floor?"

Madame Martin shrugged wearily, but Mlle. Doncoeur answered for her.

"Not a hole exactly, but you could see that the floorboards had been moved."

"Tell me, Madame Martin, have you any idea what might have been hidden under the flooring?"

"No, Monsieur."

"How long have you lived in this apartment?"

"Since my marriage, five years ago."

"And this room was part of the apartment then?"

"Yes."

"You know who lived there before you?"

"My husband. He's thirty-eight. He was thirty-three when we were married, and he had his own furniture then. He liked to have his own home to come back to when he returned to Paris from the road."

"Do you think he might have wanted to surprise Colette?"

"He is six or seven hundred kilometers from here."

"Where did you say?"

"In Bergerac. His itinerary is planned in advance and he rarely deviates from his schedule."

"For what firm does he travel?"

"He covers the central and southwest territory for Zenith watches. It's an important line, as you probably know. He has a very good job."

"There isn't a finer man on earth!" exclaimed Mlle. Doncoeur. She blushed, then added, "Except you, Monsieur l'Inspector."

"As I understand it, then, someone got into your apartment last night disguised as Father Christmas."

"According to the little girl."

"Didn't you hear anything? Is your room far from the little girl's?"

"There's a dining room between us."

"Don't you leave the connecting doors open at night?"

"It isn't necessary. Colette is not afraid, and as a rule she never wakes up. If she wants anything, she has a little bell on her night table."

"Did you go out last night?"

"I did not, Monsieur l'Inspector." Madame Martin was annoyed.

"Did you receive visitors?"

"I do not receive visitors while my husband is away."

Maigret glanced at Mlle. Doncoeur, whose expression did not change. So Madame Martin was telling the truth.

"Did you go to bed late?"

"I read until midnight. As soon as the radio played *Minuit, Chrétiens,* I went to bed."

"And you heard nothing unusual?"

"Nothing."

"Have you asked the concierge if she clicked the latch to let in any stranger last night?"

"I asked her," Mlle. Doncoeur volunteered. "She says she didn't."

"And you found nothing missing from your apartment this morning, Madame Martin? Nothing disturbed in the dining room?"

"No."

"Who is with the little girl now?"

"No one. She's used to staying alone. I can't be at home all day. I have marketing to do, errands to run . . ."

"I understand. You told me Colette is an orphan?"

"Her mother is dead."

"So her father is living. Where is he?"

"Her father's name is Paul Martin. He's my husband's

brother. As to telling you where he is—" Madame Martin sketched a vague gesture.

"When did you see him last?"

"About a month ago. A little longer. It was around All Saints' Day. He was finishing a novena."

"I beg your pardon?"

"I may as well tell you everything at once," said Madame Martin with a faint smile, "since we seem to be washing our family linen." She glanced reproachfully at Mlle. Doncoeur. "My brother-in-law, especially since he lost his wife, is not quite respectable."

"What do you mean exactly?"

"He drinks. He always drank a little, but he never used to get into trouble. He had a good job with a furniture store in the Faubourg Saint-Antoine. But since the accident—"

"The accident to his daughter?"

"No, to his wife. He borrowed a car from a friend one Sunday about three years ago and took his wife and little girl to the country. They had lunch at a roadside inn near Mantes-la-Jolie and he drank too much white wine. He sang most of the way back to Paris—until he ran into something near the Bougival bridge. His wife was killed instantly. He cracked his own skull and it's a miracle he's still alive. Colette escaped without a scratch. Paul hasn't been a man since then. We've practically adopted the little girl. He comes to see her occasionally when he's sober. Then he starts over again."

"Do you know where he lives?"

Another vague gesture. "Everywhere. We've seen him loitering around the Bastille like a beggar. Sometimes he sells papers in the street. I can speak freely in front of Mlle. Doncoeur because unfortunately the whole house knows about him."

"Don't you think he might have dressed up as Father Christmas to call on his daughter?"

"That's what I told Mlle. Doncoeur, but she insisted on coming to see you anyhow."

"Because I see no reason for him to take up the flooring," said Mlle. Doncoeur acidly.

"Or perhaps your husband returned to Paris unexpectedly."

"It's certainly something of the sort. I'm not at all disturbed. But Mlle. Doncoeur—"

Decidedly Madame Martin had not crossed the boulevard light-heartedly.

"Do you know where your husband might be staying in Bergerac?"

"Yes. At the Hotel de Bordeaux."

"You hadn't thought of telephoning him?"

"We have no phone. There's only one in the house—the people on the second floor, and they hate to be disturbed."

"Would you object to my calling the Hotel de Bordeaux?"

Madame Martin started to nod, then hesitated. "He'll think something terrible has happened."

"You can speak to him yourself."

"He's not used to my phoning him on the road."

"You'd rather he not know what's happening?"

"That's not so. I'll talk to him if you like."

Maigret picked up the phone and placed the call. Ten minutes later he was connected with the Hotel de Bordeaux in Bergerac. He passed the instrument to Madame Martin.

"Hello . . . Monsieur Martin, please . . . Yes, Monsieur Jean Martin . . . No matter. Wake him up."

She put her hand over the mouthpiece. "He's still asleep. They've gone to call him."

Then she retreated into silence, evidently rehearsing the words she was to speak to her husband.

"Hello? . . . Hello, darling . . . What? . . . Yes, Merry Christmas! . . . Yes, everything's all right . . . Colette is fine . . . No, that's not why I phoned . . . No, no, no! Nothing's wrong. Please don't worry!" She repeated each word separately. "Please . . . don't . . . worry! I just want to tell you about a strange thing that happened last night. Somebody dressed up like Father Christmas and came into Colette's room . . . No, no! He didn't hurt her. He gave her a big doll . . . Yes, *doll*! . . . And he did queer things to the floor. He removed two boards which he put

back in a hurry . . . Mlle. Doncoeur thought I should report it to the police inspector who lives across the street.
I'm there now . . . You don't understand? Neither do I . . .
You want me to put him on?" She passed the instrument
to Maigret. "He wants to speak to you."

A warm masculine voice came over the wire, the voice
of an anxious, puzzled man.

"Are you sure my wife and the little girl are all right? . . .
It's all so incredible! If it were just the doll, I might suspect
my brother. Loraine will tell you about him. Loraine is
my wife. Ask her . . . But he wouldn't have removed the
flooring . . . Do you think I'd better come home? I can get
a train for Paris at three this afternoon . . . What? . . .
Thank you so much. It's good to know you'll look out for
them."

Loraine Martin took back the phone.

"See, darling? The inspector says there's no danger. It
would be foolish to break your trip now. It might spoil
your chances of being transferred permanently to Paris."

Mlle. Doncoeur was watching her closely and there was
little tenderness in the spinster's eyes.

"I promise to wire you or phone you if there's anything
new . . . She's playing quietly with her new doll . . . No, I
haven't had time yet to give her your present. I'll go right
home and do it now."

Madame Martin hung up and declared: "You see."
Then, after a pause, "Forgive me for bothering you. It's
really not my fault. I'm sure this is all the work of some
practical joker—unless it's my brother-in-law. When he's
been drinking there's no telling what he might do."

"Do you expect to see him today? Don't you think he
might want to see his daughter?"

"That depends. If he's been drinking, no. He's very
careful never to come around in that condition."

"May I have your permission to come over and talk
with Colette a little later?"

"I see no reason why you shouldn't—if you think it
worthwhile."

"Thank you, Monsieur Maigret!" exclaimed Mlle.

Doncoeur. Her expression was half grateful, half conspiratorial. "She's such an interesting child! You'll see!"

She backed toward the door.

A few minutes later Maigret watched the two women cross the boulevard. Mlle. Doncoeur, close on the heels of Madame Martin, turned to look up at the windows of the Maigret apartment.

Mme. Maigret opened the kitchen door, flooding the dining room with the aroma of browning onions. She asked gently:

"Are you happy?"

He pretended not to understand. Luckily he had been too busy to think much about the middle-aged couple who had nobody to make a fuss over this Christmas morning.

It was time for him to shave and call on Colette.

He was just about to lather his face when he decided to make a phone call. He didn't bother with his dressing gown. Clad only in pajamas, he dropped into the easy chair by the window—*his* chair—and watched the smoke curling up from all the chimney pots while his call went through.

The ringing at the other end—in headquarters at the Quai des Orfèvres—had a different sound from all other rings. It evoked for him the long empty corridors, the vacant offices, the operator stuck with holiday duty at the switchboard. Then he heard the operator call Lucas with the words: "The boss wants you."

He felt a little like one of his wife's friends who could imagine no greater joy—which she experienced daily—than lying in bed all morning, with her windows closed and curtains drawn, and telephoning all her friends, one after the other. By the soft glow of her night-light she managed to maintain a constant state of just having awakened. "What? Ten o'clock already? How's the weather? Is it raining? Have you been out yet? Have you done all your marketing?" And as she established telephonic connection with the hurly-burly of the workaday world, she would sink more and more voluptuously into the warm softness of her bed.

"That you, Chief?"

Maigret, too, felt a need for contact with the working world. He wanted to ask Lucas who was on duty with him, what they were doing, how the shop looked on this Christmas morning.

"Nothing new? Not too busy?"

"Nothing to speak of. Routine."

"I'd like you to get me some information. You can probably do this by phone. First of all, I want a list of all convicts released from prison the last two or three months."

"Which prison?"

"All prisons. But don't bother with any who haven't served at least five years. Then check and see if any of them has ever lived on Boulevard Richard-Lenoir. Got that?"

"I'm making notes."

Lucas was probably somewhat bewildered but he would never admit it.

"Another thing. I want you to locate a man named Paul Martin, a drunk, no fixed address, who frequently hangs out around the Place de la Bastille. I don't want him arrested. I don't want him molested. I just want to know where he spent Christmas Eve. The commissaries should help you on this one."

No use trying. Maigret simply could not reproduce the idle mood of his wife's friend. On the contrary, it embarrassed him to be lolling at home in his pajamas, unshaven, phoning from his favorite easy chair, looking out at the scene of complete peace and quiet in which there was no movement except the smoke curling up from the chimney pots, while at the other end of the wire good old Lucas had been on duty since six in the morning and was probably already unwrapping his sandwiches.

"That's not quite all, old man. I want you to call Bergerac long distance. There's a traveling salesman by the name of Jean Martin staying at the Hotel de Bordeaux there. No, Jean. It's his brother. I want to know if Jean Martin got a telegram or a phone call from Paris last night or any time yesterday. And while you're about it, find out where he spent Christmas Eve. I think that's all."

"Shall I call you back?"

"Not right away. I've got to go out for a while. I'll call you when I get home."

"Something happen in your neighborhood?"

"I don't know yet. Maybe."

Mme. Maigret came into the bathroom to talk to him while he finished dressing. He did not put on his overcoat. The smoke curling slowly upward from so many chimney pots blended with the grey of the sky and conjured up the image of just as many overheated apartments, cramped rooms in which he would not be invited to make himself at home. He refused to be uncomfortable. He would put on his hat to cross the boulevard, and that was all.

The building across the way was very much like the one he lived in—old but clean, a little dreary, particularly on a drab December morning. He avoided stopping at the concierge's lodge, but noted she watched him with some annoyance. Doors opened silently as he climbed the stairs. He heard whispering, the padding of slippered feet.

Mlle. Doncoeur, who had doubtless been watching for him, was waiting on the fourth floor landing. She was both shy and excited, as if keeping a secret tryst with a lover.

"This way, Monsieur Maigret. She went out a little while ago."

He frowned, and she noted the fact.

"I told her that you were coming and that she had better wait for you, but she said she had not done her marketing yesterday and that there was nothing in the house. She said all the stores would be closed if she waited too long. Come in."

She had opened the door into Madame Martin's dining room, a small, rather dark room which was clean and tidy.

"I'm looking after the little girl until she comes back. I told Colette that you were coming to see her, and she is delighted. I've spoken to her about you. She's only afraid you might take back her doll."

"When did Madame Martin decide to go out?"

"As soon as we came back across the street, she started dressing."

"Did she dress completely?"

"I don't understand."

"I mean, I suppose she dresses differently when she goes downtown than when she merely goes shopping in the neighborhood."

"She was quite dressed up. She put on her hat and gloves. And she carried her shopping bag."

Before going to see Colette, Maigret stepped into the kitchen and glanced at the breakfast dishes.

"Did she eat before you came to see me?"

"No. I didn't give her a chance."

"And when she came back?"

"She just made herself a cup of black coffee. I fixed breakfast for Colette while Madame Martin got dressed."

There was a larder on the ledge of the window looking out on the courtyard. Maigret carefully examined its contents: butter, eggs, vegetables, some cold meat. He found two uncut loaves of fresh bread in the kitchen cupboard. Colette had eaten croissants with her hot chocolate.

"How well do you know Madame Martin?"

"We're neighbors, aren't we? And I've seen more of her since Colette has been in bed. She often asks me to keep an eye on the little girl when she goes out."

"Does she go out much?"

"Not very often. Just for her marketing."

Maigret tried to analyze the curious impression he had had on entering the apartment. There was something in the atmosphere that disturbed him, something about the arrangement of the furniture, the special kind of neatness that prevailed, even the smell of the place. As he followed Mlle. Doncoeur into the dining room, he thought he knew what it was.

Madame Martin had told him that her husband had lived in this apartment before their marriage. And even though Madame Martin had lived there for five years, it had remained a bachelor's apartment. He pointed to the two enlarged photographs standing on opposite ends of the mantelpiece.

"Who are they?"

"Monsieur Martin's father and mother."

"Doesn't Madame Martin have photos of her own parents about?"

"I've never heard her speak of them. I suppose she's an orphan."

Even the bedroom was without the feminine touch. He opened a closet. Next to the neat rows of masculine clothing, the woman's clothes were hanging, mostly severely tailored suits and conservative dresses. He did not open the bureau drawers but he was sure they did not contain the usual trinkets and knickknacks that women collect.

"Mademoiselle Doncoeur!" called a calm little voice.

"Let's talk to Colette," said Maigret.

The child's room was as austere and cold as the others. The little girl lay in a bed too large for her, her face solemn, her eyes questioning but trusting.

"Are you the inspector, Monsieur?"

"I'm the inspector, my girl. Don't be afraid."

"I'm not afraid. Hasn't Mama Loraine come home yet?"

Maigret pursed his lips. The Martins had practically adopted their niece, yet the child said "Mama Loraine," not just "Mama."

"Do you believe it was Father Christmas who came to see me last night?" Colette asked Maigret.

"I'm sure it was."

"Mama Loraine doesn't believe it. She never believes me."

The girl had a dainty, attractive little face, with very bright eyes that stared at Maigret with level persistence. The plaster cast which sheathed one leg all the way to the hip made a thick bulge under the blankets.

Mlle. Doncoeur hovered in the doorway, evidently anxious to leave the inspector alone with the girl. She said: "I must run home for a moment to make sure my lunch isn't burning."

Maigret sat down beside the bed wondering how to go about questioning the girl.

"Do you love Mama Loraine very much?" he began.

"Yes, Monsieur." She replied without hesitation and without enthusiasm.

"And your papa?"

"Which one? Because I have two papas, you know— Papa Paul and Papa Jean."

"Has it been a long time since you saw Papa Paul?"

"I don't remember. Perhaps several weeks. He promised to bring me a toy for Christmas, but he hasn't come yet. He must be sick."

"Is he often sick?"

"Yes, often. When he's sick he doesn't come to see me."

"And your Papa Jean?"

"He's away on a trip, but he'll be back for New Year's. Maybe then he'll be appointed to the Paris office and won't have to go away anymore. That would make him very happy and me, too."

"Do many of your friends come to see you since you've been in bed?"

"What friends? The girls in school don't know where I live. Or maybe they know but their parents don't let them come alone."

"What about Mama Loraine's friends? Or your papa's?"

"Nobody comes, ever."

"Ever? Are you sure?"

"Only the man to read the gas meter, or for the electricity. I can hear them, because the door is almost always open. I recognize their voices. Once a man came and I didn't recognize his voice. Or twice."

"How long ago was that?"

"The first time was the day after my accident. I remember because the doctor just left."

"Who was it?"

"I didn't see him. He knocked at the other door. I heard him talking and then Mama Loraine came and closed my door. They talked for quite a while but I couldn't hear very well. Afterward Mama Loraine said it was a man who wanted to sell her some insurance. I don't know what that is."

"And he came back?"

"Five or six days ago. It was night and I'd already turned off my light. I wasn't asleep, though. I heard someone knock, and then they talked in low voices like the first time. Mademoiselle Doncoeur sometimes comes over in the evening, but I could tell it wasn't she. I thought they were quarreling and I was frightened. I called out, and Mama Loraine came in and said it was the man about the insurance again and I should go to sleep."

"Did he stay long?"

"I don't know. I think I fell asleep."

"And you didn't see him either time?"

"No, but I'd recognize his voice."

"Even though he speaks in low tones?"

"Yes, that's why. When he speaks low it sounds just like a big bumblebee. I can keep the doll, can't I? Mama Loraine bought me two boxes of candy and a little sewing kit. She bought me a doll, too, but it wasn't nearly as big as the doll Father Christmas gave me, because she's not rich. She showed it to me this morning before she left, and then she put it back in the box. I have the big one now, so I won't need the little one and Mama Loraine can take it back to the store."

The apartment was overheated, yet Maigret felt suddenly cold. The building was very much like the one across the street, yet not only did the rooms seem smaller and stuffier, but the whole world seemed smaller and meaner over here.

He bent over the floor near the fireplace. He lifted the loose floor-boards, but saw nothing but an empty, dusty cavity smelling of dampness. There were scratches on the planks which indicated they had been forced up with a chisel or some similar instrument.

He examined the outside door and found indications that it had been forced. It was obviously an amateur's work, and luckily for him, the job had been an easy one.

"Father Christmas wasn't angry when he saw you watching him?"

"No, Monsieur. He was busy making a hole in the floor so he could go and see the little boy downstairs."

"Did he speak to you?"

"I think he smiled at me. I'm not sure, though, because of his whiskers. It wasn't very light. But I'm sure he put his finger to his lips so I wouldn't call anybody, because grown-ups aren't supposed to see Father Christmas. Did you ever see him?"

"A very long time ago."

"When you were little?"

Maigret heard footsteps in the hallway. The door opened and Madame Martin came in. She was wearing a grey tailored suit and a small beige hat and carried a brown shopping bag. She was visibly cold, for her skin was taut and very white, yet she must have hurried up the stairs, since there were two pink spots on her cheeks and she was out of breath. Unsmiling, she asked Maigret:

"Has she been a good girl?" Then, as she took off her jacket, "I apologize for making you wait. I had so many things to buy, and I was afraid the stores would all be closed later on."

"Did you meet anyone?"

"What do you mean?"

"Nothing. I was wondering if anyone tried to speak to you."

She had had plenty of time to go much further than the Rue Amelot or the Rue du Chemin-Vert where most of the neighborhood shops were located. She had even had time to go across Paris and back by taxi or the Metro.

Mlle. Doncoeur returned to ask if there was anything she could do. Madame Martin was about to say no when Maigret intervened: "I'd like you to stay with Colette while I step into the next room."

Mlle. Doncoeur understood that he wanted her to keep the child busy while he questioned the foster-mother. Madame Martin must have understood, too, but she gave no indication.

"Please come in. Do you mind if I take off my things?"

Madame Martin put her package in the kitchen. She took off her hat and fluffed out her pale blonde hair.

When she had closed the bedroom door, she said: "Mlle. Doncoeur is all excited. This is quite an event, isn't it, for an old maid—particularly an old maid who cuts out every newspaper article about a certain police inspector, and who finally has the inspector in her own house—Do you mind?"

She had taken a cigarette from a silver case, tapped the end, and snapped a lighter. The gesture somehow prompted Maigret's next question:

"You're not working, Madame Martin?"

"It would be difficult to hold a job and take care of the house and the little girl, too, even when the child is in school. Besides, my husband won't allow me to work."

"But you did work before you met him?"

"Naturally. I had to earn a living. Won't you sit down?"

He lowered himself into a rude raffia-bottomed chair. She rested one thigh against the edge of a table.

"You were a typist?"

"I have been a typist."

"For long?"

"Quite a while."

"You were still a typist when you met Martin? You must forgive me for asking these personal questions."

"It's your job."

"You were married five years ago. Were you working then? Just a moment. May I ask your age?"

"I'm thirty-three. I was twenty-eight then, and I was working for a Monsieur Lorilleux in the Palais-Royal arcades."

"As his secretary?"

"Monsieur Lorilleux had a jewelry shop. Or more exactly, he sold souvenirs and old coins. You know those old shops in the Palais-Royal. I was salesgirl, bookkeeper, *and* secretary. I took care of the shop when he was away."

"He was married?"

"And father of three children."

"You left him to marry Martin?"

"Not exactly. Jean didn't want me to go on working,

but he wasn't making very much money then and I had quite a good job. So I kept it for the first few months."

"And then?"

"Then a strange thing happened. One morning I came to work at nine o'clock as usual, and I found the door locked. I thought Monsieur Lorilleux had overslept, so I waited."

"Where did he live?"

"Rue Mazarine with his family. At half-past nine I began to worry."

"Was he dead?"

"No. I phoned his wife, who said he had left the house at eight o'clock as usual."

"Where did you telephone from?"

"From the glove shop next door. I waited all morning. His wife came down and we went to the commissariat together to report him missing, but the police didn't take it very seriously. They just asked his wife if he'd ever had heart trouble, if he had a mistress—things like that. But he was never seen again, and nobody ever heard from him. Then some Polish people bought out the store and my husband made me stop working."

"How long was this after your marriage?"

"Four months."

"Your husband was already traveling in the southwest?"

"He had the same territory he has now."

"Was he in Paris when your employer disappeared?"

"No, I don't think so."

"Didn't the police examine the premises?"

"Nothing had been touched since the night before. Nothing was missing."

"Do you know what became of Madame Lorilleux?"

"She lived for a while on the money from the sale of the store. Then she bought a little dry-goods shop not far from here, in the Rue du Pas-de-la-Mule. Her children must be grown up now, probably married."

"Do you still see her?"

"I go into her shop once in a while. That's how I know

she's in business in the neighborhood. The first time I saw her there I didn't recognize her."

"How long ago was that?"

"I don't know. Six months or so."

"Does she have a telephone?"

"I don't know. Why?"

"What kind of man was Lorilleux?"

"You mean physically?"

"Let's start with the physical."

"He was a big man, taller than you, and broader. He was fat, but flabby, if you know what I mean. And rather sloppy looking."

"How old?"

"Around fifty. I can't say exactly. He had a little salt-and-pepper mustache, and his clothes were always too big for him."

"You were familiar with his habits?"

"He walked to work every morning. He got down fifteen minutes ahead of me and cleared up the mail before I arrived. He didn't talk much. He was a rather gloomy person. He spent most of the day in the little office behind the shop."

"No romantic adventures?"

"Not that I know of."

"Didn't he try to make love to you?"

"No!" The monosyllable was tartly emphatic.

"But he thought highly of you?"

"I think I was a great help to him."

"Did your husband ever meet him?"

"They never spoke. Jean sometimes came to wait for me outside the shop, but he never came in." A note of impatience, tinged with anger, crept into her voice. "Is that all you want to know?"

"May I point out, Madame Martin, that you are the one who came to get me?"

"Only because a crazy old maid practically dragged me there so she could get a close-up look at you."

"You don't like Mlle. Doncoeur?"

"You know that we've taken in my brother-in-law's child. Believe me or not, I've done everything I can for her. I treat her the way I'd treat my own child." She paused to light a fresh cigarette, and Maigret tried unsuccessfully to picture her as a doting mother. "And now that old maid is always over here, offering to help me with the child. Every time I start to go out, I find her in the hallway, smiling sweetly, and saying, 'You mustn't leave Colette all alone, Madame Martin. Let me go in and keep her company.' I sometimes wonder if she doesn't go through my drawers when I'm out."

"You put up with her, nevertheless."

"How can I help it? Colette asks for her, especially since she's been in bed. And my husband is fond of her because when he was a bachelor, she took care of him when he was sick with pleurisy."

"Have you already returned the doll you bought for Colette's Christmas?"

She frowned and glanced at the door to the child's bedroom. "I see you've been questioning the little girl. No, I haven't taken it back for the good reason that all the big department stores are closed today. Would you like to see it?"

She spoke defiantly, expecting him to refuse, but he said nothing. He examined the cardboard box, noting the price tag. It was a very cheap doll.

"May I ask where you went this morning?"

"I did my marketing."

"Rue Amelot or Rue de Chemin-Vert?"

"Both."

"If I may be indiscreet, what did you buy?"

Furious, she stormed into the kitchen, snatched up her shopping bag, and dumped it on the dining room table. "Look for yourself!"

There were three tins of sardines, butter, potatoes, some ham, and a head of lettuce.

She fixed him with a hard, unwavering stare. She was not in the least nervous. Spiteful, rather.

"Any more questions?"

"Yes, the name of your insurance agent."

"My insurance . . ." She was obviously puzzled.

"Insurance agent. The one who came to see you."

"I'm sorry. I was at a loss for a moment because you

spoke of *my* agent as though he were really handling a policy for me. So Colette told you that, too? Actually, a man did come to see me twice, trying to sell me a policy. He was one of those door-to-door salesmen, and I thought at first he was selling vacuum cleaners, not life insurance. I had a terrible time getting rid of him."

"Did he stay long?"

"Long enough for me to convince him that I had no desire to take out a policy."

"What company did he represent?"

"He told me but I've forgotten. Something with 'Mutual' in it."

"And he came back later?"

"Yes."

"What time does Colette usually go to sleep?"

"I put out her light at 7:30, but sometimes she talks to herself in the dark until much later."

"So the second time the insurance man called, it was later than 7:30?"

"Possibly." She saw the trap. "I remember now I was washing the dishes."

"And you let him in?"

"He had his foot in the door."

"Did he call on other tenants in the building?"

"I haven't the slightest idea, but I'm sure you will inquire. Must you cross-examine me like a criminal, just because a little girl imagines she saw Santa Claus? If my husband were here—"

"By the way, does your husband carry life insurance?"

"I think so. In fact, I'm sure he does."

Maigret picked up his hat from a chair and started for the door. Madame Martin seemed surprised.

"Is that all?"

"That's all. It seems your brother-in-law promised to come and see his daughter today. If he should come, I would be grateful if you let me know. And now I'd like a few words with Mlle. Doncoeur."

There was a convent smell about Mlle. Doncoeur's apartment, but there was no dog or cat in sight, no antimacassars on the chairs, no bric-a-brac on the mantel-piece.

"Have you lived in this house long, Mlle. Doncoeur?"

"Twenty-five years, Monsieur l'Inspecteur. I'm one of the oldest tenants. I remember when I first moved in you were already living across the street, and you wore long mustaches."

"Who lived in the next apartment before Martin moved in?"

"A public works engineer. I don't remember his name, but I could look it up for you. He had a wife and daughter. The girl was a deaf-mute. It was very sad. They went to live somewhere in the country."

"Have you been bothered by a door-to-door insurance agent recently?"

"Not recently. There was one who came around two or three years ago."

"You don't like Madame Martin, do you?"

"Why?"

"I asked if you like Madame Martin?"

"Well, if I had a son—"

"Go on."

"If I had a son, I don't think I would like Madame Martin for a daughter-in-law. Especially as Monsieur Martin is such a nice man, so kind."

"You think he is unhappy with his wife?"

"I wouldn't say that. I have nothing against her, really. She can't help being the kind of woman she is."

"What kind of woman is she?"

"I couldn't say, exactly. You've seen her. You're a better judge of those things than I am. In a way, she's not like a woman at all. I'll wager she never shed a tear in her life. True, she is bringing up the child properly, decently, but she never says a kind word to her. She acts exasperated when I tell Colette a fairy tale. I'm sure she's told the girl there is no Santa Claus. Luckily Colette doesn't believe her."

"The child doesn't like her either, does she?"

"Colette is always obedient. She tries to do what's expected of her. I think she's just as happy to be left alone."

"Is she alone much?"

"Not much. I'm not reproaching Madame Martin. It's hard to explain. She wants to live her own life. She's not interested in others. She doesn't even talk much about herself."

"Have you ever met her brother-in-law—Colette's father?"

"I've seen him on the landing, but I've never spoken to him. He walks with his head down, as if he were ashamed of something. He always looks as if he slept in his clothes. No, I don't think it was he last night, Monsieur Maigret. He's not the type. Unless he was terribly drunk."

On his way out Maigret looked in at the concierge's lodge, a dark cubicle where the light burned all day.

It was noon when he started back across the boulevard. Curtains stirred at the windows of the house behind him. Curtains stirred at his own window, too. Mme. Maigret was watching for him so she would know when to put the chicken in the oven. He waved to her. He wanted very much to stick out his tongue and lick up a few of the tiny snowflakes that were drifting down. He could still remember their taste.

"I wonder if that little tike is happy over there," sighed Mme. Maigret as she got up from the table to bring the coffee from the kitchen.

She could see he wasn't listening. He had pushed back his chair and was stuffing his pipe while staring at the purring stove. For her own satisfaction she added: "I don't see how she could be happy with that woman."

He smiled vaguely, as he always did when he hadn't heard what she said, and continued to stare at the tiny flames licking evenly at the mica windows of her salamander. There were at least ten similar stoves in the house, all purring alike in ten similar dining rooms with wine and cakes on the table, a carafe of cordial waiting on the sideboard, and all the windows pale with the same hard, grey light of a sunless day.

It was perhaps this very familiarity which had been confusing his subconscious since morning. Nine times out of ten his investigations plunged him abruptly into new surroundings, set him at grips with people of a world he barely knew, people of a social level whose habits and manners he had to study from scratch. But in this case, which was not really a case since he had no official assignment, the whole approach was unfamiliar because the background was too familiar. For the first time in his career something professional was happening in his own world, in a building which might just as well be his building.

The Martins could easily have been living on his floor, instead of across the street, and it would probably have been Mme. Maigret who would look after Colette when her aunt was away. There was an elderly maiden lady living just under him who was a plumper, paler replica of Mlle. Doncoeur. The frames of the photographs of Martin's father and mother were exactly the same as those which framed Maigret's father and mother, and the enlargements had probably been made by the same studio.

Was that what was bothering him? He seemed to lack perspective. He was unable to look at people and things from a fresh, new viewpoint.

He had detailed his morning activities during dinner—a pleasant little Christmas dinner which had left him with an overstuffed feeling—and his wife had listened while looking at the windows across the street with an air of embarrassment.

"Is the concierge sure that nobody could have come in from outside?"

"She's not so sure any more. She was entertaining friends until after midnight. And after she had gone to bed, there were considerable comings and goings, which is natural for Christmas Eve."

"Do you think something more is going to happen?"

That was a question that had been plaguing Maigret all morning. First of all, he had to consider that Madame Martin had not come to see him spontaneously, but only on the insistence of Mlle. Doncoeur. If she had got up earlier, if she had been the first to see the doll and hear the story of Father Christmas, wouldn't she have kept the secret and ordered the little girl to say nothing?

And later she had taken the first opportunity to go out, even though there was plenty to eat in the house for the day. And she had been so absent-minded that she had bought butter, although there was still a pound in the cooler.

Maigret got up from the table and resettled himself in his chair by the window. He picked up the phone and called Quai des Orfèvres.

"Lucas?"

"I got what you wanted, Chief. I have a list of all prisoners released for the last four months. There aren't as many as I thought. And none of them has lived in the Boulevard Richard-Lenoir at any time."

That didn't matter any more now. At first Maigret had thought that a tenant across the street might have hidden money or stolen goods under the floor before he was arrested. His first thought on getting out of jail would be to recover his booty. With the little girl bedridden, however, the room was occupied day and night. Impersonating Father Christmas would not have been a bad idea to get into the room. Had this been the case, however, Madame Martin would not have been so reluctant to call in Maigret. Nor would she have been in so great a hurry to get out of the house afterwards on such a flimsy pretext. So Maigret had abandoned that theory.

"You want me to check each prisoner further?"

"Never mind. Any news about Paul Martin?"

"That was easy. He's known in every station house between the Bastille and the Hotel de Ville, and even on the Boulevard Saint-Michel."

"What did he do last night?"

"First he went aboard the Salvation Army barge to eat. He's a regular there one day a week and yesterday was his day. They had a special feast for Christmas Eve and he had to stand in line quite a while."

"After that?"

"About eleven o'clock he went to the Latin Quarter and opened doors for motorists in front of a night club. He

must have collected enough money in tips to get himself
a sinkful, because he was picked up dead drunk near the
Place Maubert at four in the morning. He was taken to
the station house to sleep it off, and was there until elev-
en this morning. They'd just turned him loose when I
phoned, and they promised to bring him to me when they
find him again. He still had a few francs in his pocket."

"What about Bergerac?"

"Jean Martin is taking the afternoon train for Paris. He
was quite upset by a phone call he got this morning."

"He got only one call?"

"Only one this morning. He got a call last night while
he was eating dinner."

"You know who called him?"

"The desk clerk says it was a man's voice, asking for
Monsieur Jean Martin. He sent somebody into the dining
room for Martin but when Martin got to the phone, the
caller had hung up. Seems it spoiled his whole evening.
He went out with a bunch of traveling salesmen to some
local hot-spot where there were pretty girls and what-
not, but after drinking a few glasses of champagne, he
couldn't talk about anything except his wife and daughter.
The niece he calls his daughter, it seems. He had such a
dismal evening that he went home early. Three A.M.
That's all you wanted to know, Chief?"

When Maigret didn't reply, Lucas had to satisfy his
curiosity. "You still phoning from home, Chief? What's
happening up your way? Somebody get killed?"

"I still can't say. Right now all I know is that the principals are a seven-year-old girl, a doll, and Father Christmas."

"Ah?"

"One more thing. Try to get me the home address of the
manager of Zenith Watches, Avenue de l'Opéra. You
ought to be able to raise somebody there, even on Christmas Day. Call me back."

"Soon as I have something."

Mme. Maigret had just served him a glass of Alsatian
plum brandy which his sister had sent them. He smacked
his lips. For a moment he was tempted to forget all about

the business of the doll and Father Christmas. It would be much simpler just to take his wife to the movies.

"What color eyes has she?"

It took him a moment to realize that the only person in the case who interested Mme. Maigret was the little girl.

"Why, I'm not quite sure. They can't be dark. She has blonde hair."

"So they're blue."

"Maybe they're blue. Very light, in any case. And they are very serious."

"Because she doesn't look at things like a child. Does she laugh?"

"She hasn't much to laugh about."

"A child can always laugh if she feels herself surrounded by people she can trust, people who let her act her age. I don't like that woman."

"You prefer Mlle. Doncoeur?"

"She may be an old maid but I'm sure she knows more about children than that Madame Martin. I've seen *her* in the shops. Madame Martin is one of those women who watch the scales and take their money out of their pocketbooks, coin by coin. She always looks around suspiciously, as though everybody was out to cheat her."

The telephone rang as Mme. Maigret was repeating, "I don't like that woman."

It was Lucas calling, with the address of Monsieur Arthur Godefroy, general manager in France for Zenith Watches. He lived in a sumptuous villa at Saint-Cloud, and Lucas had discovered that he was at home. He added:

"Paul Martin is here, Chief. When they brought him in, he started crying. He thought something had happened to his daughter. But he's all right now—except for an awful hangover. What do I do with him?"

"Anyone around who can come up here with him?"

"Torrence just came on duty. I think he could use a little fresh air. He looks as if he had a hard night, too. Anything more from me, Chief?"

"Yes. Call Palais-Royal station. About five years ago a man named Lorilleux disappeared without a trace. He sold jewelry and old coins in the Palais-Royal arcades. Get me all the details you can on his disappearance."

Maigret smiled as he noted that his wife was sitting opposite him with her knitting. He had never before worked on a case in such domestic surroundings.

"Do I call you back?" asked Lucas.

"I don't expect to move an inch from my chair."

A moment later Maigret was talking to Monsieur Godefroy, who had a decided Swiss accent. The Zenith manager thought that something must have happened to Jean Martin for anyone to be making inquiries about him on Christmas Day.

"Most able. Most devoted. I'm bringing him into Paris to be assistant manager next year—next week, that is. Why do you ask? Has anything—? Be still, you!" He paused to quiet the juvenile hubbub in the background. "You must excuse me. All my family is with me today and—"

"Tell me, Monsieur Godefroy, has anyone called your office these last few days to inquire about Monsieur Martin's current address?"

"Yesterday morning, as a matter of fact. I was very busy with the holiday rush, but he asked to speak to me personally. I forget what name he gave. He said he had an extremely important message for Jean Martin, so I told him how to get in touch with Martin in Bergerac."

"He asked you nothing else?"

"No. He hung up at once. Is anything wrong?"

"I hope not. Thank you very much, Monsieur."

The screams of children began again in the background and Maigret said goodbye.

"Were you listening?"

"I heard what you said. I didn't hear his answers."

"A man called the office yesterday morning to get Martin's address. The same man undoubtedly called Bergerac that evening to make sure Martin was still there, and therefore would not be at his Boulevard Richard-Lenoir address for Christmas Eve."

"The same man who appeared last night as Father Christmas?"

"More than likely. That seems to clear Paul Martin. He would not have to make two phone calls to find out where his brother was. Madame Martin would have told him."

"You're really getting excited about this case. You're delighted that it came up, aren't you? Confess!" And while Maigret was racking his brain for excuses, she added: "It's quite natural. I'm fascinated, too. How much longer do you think the child will have to keep her leg in a cast?"

"I didn't ask."

"I wonder what sort of complications she could have had?"

Maigret looked at her curiously. Unconsciously she had switched his mind onto a new track.

"That's not such a stupid remark you just made."

"What did I say?"

"After all, since she's been in bed for two months, she should be up and around soon, barring really serious complications."

"She'll probably have to walk on crutches at first."

"That's not the point. In a few days then, or a few weeks at most, she will no longer be confined to her room. She'll go for a walk with Madame Martin. And the coast will be clear for anyone to enter the apartment without dressing up like Father Christmas."

Mme. Maigret's lips were moving. While listening to her husband and watching his face, she was counting stitches.

"First of all, the presence of the child forced our man to use trickery. She's been in bed for two months—two months for him to wait. Without the complications the flooring could have been taken up several weeks ago. Our man must have had urgent reasons for acting at once, without further delay."

"Monsieur Martin will return to Paris in a few days?"

"Exactly."

"What do you suppose the man found underneath the floor?"

"Did he really find anything? If not, his problem is still

as pressing as it was last night. So he will take further action."

"What action?"

"I don't know."

"Look, Maigret, isn't the child in danger? Do you think she's safe with that woman?"

"I could answer that if I knew where Madame Martin went this morning on the pretext of doing her shopping." He picked up the phone again and called Police Judiciaire.

"I'm pestering you again, Lucas. I want you to locate a taxi that picked up a passenger this morning between nine and ten somewhere near Boulevard Richard-Lenoir. The fare was a woman in her early thirties, blonde, slim but solidly built. She was wearing a grey suit and a beige hat. She carried a brown shopping bag. I want to know her destination. There couldn't have been so many cabs on the street at that hour."

"Is Paul Martin with you?"

"Not yet."

"He'll be there soon. About that other thing, the Lorilleux matter, the Palais-Royal boys are checking their files. You'll have the data in a few minutes."

Jean Martin must be catching his train in Bergerac at this moment. Little Colette was probably taking her nap. Mlle. Doncoeur was doubtless sitting behind her window curtain, wondering what Maigret was up to.

People were beginning to come out now, families with their children, the children with their new toys. There were certainly queues in front of the cinemas.

A taxi stopped in front of the house. Footsteps sounded in the stairway. Mme. Maigret went to the door. The deep bass voice of Torrence rumbled: "You there, Chief?"

Torrence came in with an ageless man who hugged the walls and looked humbly at the floor. Maigret went to the sideboard and filled two glasses with plum brandy.

"To your health," he said.

The man looked at Maigret with surprised, anxious eyes. He raised a trembling, hesitant hand.

"To your health, Monsieur Martin. I'm sorry to make

you come all the way up here, but you won't have far to
go now to see your daughter."

"Nothing has happened to her?"

"No, no. When I saw her this morning she was playing
with her new doll. You can go, Torrence. Lucas must
need you."

Mme. Maigret had gone into the bedroom with her knitting. She was sitting on the edge of the bed, counting her
stitches.

"Sit down, Monsieur Martin."

The man had touched his lips to the glass and set it
down. He looked at it uneasily.

"You have nothing to worry about. Just tell yourself
that I know all about you."

"I wanted to visit her this morning," the man sighed. "I
swore I would go to bed early so I could wish her a Merry
Christmas."

"I know that, too."

"It's always the same. I swear I'll take just one drink,
just enough to pick me up."

"You have only one brother, Monsieur Martin?"

"Yes, Jean. He's six years younger than I am. He and
my wife and my daughter were all I had to love in this
world.

"You don't love your sister-in-law?"

He shivered. He seemed both startled and embarrassed.

"I have nothing against Loraine."

"You entrusted your child to her, didn't you?"

"Well, yes, that is to say, when my wife died and I began to slip."

"I understand. Is your daughter happy?"

"I think so, yes. She never complains."

"Have you ever tried to get back on your feet?"

"Every night I promise myself to turn over a new leaf,
but next day I start all over again. I even went to see a
doctor. I followed his advice for a few days. But when I
went back, he was very busy. He said I ought to be in a
special sanatorium."

He reached for his glass, then hesitated. Maigret picked
up his own glass and took a swallow to encourage him.

"Did you ever meet a man in your sister-in-law's apartment?"

"No, I think she's above reproach on that score."

"Do you know where your brother first met her?"

"In a little restaurant in the Rue Beaujolais where he used to eat when he was in Paris. It was near the shop where Loraine was working."

"Did they have a long engagement?"

"I can't say. Jean was on the road for two months and when he came back he told me he was getting married."

"Were you his best man?"

"Yes. Loraine has no family in Paris. She's an orphan. So her landlady acted as her witness. Is there something wrong?"

"I don't know yet. A man entered Colette's room last night dressed as Father Christmas. He gave your girl a doll and lifted two loose boards from the floor."

"Do you think I'm in fit condition to see her?"

"You can go over in a little while. If you feel like it you can shave here. Do you think your brother would be likely to hide anything under the floor?"

"Jean? Never!"

"Even if he wanted to hide something from his wife?"

"He doesn't hide things from his wife. You don't know him. He's one of those rare humans—a scrupulously honest man. When he comes home from the road, she knows exactly how much money he has left, to the last centime."

"Is she jealous?"

Paul Martin did not reply.

"I advise you to tell me what you know. Remember that your daughter is involved in this."

"I don't think that Loraine is especially jealous. Not of women, at least. Perhaps about money. At least that's what my poor wife always said. She didn't like Loraine."

"Why not?"

"She used to say that Loraine's lips were too thin, that she was too polite, too cold, always on the defensive. My wife always thought that Loraine set her cap for Jean because he had a good job with a future and owned his own furniture."

"Loraine had no money of her own?"

"She never speaks of her family. I understand her father died when she was very young and her mother did housework somewhere in the Glacière quarter. My poor wife used to say, 'Loraine knows what she wants.' "

"Do you think she was Lorilleux's mistress?"

Paul Martin did not reply. Maigret poured him another finger of plum brandy. Martin gave him a grateful look, but he did not touch the glass. Perhaps he was thinking that his daughter might notice his breath when he crossed the street later on.

"I'll get you a cup of coffee in a moment. Your wife must have had her own ideas on the subject."

"How did you know? Please note that my wife never spoke disparagingly of people. But with Loraine it was almost pathological. Whenever we were to meet my sister-in-law, I used to beg my wife not to show her antipathy. It's funny that you should bring all that up now, at this time in my life. Do you think I did wrong in letting her take Colette? I sometimes think so. But what else could I have done?"

"You didn't answer my question about Loraine's former employer."

"Oh, yes. My wife always said it was very convenient for Loraine to have married a man who was away from home so much."

"You know where she lived before her marriage?"

"In a street just off Boulevard Sébastopol, on the right as you walk from Rue de Rivoli toward the Boulevard. I remember we picked her up there the day of the wedding."

"Rue Pernelle?"

"That's it. The fourth or fifth house on the left side of the street in a quiet rooming house, quite respectable. People who work in the neighborhood live there. I remember there were several little actresses from the Châtelet."

"Would you like to shave, Monsieur Martin?"

"I'm ashamed. Still, since my daughter is just across the street—"

"Come with me."

Maigret took him through the kitchen so he wouldn't have to meet Mme. Maigret in the bedroom. He set out the necessary toilet articles, not forgetting a clothes brush.

When he returned to the dining room, Mme. Maigret poked her head through the door and whispered: "What's he doing?"

"He's shaving."

Once more Maigret reached for the telephone. He was certainly giving poor Lucas a busy Christmas Day.

"Are you indispensable at the office?"

"Not if Torrence sits in for me. I've got the information you wanted."

"In just a moment. I want you to jump over to Rue Pernelle. There's a rooming house a few doors down from the Boulevard Sébastopol. If the proprietor wasn't there five years ago, try to dig up someone who lived there then. I want everything you can find out on a certain Loraine."

"Loraine who?"

"Just a minute. I didn't think of that."

Through the bathroom door he asked Martin for the maiden name of his sister-in-law. A few seconds later he was on the phone again.

"Loraine Boitel," he told Lucas. "The landlady of this rooming house was witness at her marriage to Jean Martin. Loraine Boitel was working for Lorilleux at the time. Try to find out if she was more than a secretary to him, and if he ever came to see her. And work fast. This may be urgent. What have you got on Lorilleux?"

"He was quite a fellow. At home in the Rue Mazarine he was a good respectable family man. In his Palais-Royal shop he not only sold old coins and souvenirs of Paris, but he had a fine collection of pornographic books and obscene pictures."

"Not unusual for the Palais-Royal."

"I don't know what else went on there. There was a big divan covered with red silk rep in the back room, but the investigation was never pushed. Seems there were a lot of important names among his customers."

"What about Loraine Boitel?"

"The report barely mentions her, except that she waited all morning for Lorilleux the day he disappeared. I was on the phone about this when Langlois of the Financial Squad came into my office. The name Lorilleux rang a bell in the back of his mind and he went to check his files. Nothing definite on him, but he'd been making frequent trips to Switzerland and back, and there was a lot of gold smuggling going on at that time. Lorilleux was stopped and searching at the frontier several times, but they never found anything on him."

"Lucas, old man, hurry over to Rue Pernelle. I'm more than ever convinced that this is urgent."

Paul Martin appeared in the doorway, his pale cheeks close-shaven.

"I don't know how to thank you. I'm very much embarrassed."

"You'll visit your daughter now, won't you? I don't know how long you usually stay, but today I don't want you to leave until I come for you."

"I can't very well stay all night, can I?"

"Stay all night if necessary. Manage the best you can."

"Is the little girl in danger?"

"I don't know, but your place today is with your daughter."

Paul Martin drank his black coffee avidly, and started for the stairway. The door had just closed after him when Mme. Maigret rushed into the dining room.

"You can't let him go to see his daughter empty-handed on Christmas Day!"

"But—" Maigret was about to say that there just didn't happen to be a doll around the house, when his wife thrust a small shiny object into his hands. It was a gold thimble which had been in her sewing basket for years but which she never used.

"Give him that. Little girls always like thimbles. Hurry!"

He shouted from the landing: "Monsieur Martin! Just a minute, Monsieur Martin!"

He closed the man's fingers over the thimble. "Don't tell a soul where you got this."

Before re-entering the dining room he stood for a moment on the threshold, grumbling. Then he sighed: "I hope you've finished making me play Father Christmas."

"I'll bet she likes the thimble as well as a doll. It's something grown-ups use, you know."

They watched the man cross the boulevard. Before going into the house, he turned to look up at Maigret's windows, as if seeking encouragement.

"Do you think he'll ever be cured?"

"I doubt it."

"If anything happens to that woman, to Madame Martin—"

"Well?"

"Nothing. I was thinking of the little girl. I wonder what would become of her."

Ten minutes passed. Maigret had opened his newspaper and lighted his pipe. His wife had settled down again with her knitting. She was counting stitches when he exhaled a cloud of smoke and murmured: "You haven't even seen her."

Maigret was looking for an old envelope, on the back of which he had jotted down a few notes summing up the day's events. He found it in a drawer into which Mme. Maigret always stuffed any papers she found lying around the house.

This was the only investigation, he mused, which he had ever conducted practically in its entirety from his favorite armchair. It was also unusual in that no dramatic stroke of luck had come to his aid. True, luck had been on his side, in that he had been able to muster all his facts by the simplest and most direct means. How many times had he deployed scores of detectives on an all-night search for some minor detail. This might have happened, for instance, if Monsieur Arthur Godefroy of Zenith had gone home to Zurich for Christmas, or if he had been out of reach of a telephone. Or if Monsieur Godefroy had been unaware of the telephone inquiry regarding the where-abouts of Jean Martin.

When Lucas arrived shortly after four o'clock, his nose red and his face pinched with the cold, he too could report the same kind of undramatic luck.

A thick yellow fog, unusual for Paris, had settled over the city. Lights shone in all the windows, floating on the murk like ships at sea or distant beacons. Familiar details had been blotted out so completely that Maigret half-expected to hear the moan of foghorns.

For some reason, perhaps because of some boyhood memory, Maigret was pleased to see the weather thicken. He was also pleased to see Lucas walk into his apartment, take off his overcoat, sit down, and stretch out his frozen hands toward the fire.

In appearance, Lucas was a reduced-scale model of Maigret—a head shorter, half as broad in the shoulders, half as stern in expression although he tried hard. Without conscious imitation but with conscious admiration, Lucas had copied his chief's slightest gestures, postures, and changes of expression—even to the ceremony of inhaling the fragrance of the plum brandy before touching his lips to the glass.

The landlady of the rooming house in the Rue Pernelle had been killed in a subway accident two years earlier, Lucas reported. Luckily, the place had been taken over by the former night watchman, who had been in trouble with the police on morals charges.

"So it was easy enough to make him talk," said Lucas, lighting a pipe much too large for him. "I was surprised that he had the money to buy the house, but he explained that he was front man for a big investor who had money in all sorts of enterprises but didn't like to have his name used."

"What kind of dump is it?"

"Looks respectable. Clean enough. Office on the mez-zanine. Rooms by the month, some by the week, and a few on the second floor by the hour."

"He remembers Loraine?"

"Very well. She lived there more than three years. I got

the impression he didn't like her because she was tight-fisted."

"Did Lorilleux come to see her?"

"On my way to the Rue Pernelle I picked up a photo of Lorilleux at the Palais-Royal station. The new landlord recognized him right away."

"Lorilleux went to her room often?"

"Two or three times a month. He always had baggage with him, he always arrived around one o'clock in the morning, and always left before six. I checked the time-tables. There's a train from Switzerland around midnight and another at six in the morning. He must have told his wife he was taking the six o'clock train."

"Nothing else?"

"Nothing, except that Loraine was stingy with tips, and always cooked her dinner on an alcohol burner, even though the house rules said no cooking in the rooms."

"No other men?"

"No. Very respectable except for Lorilleux. The land-lady was witness at her wedding."

Maigret glanced at his wife. He had insisted she remain in the room when Lucas came. She stuck to her knitting, trying to make believe she was not there.

Torrence was out in the fog, going from garage to garage, checking the trip-sheets of taxi fleets. The two men waited serenely, deep in their easy chairs, each holding a glass of plum brandy with the same pose. Maigret felt a pleasant numbness creeping over him.

His Christmas luck held out with the taxis, too. Some-times it took days to run down a particular taxi driver, particularly when the cab in question did not belong to a fleet. Cruising drivers were the hardest to locate; they sometimes never even read the newspapers. But shortly before five o'clock, Torrence called from Saint-Ouen.

"I found one of the taxis," he reported.

"One? Was there more than one?"

"Looks that way. This man picked up the woman at the corner of Boulevard Richard-Lenoir and Boulevard Voltaire this morning. He drove her to Rue de Maubeuge, opposite the Gare du Nord, where she paid him off."

"Did she go into the railway station?"

"No. The chauffeur says she went into a luggage shop that keeps open on Sundays and holidays. After that he doesn't know."

"Where's the driver now?"

"Right here in the garage. He just checked in."

"Send him to me, will you? Right away. I don't care how he gets here as long as it's in a hurry. Now I want you to find me the cab that brought her home."

"Sure, Chief, as soon as I get myself a coffee with a stick in it. It's damned cold out here."

Maigret glanced through the window. There was a shadow against Mlle. Doncoeur's curtains. He turned to Lucas.

"Look in the phone book for a luggage shop across from the Gare du Nord."

Lucas took only a minute to come up with a number, which Maigret dialed.

"Hello, this is the Police Judiciaire. Shortly before ten this morning a young woman bought something in your shop, probably a valise. She was a blonde, wearing a grey suit and beige hat. She carried a brown shopping bag. Do you remember her?"

Perhaps trade was slack on Christmas Day. Or perhaps it was easier to remember customers who shopped on Christmas. In any case, the voice on the phone replied:

"Certainly, I waited on her myself. She said she had to leave suddenly for Cambrai because her sister was ill, and she didn't have time to go home for her bags. She wanted a cheap valise, and I sold her a fiber model we have on sale. She paid me and went into the bar next door. I was standing in the doorway and a little later I saw her walking toward the station, carrying the valise."

"Are you alone in your shop?"

"I have one clerk on duty."

"Can you leave him alone for half an hour? Fine! Then jump in a taxi and come to this address. I'll pay the fare, of course."

"And the return fare? Shall I have the cab wait?"

"Have him wait, yes."

According to Maigret's notes on the back of the envelope, the first taxi driver arrived at 5:50 P.M. He was somewhat surprised, since he had been summoned by the police, to find himself in a private apartment. He recognized Maigret, however, and made no effort to disguise his curious interest in how the famous inspector lived.

"I want you to climb to the fourth floor of the house just across the street. If the concierge stops you, tell her you're going to see Madame Martin."

"Madame Martin. I got it."

"Go to the door at the end of the hall and ring the bell. If a blonde opens the door and you recognize her, make some excuse—you're on the wrong floor, anything you think of. If somebody else answers, ask to speak to Madame Martin personally."

"And then?"

"Then you come back here and tell me whether or not she is the fare you drove to Rue de Maubeuge this morning."

"I'll be right back, Inspector."

As the door closed, Maigret smiled in spite of himself.

"The first call will make her worry a little. The second, if all goes well, will make her panicky. The third, if Torrence has any luck—"

Torrence, too, was having his run of Christmas luck. The phone rang and he reported:

"I think I've found him, Chief. I dug up a driver who picked up a woman answering your description at the Gare du Nord, only he didn't take her to Boulevard Richard-Lenoir. He dropped her at the corner of Boulevard Beaumarchais and the Rue du Chemin-Vert."

"Send him to me."

"He's a little squiffed."

"No matter. Where are you?"

"The Barbès garage."

"Then it won't be much out of your way to stop by the Gare du Nord. Go to the check room. Unfortunately it won't be the same man on duty, but try to find out if a small new valise was checked between 9:30 and 10 this morning. It's made of fiber and shouldn't be too heavy.

Get the number of the check. They won't let you take the
valise without a warrant, so try to get the name and address of the man on duty this morning."

"What next?"

"Phone me. I'll wait for your second taxi driver. If he's
been drinking, better write down my address for him, so
he won't get lost."

Mme. Maigret was back in the kitchen, preparing the
evening meal. She hadn't dared ask whether Lucas would
eat with them.

Maigret wondered if Paul Martin was still across the
street with his daughter. Had Madame Martin tried to get
rid of him?

The bell rang again. Two men stood at the door.

The first driver had come back from Madame Martin's
and had climbed Maigret's stairs behind the luggage
dealer.

"Did you recognize her?"

"Sure. She recognized me, too. She turned pale. She ran
to close a door behind her, then she asked me what I
wanted."

"What did you tell her?"

"That I had the wrong floor. I think maybe she wanted
to buy me off, but I didn't give her a chance. But she was
watching from the window when I crossed the street. She
probably knows I came here."

The luggage dealer was baffled and showed it. He was
a middle-aged man, completely bald and equally obse-
quious. When the driver had gone, Maigret explained
what he wanted, and the man objected vociferously.

"One just doesn't do this sort of thing to one's customers," he repeated stubbornly. "One simply does not in-
form on one's customers, you know."

After a long argument he agreed to call on Madame
Martin. To make sure he didn't change his mind, Maigret
sent Lucas to follow him.

They returned in less than ten minutes.

"I call your attention to the fact that I have acted under
your orders, that I have been compelled—"

"Did you recognize her?"

"Will I be forced to testify under oath?"

"More than likely."

"That would be very bad for my business. People who buy luggage at the last minute are very often people who dislike public mention of their comings and goings."

"You may not have to go to court. Your deposition before the examining magistrate may be sufficient."

"Very well. It was she. She's dressed differently, but I recognized her all right."

"Did she recognize you?"

"She asked immediately who had sent me."

"What did you say?"

"I . . . I don't remember. I was quite upset. I think I said I had rung the wrong bell."

"Did she offer you anything?"

"What do you mean? She didn't even offer me a chair. Luckily. It would have been most unpleasant."

Maigret smiled, somewhat incredulously. He believed that the taxi driver had actually run away from a possible bribe. He wasn't so sure about this prosperous-looking shopkeeper who obviously begrudged his loss of time.

"Thank you for your cooperation."

The luggage dealer departed hastily.

"And now for Number Three, my dear Lucas."

Mme. Maigret was beginning to grow nervous. From the kitchen door she made discreet signs to her husband, beckoning him to join her. She whispered: "Are you sure the father is still across the street?"

"Why?"

"I don't know. I can't make out exactly what you're up to, but I've been thinking about the child, and I'm a little afraid."

Night had long since fallen. The families were all home again. Few windows across the street remained dark. The silhouette of Mlle. Doncoeur was still very much in evidence.

While waiting for the second taxi driver, Maigret decided to put on his collar and tie. He shouted to Lucas:

"Pour yourself another drop. Aren't you hungry?"

"I'm full of sandwiches, Chief. Only one thing I'd like when we go out: a tall beer, right from the spigot."

The second driver arrived at 6:20. At 6:35 he had returned from across the street, a gleam in his eye.

"She looks even better in her negligee than she does in her street clothes," he said thickly. "She made me come in and she asked who sent me. I didn't know what to say, so I told her I was a talent scout for the Folies Bergère. Was she furious! She's a fine hunk of woman, though, and I mean it. Did you get a look at her legs?"

He was in no hurry to leave. Maigret saw him ogling the bottle of plum brandy with envious eyes, and poured him a glass—to speed him on his way.

"What are you going to do next, Chief?" Lucas had rarely seen Maigret proceed with such caution, preparing each step with such care that he seemed to be mounting an attack on some desperate criminal. And yet the enemy was only a woman, a seemingly insignificant little housewife.

"You think she'll still fight back?"

"Fiercely. And what's more, in cold blood."

"What are you waiting for?"

"The phone call from Torrence."

As if on cue, the telephone rang. Torrence, of course.

"The valise is here all right. It feels practically empty. As you predicted, they won't give it to me without a warrant. The check-room attendant who was on duty this morning lives in the suburbs, near La Varenne-Saint-Hilaire." A snag at last? Or at least a delay? Maigret frowned. But Torrence continued. "We won't have to go out there, though. When he finishes his day's work here, he plays cornet in a *bal musette* in the Rue de Lappe."

"Go get him for me."

"Shall I bring him to your place?"

Maigret hesitated, thinking of Lucas's yearning for a glass of draft beer.

"No, I'll be across the street. Madame Martin's apartment, fourth floor."

He took down his heavy overcoat. He filled his pipe.

"Coming?" he said to Lucas.

Mme. Maigret ran after him to ask what time he'd be home for dinner. After a moment of hesitation, he smiled.

"The usual time," was his not very reassuring answer.

"Look out for the little girl, will you?"

At ten o'clock that evening the investigation was still blocked. It was unlikely that anyone in the whole building had gone to sleep, except Colette. She had finally dozed off, with her father sitting in the dark by her bedside.

Torrence had arrived at 7:30 with his part-time musician and checkroom attendant, who declared:

"She's the one. I remember she didn't put the check in her handbag. She slipped it into a big brown shopping bag." And when they took him into the kitchen he added, "That's the bag. Or one exactly like it."

The Martin apartment was very warm. Everyone spoke in low tones, as if they had agreed not to awaken the child. Nobody had eaten. Nobody, apparently, was even hungry. On their way over, Maigret and Lucas had each drunk two beers in a little cafe on the Boulevard Voltaire.

After the cornetist had spoken his piece, Maigret took Torrence aside and murmured fresh instructions.

Every corner of the apartment had been searched. Even the photos of Martin's parents had been taken from their frames, to make sure the baggage check had not been secreted between picture and backing. The dishes had been taken from their shelves and piled on the kitchen table. The larder had been emptied and examined closely. No baggage check.

Madame Martin was still wearing her pale blue negligee. She was chain-smoking cigarettes. What with the smoke from the two men's pipes, a thick blue haze swirled about the lamps.

"You are, of course, free to say nothing and answer no questions. Your husband will arrive at 11:17. Perhaps you will be more talkative in his presence."

"He doesn't know any more than I do."

"Does he know as much?"

"There's nothing to know. I've told you everything."

She had sat back and denied everything, all along the

line. She had conceded only one point. She admitted that
Lorilleux had dropped in to see her two or three times
at night when she lived in the Rue Pernelle. But she
insisted there had been nothing between them, nothing
personal.

"In other words, he came to talk business—at one
o'clock in the morning?"

"He used to come to town by a late train, and he didn't
like to walk the streets with large sums of money on him.
I already told you he might have been smuggling gold,
but I had nothing to do with it. You can't arrest me for his
activities."

"Did he have large sums of money on him when he disappeared?"

"I don't know. He didn't always take me into his confidence."

"But he did come to see you in your room at night?"

Despite the evidence, she clung to her story of the
morning's marketing. She denied ever having seen the
two taxi drivers, the luggage dealer, or the checkroom attendant.

"If I had really left a package at the Gare du Nord, you
would have found the check, wouldn't you?"

She glanced nervously at the clock on the mantel, obviously thinking of her husband's return.

"Admit that the man who came last night found nothing
under the floor because you changed the hiding place."

"I know of nothing that was hidden under the floor."

"When you learned of his visit, you decided to move
the treasure to the checkroom for safekeeping."

"I haven't been near the Gare du Nord. There must be
thousands of blondes in Paris who answer my description."

"I think I know where we'll find the check."

"You're so very clever."

"Sit over here at this table," Maigret produced a foun-
tain pen and a sheet of paper. "Write your name and
address."

She hesitated, then obeyed.

"Tonight every letter mailed in this neighborhood will

be examined, and I'll wager we will find one addressed in your handwriting, probably to yourself."

He handed the paper to Lucas with an order to get in touch with the postal authorities. Much to his surprise, the woman reacted visibly.

"You see, it's a very old trick, Little One." For the first time he called her "Little One," the way he would have done if he were questioning her in his office, Quai des Orfèvres.

They were alone now. Maigret slowly paced the floor, while she remained seated.

"In case you're interested," Maigret said slowly, "the thing that shocks me most about you is not what you have done but the cold-blooded way you have done it. You've been dangling at the end of a slender thread since early this morning, and you still haven't blinked an eye. When your husband comes home, you'll try to play the martyr. And yet you know that sooner or later we'll discover the truth."

"But I've done nothing wrong."

"Then why do you lie?"

She did not reply. She was still far from the breaking point. Her nerves were calm, but her mind was obviously racing at top speed, seeking some avenue of escape.

"I'm not saying anything more," she declared. She sat down and pulled the hem of her negligee over her bare knees.

"Suit yourself." Maigret made himself comfortable in a chair opposite her.

"Are you going to stay here all night?" she asked.

"At least until your husband gets home."

"Are you going to tell him about Monsieur Lorilleux's visits to my room?"

"If necessary."

"You're a cad! Jean knows nothing about all this. He had no part in it."

"Unfortunately he is your husband."

When Lucas came back, they were staring at each other in silence.

"Janvier is taking care of the letter, Chief. I met Torrence downstairs. He says the man is in that little bar, two doors down from your house."

She sprang up. "What man?"

Maigret didn't move a muscle. "The man who came here last night. You must have expected him to come back, since he didn't find what he was looking for. And he might be in a different frame of mind this time."

She cast a dismayed glance at the clock. The train from Bergerac was due in twenty minutes. Her husband could be home in forty. She asked: "You know who this man is?"

"I can guess. I could go down and confirm my suspicion. I'd say it is Lorilleux and I'd say he is very eager to get back his property."

"It's not his property!"

"Let's say that, rightly or wrongly, he considers it his property. He must be in desperate straits, this man. He came to see you twice without getting what he wanted. He came back a third time disguised as Father Christmas. And he'll come back again. He'll be surprised to find you have company. I'm convinced that he'll be more talkative than you. Despite the general belief, men always speak more freely than women. Do you think he is armed?"

"I don't know."

"I think he is. He is tired of waiting. I don't know what story you've been telling him, but I'm sure he's fed up with it. The gentleman has a vicious face. There's nothing quite as cruel as a weakling with his back up."

"Shut up!"

"Would you like us to go so that you can be alone with him?"

The back of Maigret's envelope contained the following note: "10:38 P.M.—she decides to talk."

It was not a very connected story at first. It came out in bits and pieces, fragments of sentences interlarded with venomous asides, supplemented by Maigret's own guesses, which she either confirmed or amended.

"What do you want to know?"

"Was it money that you left in the checkroom?"

"Bank notes. Almost a million."

"Did the money belong to Lorilleux?"

"No more to him than to me."

"To one of his customers?"

"Yes. A man named Julian Boissy."

"What became of him?"

"He died."

"How?"

"He was killed."

"By whom?"

"By Monsieur Lorilleux."

"Why?"

"Because I gave him to understand that if he could raise enough money—real money—I might run away with him."

"You were already married?"

"Yes."

"You're not in love with your husband?"

"I despise mediocrity. All my life I've been poor. All my life I've been surrounded by people who have had to scrimp and save, people who have had to sacrifice and count centimes. I've had to scrimp and sacrifice and count centimes myself." She turned savagely on Maigret, as if he had been responsible for all her troubles. "I just didn't want to be poor any more."

"Would you have gone away with Lorilleux?"

"I don't know. Perhaps for a while."

"Long enough to get your hands on his money?"

"I hate you!"

"How was Boissy murdered?"

"Monsieur Boissy was a regular customer of long standing."

"Pornographic literature?"

"He was a lascivious old goat, sure. So are all men. So is Lorilleux. So are you, probably. Boissy was a widower. He lived alone in a hotel room. He was very rich and very stingy. All rich people are stingy."

"That doesn't work both ways, does it? You, for instance, are not rich."

"I would have been rich."

"If Lorilleux had not come back. How did Boissy die?"

"The devaluation of the franc scared him out of his wits. Like everybody else at that time, he wanted gold. Monsieur Lorilleux used to shuttle gold in from Switzerland pretty regularly. And he always demanded payment in advance. One afternoon Monsieur Boissy came to the shop with a fortune in currency. I wasn't there. I had gone out on an errand."

"You planned it that way?"

"No."

"You had no idea what was going to happen?"

"No. Don't try to put words in my mouth. When I came back, Lorilleux was packing the body into a big box."

"And you blackmailed him?"

"No."

"Then why did he disappear after having given you the money?"

"I frightened him."

"You threatened to go to the police?"

"No. I merely told him that our neighbors in the Palais-Royal had been looking at me suspiciously and that I thought he ought to put the money in a safe place for a while. I told him about the loose floorboard in my apartment. He thought it would only be for a few days. Two days later he asked me to cross the Belgian frontier with him."

"And you refused?"

"I told him I'd been stopped and questioned by a man who looked like a police inspector. He was terrified. I gave him some of the money and promised to join him in Brussels as soon as it was safe."

"What did he do with the corpse?"

"He put the box in a taxi and drove to a little country house he owned on the banks of the Marne. I suppose he either buried it there or threw it into the river. Nobody ever missed Monsieur Boissy."

"So you sent Lorilleux to Belgium without you. How did you keep him away for five years?"

"I used to write him, general delivery. I told him the police were after him, and that he probably would read nothing about it in the papers because they were setting a trap for him. I told him the police were always coming back to question me. I even sent him to South America."

"He came back two months ago?"

"About. He was at the end of his rope."

"Didn't you send him any money?"

"Not much."

"Why not?"

She did not reply. She looked at the clock.

"Are you going to arrest me? What will be the charge? I didn't kill Boissy. I wasn't there when he was killed. I had nothing to do with disposing of his body."

"Stop worrying about yourself. You kept the money because all your life you wanted money—not to spend, but to keep, to feel secure, to feel rich and free from want."

"That's my business."

"When Lorilleux came back to ask for money, or to ask you to keep your promise and run away with him, you used Colette as a pretext. You tried to scare him into leaving the country again, didn't you?"

"He stayed in Paris, hiding." Her upper lip curled slightly. "What an idiot! He could have shouted his name from the housetops and nobody would have noticed."

"The business of Father Christmas wasn't idiotic."

"No? The money wasn't under the floorboard any longer. It was right here under his nose, in my sewing basket."

"Your husband will be here in ten or fifteen minutes. Lorilleux across the street probably knows it. He's been in touch with Bergerac by phone, and he can read a timetable. He's surely armed. Do you want to wait here for your two men?"

"Take me away! I'll slip on a dress—"

"The checkroom stub?"

"General delivery, Boulevard Beaumarchais."

She did not close the bedroom door after her. Brazenly she dropped the negligee from her shoulders and sat on the edge of the bed to pull on her stockings. She selected a woolen dress from the closet, tossed toilet articles and lingerie into an overnight bag.

"Let's hurry!"

"Your husband?"

"That fool? Leave him for the birds."

"Colette?"

She shrugged.

Mlle. Doncoeur's door opened a crack as they passed.

Downstairs on the sidewalk she clung fearfully to the two men, peering into the fog.

"Take her to the Quai des Orfèvres, Lucas. I'm staying here."

She held back. There was no car in sight, and she was obviously frightened by the prospect of walking into the night with only Lucas to protect her. Lucas was not very big.

"Don't be afraid. Lorilleux is not in this vicinity."

"You lied to me! You—you—"

Maigret went back into the house.

The conference with Jean Martin lasted two hours.

When Maigret left the house at one thirty, the two brothers were in serious conversation. There was a crack of light under Mlle. Doncoeur's door, but she did not open the door as he passed.

When he got home, his wife was asleep in a chair in the dining room. His place was still set. Mme. Maigret awoke with a start.

"You're alone?" When he looked at her with amused surprise, she added, "Didn't you bring the little girl home?"

"Not tonight. She's asleep. You can go for her tomorrow morning."

"Why, then we're going to—"

"No, not permanently. Jean Martin may console himself with some decent girl. Or perhaps his brother will get back on his feet and find a new wife."

"In other words, she won't be ours?"

"Not in fee simple, no. Only on loan. I thought that would be better than nothing. I thought it would make you happy."

"Why, yes, of course. It will make me very happy. But . . . but . . ."

She sniffed once and fumbled for her handkerchief. When she couldn't find it, she buried her face in her apron.

—translated by Lawrence G. Blochman

APPALACHIAN BLACKMAIL
by Jacqueline Vivelo

My great-aunt Molly Hardison was a wealthy woman. By the standards of the coal mining town that was home to my family, she was fabulously rich. We didn't have any particular claim on her; she had nearer relatives. Still, she never forgot us children—and there were eight of us—at Christmastime. Once in every two or three years, she would come and spend the holiday with us.

Mama said Christmas with us was more like Aunt Molly's own childhood holidays than Christmas at her grand house or with her sons and their snooty wives.

We were poor all the time, and some years we were poorer than others. Nevertheless, at Christmas our house would be filled with evergreen boughs, pine cones, and red ribbons. Mama would keep hot cider simmering on the back of the woodstove so the house always smelled of cinnamon and cloves. No matter how bad things were, Papa could take his hunting dog, first Ol' Elsie and then later her son Ol' Ben, and bring in game. He brought home quail by the dozens, deer, wild turkeys.

Sometimes he'd be the only person we knew who had found a turkey, but he'd always get ours for the holiday. I think he was smart in the ways of turkeys. I was his tomboy and counted myself in on his discussions about hunting with my brothers. Papa would follow a goodsized turkey gobbler for weeks, learning its ways and finding its roosts. Turkeys like to move around, which is why they fool so many hunters, and they almost always have more than one roost.

I listened to all my father could tell us about hunting and would have gone with him when he began to take Joe and Cliff, but Mama put her foot down. I had to content myself with taking care of the hunting dog.

"Maybe someday, Betsy," Papa consoled me. "You'd make a fine hunter."

In any case, our house looked and smelled good at Christmas. It was filled with all the food a resourceful country family could provide. In our neck of the woods that was better than most city families, poor or rich, could do.

So, fairly regularly Aunt Molly would come and spend Christmas in our bustling, over-crowded house. Whether she was there or not, she always sent presents. Her sister, our own grandmother, was dead, which made her something of a stand-in. But we children understood that presents for Christmas and our birthdays would be all we could expect from Aunt Molly, except, of course, for my sister Molly.

I don't think any scheming was involved on my mother's part. I think she just liked the name Molly. She named her first daughter for her mother and her second daughter for her aunt. It didn't hurt that both Mollys happened to be green-eyed redheads. Our Molly was the only redhead among the eight of us and the only one with green eyes. We understood, all of us from oldest to youngest, that our Molly was special to Aunt Molly.

Aunt Molly made it clear that something more than seasonal presents would come Molly's way. I was five the Christmas that Aunt Molly first brought her ruby and diamond necklace with her. Molly was twelve that year when our great-aunt put that magnificent necklace on her for the first time.

"It isn't yours yet, but it will be. I'm not having it go to either of my daughters-in-law. It'll be yours."

We were all in awe of those old stones that glowed with fire. Even the boys took a look, rolled their eyes, and murmured, "Wowee."

"When?" my sister Amanda, oldest of all and most practical, asked.

Aunt Molly fairly cackled.

"When? Well, you see, she'll get to keep it when she marries. Marriage," Great-aunt Molly said, "is the only choice open to a girl. It's the only way to live."

From then on, every Christmas that Aunt Molly spent with us included another look at the necklace and another review of what Molly had to do to get it.

When my sister Amanda was nineteen, she married Dr. Harvey Brittaman, a young G. P. who had just taken up practice in our area. Great-aunt Molly gave them a full set of fine dishes, a hundred and two pieces.

Everybody agreed that none of the rest of us girls was likely to do any better than Amanda had. After all, a doctor!

Sister Molly was seventeen that year. I always thought she was the best-looking of all of us, though later on my little sister Cindy turned out to be a beauty, too. Molly had creamy fair skin without freckles and deep dark red hair. She was slim and tall and wore her hair long. She liked nothing in the world better than reading and carried a book with her everywhere. She would sit on a damp hillside and read until someone, usually me, went and told her to come home.

She had lots of admirers in high school, but two were the frontrunners. Malcolm Bodey was a football player, and Jerry Rattagan edited the school newspaper. Malcolm was planning to go into the mines like the rest of his family. Jerry was going on to the state university.

"You wait for the older men," Aunt Molly told sister Molly when she came for Amanda's wedding. "These boys are fine, but someone better will come along."

That wedding started me thinking. I was ten at the time. I thought about losing Amanda. I thought about marrying in general. I thought about me. I tried to picture me marrying one of the boys I knew, and it was an awful thought. I decided to try again to persuade Mama to let Papa teach me to hunt. I figured what I'd really like was to be a woodsman and live alone in a cabin in the woods. In our house I never had any time or any place alone.

Then I thought about Molly, Molly and the ruby and diamond necklace. For the first time I saw that the necklace hadn't been anything but trouble. For one thing, it had turned my sister Amanda bitter. Here she was, the oldest and the first married, but she wasn't getting the necklace. Aunt Molly had given her Royal Doulton china worth a king's ransom, but it didn't take away the sting. Amanda bore the brunt of the sense of rejection, but I suddenly saw that it was there for all of us, boys as well as girls.

A year later Molly graduated from high school and went to work at Lacy's drugstore. She didn't talk to any of us about what she wanted, but it was easy to see she was unhappy. Malcolm was determined to marry her, and it seemed to me she was weakening.

I felt like there was something about Molly I was missing, so out on the hillside one day I just asked her outright, "How do you really feel about that necklace Aunt Molly's going to give you when you get married?"

Well, she told me. I guess nobody had ever asked her that question before. She spilled out her feelings, her hopes, her wishes—everything in one long outburst. "Didn't you know?" she asked. "Didn't you guess? You're the one who's always watching everybody. I thought you didn't miss a thing—not that I expected anybody else to guess. But I thought you would."

I felt pretty stupid. Once she told me, it seemed obvious.

That next Christmas was one that Aunt Molly spent with us. She showed up two days before Christmas, in time to put her presents under the tree and to help with some of the cooking. Her coming brought back all the things I'd been thinking about when Amanda was married. When you're eleven-going-on-twelve, you're plagued by weighty thoughts.

My brother Cliff was my confidant in the family, but he'd picked that moment to have a chest cold or flu of some sort. He had been moved into the little room at the head of the stairs that was used as a sickroom whenever Mama suspected one of us had something contagious. We were only supposed to pass notes to each other, sending them in on the food trays.

I stood my serious thoughts all on my own for as long as I could, then went and knocked on the sickroom door.

"Who is it?" If a toad had a voice, it might sound all croupy like Cliff's that day.

"It's Betsy. I'm coming in."

I went to the far end of the bed and sat by Cliff's feet. He didn't say you shouldn't be here. He just said, "I can't talk so good."

"Well, you can listen." And I told him all the things I had thought about marriage, about the necklace, and about Molly. While I was talking, some things that had never entered my mind before seemed clear. Cliff croaked that since he wasn't the marrying type and I wasn't either, maybe we could both be hunters.

I felt a lot better after that. I wasn't weird after all. I slipped out of his room before Mama showed up with his lunch.

After supper that night we all gathered in the parlor. Cliff, his chest wrapped with flannel cloths that smelled of camphor, was bundled into a chair by the fireplace, Ol' Ben asleep at his feet. Even Amanda was with us. Her husband Harvey was there, too, but the two youngest children didn't know that because Harvey was dressed as Santa Claus and carried a big bag of toys.

He distributed presents, and we all opened them. There would be more in the morning under the tree, but we liked to spread Christmas out as far as we could.

Christmas Eve was always the time Aunt Molly asked Molly to wear the ruby and diamond necklace, "for a while, so I can see it on you, child." Aunt Molly laid it out on the table, and we all saw that it was still as impressive as ever. It seemed to catch the lights of the Christmas tree and the glow of the candles, not only reflecting but matching with light of its own.

Just as Aunt Molly said, "Come here, my dear, and let me put this on you," Cliff had a fit of coughing. Everyone's attention turned from the necklace to Cliff.

Aunt Molly laid the necklace down and stood up to look over the back of Cliff's chair. One younger child climbed on each arm of the chair, Cindy on one side and

Tommy on the other. Harvey, who was a doctor first and Santa second, tossed his sack to one side and clumped across the room in oversized shoes. Someone tramped on Ol' Ben's tail in an effort to get to Cliff, and I led the dog, drugged by food and the warmth of the fire, toward the door.

"He's all right. Move back, everyone," Papa said. "Don't open that door," he added to me. "I don't want a draft through here until I get another blanket."

I slapped Ol' Ben on the bottom and sent him off to his box in the kitchen.

The little ones scrambled back to their presents. Aunt Molly, with a hand pressed to her bosom, turned back to the table. Mama picked up a bottle of cough medicine and then almost dropped it as Aunt Molly screamed.

"Who picked up the necklace? Molly, do you have it already?"

Looks of bewilderment met her questions. "Don't go out!" she commanded Santa Claus, who was trying to slip out the door with his empty sack to change back into his identity as Dr. Brittaman. "Don't anyone move out of this room until I find the necklace."

"You can't suspect Santa Claus!" my brother James shouted, which was a cue for a good bit of silly chatter that had a bad effect on Aunt Molly's temper. She was much more thorough and more demanding in her search than she might have been otherwise.

Mama and Papa kept trying to make light of it. Of course the necklace was there. It had to be. None of us would take it. Aunt Molly said she would have granted that an hour earlier but the fact was someone *had*.

Our Santa Claus suggested we quarter the room and search it inch by inch with Aunt Molly supervising each stage of the search until the necklace turned up. That search was classic, something to pass into legend within our family. First, there were twelve people in the room, counting Aunt Molly herself, and someone insisted she should not be exempt from being searched. Santa and his sack were checked. Even Cliff agreed to be searched, his chair, his blankets, his clothes, his flannel wraps, every inch of the space around him.

Every branch of the tree was examined, every present inspected for signs of tampering. Two of them had to be opened and then repackaged because young hands had been scrabbling at them. But neither one contained the necklace. Chairs were overturned. The hanging light fixture was checked. It became a game to suggest new possibilities.

Maybe because he had been caught trying to get out the door, Harvey went to extremes to see that he and his props were cleared of suspicion. He also made sure every suggestion, no matter how unreasonable, was followed up. The windows were tested, even though everyone knew no one had opened a door or window. An icy wind was blowing, and it was snowing outside. Opening up just long enough to toss something out would have let in a blast the rest would have noticed, not to mention that the necklace would have been lost in the snow.

Aunt Molly had never seemed the least bit pitiful to anyone before that night. Now she looked like a broken woman. Her face was blotchy, and her shoulders sagged. I felt truly sorry for her. Like everyone else that night, I wanted to find her necklace and restore it to her, but it just wasn't possible.

Mama put her arm around her and told her she'd walk her up to her room. At the door, Aunt Molly turned and, looking at Molly, said, "I'm sorry, dear."

"We'll find it," Mama told Aunt Molly. "We'll still find it."

Papa, Amanda, and Dr. Brittaman were all shaking their heads behind Mama and Aunt Molly's backs. I knew what they were thinking. That necklace had just plain vanished, and it didn't seem likely it could ever be found. If it wasn't in that room, well, it just wasn't anywhere.

Papa carried Cliff back to his bed. The rest of us also began to get ready to sleep. Somehow no one knew quite what to say to Molly.

We shuffled through nighttime rituals in uneasy silence. This was no way to go to bed on Christmas Eve.

Aunt Molly was hurt, and to all appearances, we had a thief in our family. A dull misery settled around my heart.

You wouldn't think a holiday could recover from a disaster like that, but the next day was one of the best Christmases of our lives. Strangely enough, it was all due to Aunt Molly, too. Several times during breakfast I saw her fingering a small piece of folded paper. She opened her presents with the rest of us and sounded sincerely grateful for her box of handkerchiefs, bottle of toilet water, book of poetry, and the handmade gifts from the younger children. If she was grieving, she was doing it bravely. It seemed to me she just looked thoughtful.

In the middle of the afternoon when the younger children were playing and Amanda and Harvey had gone home, Aunt Molly said she had something to say. She gathered Mama and Papa and Molly around the table. I hung around to hear what was going on.

"I've been doing some thinking since last night," she told them. "No, don't interrupt," she cautioned as my mother began to speak. "I think I wanted to arrange for my namesake to have my life all over again, a thing that's not possible, not even reasonable." She stopped and sighed.

"It's all right about the necklace. I mean, it isn't all right that you lost it," Molly told her, "but it's all right that it isn't coming to me."

Aunt Molly ignored her and continued, "I'd like to see this young woman go on with her studies. Toward that end, I want to pay her way to college." At a sign of protest from my father, Aunt Molly said dryly, "Believe me, four years' tuition will be less than the value of that necklace. You will not, of course, get the necklace," she added to Molly.

"Thank you," said Molly, her eyes wet and shining.

Molly walked on air for the rest of the day. Aunt Molly beamed. My parents kept exchanging smiles. The rest of us were infected by their joy, so it felt like Christmas morning all day and half the night.

* * *

I worked it out the other day that Aunt Molly on that Christmas was about the age I am now. I, of course, am not old at all, though she seemed old to me then. She just recently died, having lived into her nineties. Her large estate was divided among her children and grandchildren, but her will made provision for a sealed manila envelope to be delivered to me.

When I opened the envelope, I found a correctly folded letter on thick creamy stationery together with a yellowed slip of paper folded into a square. I opened the slip of paper first and read the message:

> *You can have you mizerable necklace back if you promise Molly don't haf to git married. She don't want a husban. She wants to go to collige.*

I wouldn't have believed the spelling could have been that bad. I unfolded the accompanying letter and read:

Dear Betsy,

I don't know how many years will pass before you get this back, but I want to return your note to you.

For days I was baffled by the disappearing stunt you pulled. No one had left the room, yet the necklace wasn't in the room, I told myself. Continuing to puzzle over the problem, I repeated that paradox endlessly. Finally I varied it a bit and said, "Not one creature went out of the room." I stopped as I reached that point because I realized a "creature" had left—that smelly old hound. Then I knew my ruby and diamond necklace must have gone out of the room with the dog. He was wearing it there in his box by the kitchen stove all the time we were searching, wasn't he? Of course, I also remembered that you were the one who sent the dog out of the room while Cliff kept the rest of us distracted. What a determined child you must have been to hold out against all that adult energy!

You always were a clever child, Betsy.

Aunt Molly'd gone home that year with her necklace. Late on Christmas afternoon, it showed up without explanation on her bed. She made sure everyone saw it one last time, then after that holiday never mentioned it again.

When the new semester began a few weeks after Christmas, my sister Molly started college.

GRIST FOR THE MILLS
OF CHRISTMAS
by James Powell

The tabloid press dubbed the corner of southern Ontario
bounded by Windsor, Sarnia, and St. Thomas "The Christmas Triangle" after holiday travelers began vanishing
there in substantial numbers. When the disappearances
reached twenty-seven, Wayne Sorley, editor-at-large
of *The Traveling Gourmet* magazine, ever on the alert
for offbeat articles, penciled in a story on "Bed-and-
Breakfasting Through the Triangle of Death" for an upcoming Christmas number, intending to combine seasonal
decorations and homey breakfast recipes (including a side
article on "Muffins from Hell") with whatever details of
the mysterious triangle came his way.

So when the middle of December rolled around, Sorley
flew to Detroit, rented a car, and drove across the border
into snow, wind, and falling temperatures.

He quickly discovered the bed-and-breakfast people
weren't really crazy about the Christmas Triangle slant.
Some thought it was bad for business. Few took the disappearances as lightly as Sorley did. To make matters
worse, his reputation had preceded him. The current issue
of *The Traveling Gourmet* contained his "Haunted Inns of
the Coast of Maine" and his side article "Cod Cakes from
Hell," marking him as a dangerous guest to have around.
Some places on Sorley's itinerary received him grudg-
ingly. Others claimed no record of his reservations and
threatened to loose the dog on him if he didn't go away.

On the evening of the twenty-third of December, and
well behind schedule, Sorley arrived at the last bed-and-
breakfast on his prearranged itinerary to find a hand-
written notice on the door. "Closed by the Board of

Health." Shaking his fist at the dark windows, Sorley decided then and there to throw in the towel. To hell with the damn Christmas Triangle! So he found a motel for the night, resolving to get back across the border and catch the first available flight for New York City. But he awoke late to find a fresh fall of snow and a dead car battery.

It was midafternoon before Sorley, determined as ever, was on the road again. By six o'clock the snow was coming down heavily and aslant and he was still far from his destination. He drove on wearily. What he really needed now, he told himself, was a couple of weeks in Hawaii. How about an article on "The Twelve Luaus of Christmas"? This late they'd have to fake it. But what the hell, in Hawaii they have to fake the holidays anyway.

Finally Sorley couldn't take the driving anymore and turned off the highway to find a place for the night. That's when he saw the "Double Kay B & B" sign with the shingle hanging under it that said "Vacancy." On the front lawn beside the sign stood a fine old pickle-dish sleigh decorated with Christmas tree lights. Plastic reindeer lit electrically from within stood in the traces. Sorley pulled into the driveway and a moment later was up on the porch ringing the bell.

Mrs. Kay was a short, stoutish, white-haired woman with a pleasant face which, except for an old scar from a sharp-edged instrument across the left cheekbone, seemed untouched by care. She ushered Sorley inside and down a carpeted hallway and up the stairs. The house was small, tidy, bright, and comfortably arranged. Sorley couldn't quite find the word to describe it until Mrs. Kay showed him the available bedroom. The framed naval charts on the walls, the boat in a bottle, and the scrimshawed narwhal tusk on the mantel gave him the word he was looking for. The house was ship-shape.

Sorley took the room. But when he asked Mrs. Kay to recommend a place to eat nearby she insisted he share their dinner. "After all, it's Christmas Eve," she said. "You just freshen up, then, and come downstairs." Sorley smiled his thanks. The kitchen smells when she led him through the house had been delicious.

Sorley went back out to his car for his suitcase. The wind had ratcheted up its howl by several notches and was chasing streamers of snow down the road and across the drifts. But that was all right. He wasn't going anywhere. As he started back up the walk someone inside the house switched off the light on the bed-and-breakfast sign.

Sorley came out of his room pleased with his luck. Here he was settled in for the night with a roof over his head and a hot meal and a warm bed in the bargain. Suddenly Sorley felt eyes watching him, a sensation as strong as a torch on the nape of his neck. But when he looked back over his shoulder the hall was empty. Or had something tiny just disappeared behind the lowboy against the wall? Frowning, he turned his head around. As he did he caught the glimpse of a scurry, not the thing itself, but the turbulence of air left in the wake of some small creature vanishing down the stairs ahead of him. A mouse, perhaps. Or, if they were seagoing people, maybe the Kays kept rats. Sorely made a face. Then, shaking his head at his overheated imagination, he went downstairs.

Mrs. Kay fed him at a dining room table of polished wood with a single place setting. "I've already eaten," she explained. "I like my supper early. And Father, Mr. Kay, never takes anything before he goes to work. He'll just heat his up in the microwave when he gets home." The meal was baked finnan haddie. Creamed smoke haddock was a favorite Sorley had not seen for a long time. She served it with a half bottle of Alsatian Gewurtztraminer. There was Stilton cheese and a fresh pear for dessert. "Father hopes you'll join him later in the study for an after-dinner drink," said Mrs. Kay.

The study was a book-lined room decorated once again with relics and artifacts of the sea. The light came from a small lamp on the desk by the door and the fire burning in the grate. A painting of a brigantine under sail in a gray sea hung above the mantel. Mr. Kay, a tall, thin man with a long, sallow, clean-shaven face, heavy white eyebrows, and patches of white hair around his ears, rose from one of two wing-backed chairs facing the fire. As he shook his guest's hand he examined him and seemed pleased with what he saw. "Welcome, Mr. Sorley." Here was a voice that might once have boomed in the teeth of a gale. "Come sit by the fire."

Before sitting, Sorley paused to admire a grouping of three small statues on the mantel. They were realistic representations of pirates, each with a tarred pigtail and a brace of pistols, all three as ugly as sin and none more than six inches tall. A peglegged pirate. Another with a hook for a hand. The third wore a black eye patch. Seeing his interest, Mr. Kay took peg leg down and displayed it in his palm. "Nicely done, are they not? I'm something of a collector in the buccaneer line. Most people's family trees are hung about with horse thieves. Pirates swing from mine." He set the statue back on the mantel. "And I'm not ashamed of it. With all this what-do-you-call-it going round, this historical revisionism, who knows what's next? Take Christopher Columbus, eh? He started out a saint. Today he's worse than a pirate. Some call him a devil. And Geronimo has gone from devil incarnate to the noble leader of his people. But here, Mr. Sorley. Forgive my running on. Sit down and join me in a hot grog."

Sorley's host poured several fingers of a thick dark rum from a heavy green bottle by his foot, added water from the electric teakettle steaming on the hearth, urging as he passed him the glass, "Wrap yourself around that."

The drink was strong. It warmed Sorley's body like the sun on a cold spring day. "Thank you," he said. "And thanks for the excellent meal."

"Oh, we keep a good table, Mother and I. We live well. Not from the bed-and-breakfast business, I can tell you that. After all, we only open one night a year and accept only a single guest."

When Sorley expressed his surprise, Mr. Kay explained, "Call it a tradition. I mean, we certainly don't need the money. I deal in gold coins—you know, doubloons, moidore—obtained when the price was right. A steal, you might say. So, yes, we live well." He looked at his guest. "And what do you do for a living, Mr. Sorley?"

Sorley wasn't listening. For a moment he thought he'd noticed something small move behind Mr. Kay, back there in the corner where two eight-foot-long bamboo poles were leaning, and was watching to catch sight of it again. When Mr. Kay repeated his question Sorley told him what he did and briefly related his adventures connected with the aborted article.

Mr. Kay laughed like thunder, slapped his knees, and said, "Then we are indeed well met. If you like, I'll tell you the whole story about the Christmas Triangle. What an evening we have ahead of us, Mr. Sorley. Outside a storm howls and butts against the windows. And here we sit snug by the fire with hot drinks in our fists, a willing taleteller and . . ."

". . . an eager listener," said Sorley, congratulating himself once again on how well things had worked out. He might get his article yet.

Mr. Kay toasted his guest silently, thought for a moment, and then began. "Now years ago, when piracy was in flower, a gangly young Canadian boy named Scattergood Crandal who had run off to join the pirate trade in the Caribbean finally earned his master-pirate papers and set out on a life's journey in buccaneering. But no pantywaist, warm-water pirating for him, no rummy palm-tree days under blue skies. Young Crandal dreamed of home, of cool gray summers plundering the shipping lanes of the Great Lakes, of frosty winter raiding parties skating up frozen rivers with mufflers around their necks and cutlasses in their teeth, surprising sleeping townspeople under their eiderdowns.

"So with his wife's dowry Crandal bought a ship, the *Olson Nickelhouse,* and sailed north with his bride, arriving in the Thousand Islands just as winter was closing the St. Lawrence. The captain and his wife and crew spent a desperate four months caught in the ice. Crandal gave the men daily skating lessons. But they were slow learners and there were to be no raiding parties that winter. By the end of February, with supplies running low, the men ate the captain's parrot. And once having eaten talkative flesh, it was a small step to utter cannibalism. One snowy day Crandal came upon them dividing up the carcasses of three ice fishermen. He warned them, 'Don't do it, you fellows. Eating human flesh'll stunt your growth and curl your toes!' But it was too late. Those men were already slaves to that vile dish whose name no menu dares speak."

As Mr. Kay elaborated on the hardships of that first year he took his guest's glass, busied himself with the rum and hot water, and made them both fresh drinks. For his part, Sorley was distracted by bits of movement on the edges of his vision. But when he turned to look, there was never anything there. He decided it was only the jitters brought on by fatigue from his long drive in bad weather. That and the play of light from the fire.

"Now Crandal knew terror was half the pirate game," continued Mr. Kay. "So the loss of the parrot hit him hard. You see, Mr. Sorley, this Canadian lad had never mastered the strong language expected from pirate captains and counted on the parrot to hold up that end of things. The blue jay he later trained to stride his shoulder hadn't quite the same effect and was incredibly messy. Still, pirates know to go with the best they have. So he had these flyers printed up announcing that Captain Crandal, his wife (for Mrs. Crandal was no slouch with the cutlass on boarding parties), and his cannibal crew, pirates late of the Caribbean, were now operating locally, vowing Death and Destruction to all offering resistance. At the bottom he included a drawing of his flag, a skeleton with a cutlass in one bony hand and in the other a frying pan to underscore the cannibal reference.

"Well, the flyer and flag made Crandal the hit of the season when things started up again on the Lakes that spring. In fact, the frying pan and Crandal's pale, beanpole appearance and his outfit of pirate black earned him the nickname Death-Warmed-Over. And as Death-Warmed-Over the Pirate he so terrorized the shipping lanes that soon the cold booty was just rolling in, cargoes of mittens and headcheese, sensible swag of potatoes and shoes, and vast plunder in the hardware line, anvils, door hinges, and barrels of three-penny nails which Crandal sold for gold in the colorful and clamorous thieves' bazaars of Rochester and Detroit."

"How about Niagara Falls?" asked Sorley, to show he knew how to play along with a tall tale. He was amused to detect a slur in his voice from the rum.

"What indeed?" smiled Mr. Kay, happy with the question. He rose and lifted the painting down from its nail above the mantel and rested it across Sorley's knees. "See those iron rings along the water line? We fitted long poles through them, hoisted the *Olson Nickelhouse* out of the water, and made heavy portage of her around the falls."

As Mr. Kay replaced the painting Sorley noticed that the group of three pirates on the mantel had rearranged themselves. Or was the strong drink and the heat from the fire affecting his concentration?

"Well," said Mr. Kay, "as cream rises, soon Crandal was Pirate King with a pirate fleet at his back. And there was no manjack on land or sea that didn't tremble at the mention of Death-Warmed-Over. Or any city either. Except for one.

"One city on the Canadian side sat smugly behind the islands in its bay and resisted Crandal's assaults. Its long Indian name with a broadside of o's in it translated out as 'Gathering Place for Virtuous Moccasins.' But Crandal called it 'Goody Two-Shoes City' because of its reek of self-righteousness. Oh, he hated the world as a pirate must and wished to do creation all the harm he could. But Goody Two-Shoes City he hated with a special passion. Early on he even tried a Sunday attack to catch the city by surprise. But the inhabitants came boiling out of the churches and up onto the battlements to pepper him with cannonballs with such a will that, if their elected officials hadn't decided they were enjoying themselves too much on the Sabbath and ordered a cease-fire, they might have blown the *Olson Nickelhouse* out of the water."

Here Mr. Kay broke off his narrative to poke the fire and then to stare into the flames. As he did, Sorley once again had the distinct impression he was being watched. He turned and was startled to find another grouping of little pirate statues he hadn't noticed before on a shelf right at the level of his eye in the bookcase beside the fireplace. They held drawn dirks and cutlasses in their earnest little hands and had pistols stuck in their belts. And, oh, what ugly little specimens they were!

"Then, early one December," Mr. Kay continued, "Crandal captured a cargo of novelty items from the toy mines of Bavaria. Of course, in those days toys were quite unknown. Parents gave their children sensible gifts like socks or celluloid collars or pencil boxes at Christmas. Suddenly Crandal broke into a happy hornpipe on the frosty deck, for it had come to him how he could harm Goody Two-Shoes City and make it curse his name forever. But he would need a disguise to get by the guards at the city gate who had strict orders to keep a sharp eye out for Death-Warmed-Over. So he changed his black outfit for a red one with a pillow for fatness, rouge for his gray cheeks, a white beard to make him look older, and a jolly laugh to cover his pirate gloom. Then, on Christmas Eve, he put the *Olson Nickelhouse* in close to shore and sneaked into Goody Two-Shoes City with a wagonload of toys crated up like hymnals. That night he crept across the rooftops and down chimneys and by morning every boy and girl had a real toy under the Christmas tree.

"Well, of course, the parents knew right away who'd done the deed and what Crandal was up to. Next Christmas, they knew, they'd have to go and buy a toy in case Crandal didn't show up again or risk a disappointed child. But suppose he came next year, too? Well, that would mean that the following year the parents would have to buy two toys. Then three. And on and on until children no longer knew the meaning of the word 'enough.'

" 'Curse Crandal and the visit from the *Olson Nickelhouse,*' the parents muttered through clenched teeth. But their eavesdropping children misheard and thought they said 'Kris Kringle' and something about a visit from 'Old Saint Nicholas.' As if a saint would give a boy a toy drum or saxophone to drive his father mad with, as if a saint would give a girl a Little Dolly Clotheshorse doll and set her dreaming over fashion magazines when she should be helping her mother in the kitchen." Mr. Kay laughed until the tears came to his eyes. "Well, the Pirate King knew he'd hit upon a better game than making fat landlubbers walk an icy gangplank over cold gray water And since the Crandals had salted away a fortune in gold coins they settled down here and started a reindeer farm so Crandal could Kringle full-time with the missus as Mrs. Kringle and the crew as his little helpers." Mr. Kay looked up. "Isn't that right, Mother?"

Mrs. Kay had appeared in the doorway with a red costume and a white beard over her arm and a pair of boots in her hand. "That's right, Father. But it's time to get ready. I've loaded the sleigh and harnessed the reindeer."

Mr. Kay got to his feet. "And here's the wonderfully strange and miraculous thing, Mr. Sorley. As the years passed we didn't age. Not one bit. What did you call it, Mother?"

"The Tinker Bell Effect," said Mrs. Kay, putting down the boots and holding up the heavily padded red jumpsuit trimmed with white for Mr. Kay to step into.

"If children believe in you," explained Mr. Kay, as he did up the Velcro fasteners, "why then you're eternal and evergreen. Plus you can fly through the air and so can your damn livestock!"

Mrs. Kay laughed a fine contralto laugh. "And somewhere along the line children must have started believing in Santa's little helpers, too," she said. "Because our pirate crew didn't age either. They just got shorter."

Mr. Kay nodded. "Which fitted in real well with their end of the operation."

"The toy workshop?" asked Sorley.

Mr. Kay smiled and shook his head. "No, that's only a myth. We buy our toys, you see. Not that Mother and I were going to spend our own hard-earned money for the damn stuff. No, the crew's little fingers make the counterfeit plates to print what cash we need to buy the toys. Electronic ones, mostly. Wonderful for stunting the brain, cramping the soul, and making ugly noises that just won't quit."

"Hold it." Sorley wagged a disbelieving finger. "You're

telling me you started out as Death-Warmed-Over the Pirate and now you're Santa Claus?"

"Mr. Sorley, I'm as surprised as you how things worked out. Talk about revisionism, eh? Yesterday's yo-ho-ho is today's ho-ho-ho." Mr. Kay stood back and let his wife attach his white beard with its built-in red plastic cheeks.

"But where does the Christmas Triangle business fit in?" demanded Sorley. "We've got twenty-seven people who disappeared around here last year alone."

"Copycats," insisted Mr. Kay. "As I said, Mother and I only take one a year, what we call our Gift from the Night. But of course, when the media got onto it the copycats weren't far behind. Little Mary Housewife can't think of a present for Tommy Tiresome who has everything, so she gives him a slug from a thirty-eight between the eyes and buries him in the basement, telling the neighbors he went to visit his mother in Sarnia. Little Billy Bank Manager with a shortage in the books and a yen for high living in warmer climes vanishes into the Christmas Triangle with a suitcase of money from the vault and reemerges under another name in Rio. And so on and so on. Copycats."

"Father's right. We only take one," said Mrs. Kay. "That's what our agreement calls for."

Mr. Kay nodded. "Last year it was an arrogant young bastard from the SPCA investigating reports on mistreated reindeer. Tell me my business, would he?" Mr. Kay's chest swelled and his eyes flashed. "Well, Mother and I harnessed him to the sleigh right between Dancer and Prancer. And his sluggard backside got more than its share of the lash that Christmas Eve, let me tell you. He was blubbering like a baby by the time I turned him over to my scurvy crew."

"I don't understand," said Sorley. But he was beginning to. He stood up slowly, utterly clearheaded and sober. "You mean your cannibal crew ate him?" he demanded in a horrified voice.

"Consider the fool from the SPCA part of our employee benefits package," shrugged Mr. Kay. "Oh, all right," he conceded when he saw Sorley's outrage, "so my little

shipmates are evil. Evil. They've got wolfish little teeth
and pointed carnivore ears. And don't think those missing
legs and arms were honestly come by in pirate combat.
Not a bit of it. There's this game they play. Like strip
poker but without the clothes. They're terrible, there's no
denying it. But you know, few of us get to pick the people
we work with. Besides, I don't give a damn about naughty
or nice."

Sorley's voice was shrill and outraged. "But this is
hideous. Hideous. I'll go to the police."

"Go, then," said Mr. Kay. "Be our guest. Mother and I
won't stand in your way."

"You'd better not try!" warned Sorley defiantly, intending to storm from the room. But when he tried he found
his shoelaces were tied together. He fell forward like a
dead weight and struck his head, blacking out for a moment. When he regained consciousness he was lying on
his stomach with his thumbs lashed together behind his
back. Before Sorley's head cleared he felt something being shoved up the back of his pant legs, over his buttocks,
and up under his belt. When they emerged out beyond the
back of his shirt collar he saw they were the bamboo poles
that had been leaning in the corner.

Before Sorley could try to struggle free, a little pirate
appeared close to his face, a grizzled thing with a hook for
an arm, little curly-toed shoes and a bandanna pulled
down over the pointed tops of its ears. With a cruel smile
it placed the point of its cutlass a menacing fraction of an
inch from Sorley's left eyeball and in language no less
vile because of the tiny voice that uttered it, the creature
warned him not to move.

Mrs. Kay was smiling down at him. "Now don't trouble
yourself over your car, Mr. Sorley. I'll drive into the city
later tonight and park it where the car strippers can't miss
it. Father'll pick me up in the sleigh on his way back."

Mr. Kay had been stamping his boots to get them on
properly. Now he said, "Give us a kiss, Mother. I'm on
my way." Then the toes of the boots hove into view on the
edge of Sorley's vision. "Good-bye, Mr. Sorley," said his

host. "Thanks for coming. Consider yourself grist for the mills of Christmas."

As soon as Mr. Kay left the room, Sorley heard little feet scramble around him and more little pirates rushed to man the ends of the bamboo poles in front of him. At a tiny command the crew put the cutlasses in their teeth and, holding their arms over their heads, hoisted Sorley up off the floor. He hung there helplessly, suspended front and back.

The little pirates lugged Sorley out into the hall and headed down the carpet toward the front door. He didn't know where they were taking him. But their progress was funereally slow, and, swaying there, Sorley conceived a frantic plan of escape. He knew his captors were tiring under their load. If they had to set him down to rest, he would dig in with his toes and, somehow, work his way to his knees. At least there he'd stand a chance.

Sorley heard sleigh bells. He raised his chin. Through the pane of beveled glass in the front door he saw the sleigh on the lawn rise steeply into the night, Christmas tree lights and all, and he heard Mr. Kay's booming "Yo-ho-ho-ho."

Suddenly Sorley's caravan stopped. He got ready, waiting for them to put him down. But they were only adjusting their grips. The little pirates turned him sideways and Sorley saw the open door and the top of the cellar steps and smelled the darkness as musty as a tomb. Then he felt the beginning of their big heave-ho. It was too damn late to escape now. Grist for the mills of Christmas? Hell, he was meat for the stew pots of elfdom.

INSPECTOR TIERCE AND
THE CHRISTMAS VISITS
by Jeffry Scott

Coppers are only human, Jill Tierce told herself, without much conviction, after Superintendent Haggard's invitation to a quiet drink after work. Actually he'd passed outside the open door of her broom-closet office, making Jill start by booming, "Heads up, girlie! Pub call, I'm buying. Back in five . . ." before bustling away, rubbing his hands.

Taking acceptance for granted was very Lance Haggard, and so was the empty, outward show of bonhomie, but there you were.

Unless forced to behave otherwise, Superintendent Haggard generally did no more than nod to Inspector Tierce in passing. This hadn't broken her heart. He had a reputation: it was whispered that he pulled strokes. Nothing criminal, he wasn't bent, but he had a knack of pilfering credit for ideas or successes, coupled with deft evasive action if his own projects went wrong.

Refusing to waste time on Jill Tierce owed less to sexism than to the fact that she was of no present use to him. Leg mangled on duty, she was recovering slowly. Fighting against being invalided out of the Wessex-Coastal Force, lying like a politician about miracles of surgery and physiotherapy, and disguising her limp by willpower, she had won a partial victory. Restricted to light duties on a part-time basis, she was assigned to review dormant cases—and Lance Haggard, skimming along the fast track, wasn't one to waste time on history.

It wasn't professional, then, and she doubted a pass. Superintendent Haggard was a notoriously faithful husband. Moreover, Inspector Tierce was clearsighted about her looks: too sharp-featured for prettiness, and the sort of pale hair that may deserve the label but escapes being called blonde.

What was he up to? Then she'd glanced out of the smeary window at her elbow and seen strings of colored lights doubly blurred by the glass and another flurry of snow. There was the explanation, Christmas spirit. She smiled wryly. The superintendent probably kept a checklist of seasonal tasks, so many off-duty hours per December week devoted to stroking inferiors who might mature into rivals or allies. She supposed she ought to feel flattered.

A police cadet messenger tapped at the door and placed a file on Jill's desk without leaving the corridor, by leaning in and reaching. He had a lipstick smudge in the lee of one earlobe. Mistletoe had been hung in the canteen at lunchtime, only five days to the twenty-fifth now.

Big deal, she thought sourly.

The new file was depressingly fat. She transferred it from the in tray to the bottom of the pending basket, noting that the covers were quite crisp though the buff cardboard jacket had begun to fade. More than a year old, Inspector Tierce estimated. Then Superintendent Haggard was back, jingling his car keys impatiently.

He drove a mile or so out of town, to a Dickensian pub by the river. The saloon bar evoked a sporting squire's den, Victorian-vintage trophy fish in glass cases on the walls, no jukebox, and just token sprigs of non-plastic holly here and there. "Quiet and a bit classy," Lance Haggard commented. "I stumbled on this place last summer, thought it would suit you."

Sure you did, she jeered, not aloud. Apart from an older man and younger woman murmuring in a snug corner (boss courting a soon-to-be-even-more-personal assistant, Jill surmised cattily) they had the bar to themselves. "Done all your Christmas shopping?" Haggard inquired. "Going anywhere for the break, or spending it with Mum and Dad?"

Satisfied that small-talk obligations were discharged, he continued before she could match banality with banality,

"I've had a file passed to you, luv. Before you drown in details, seemed a good idea to talk you through it."

Despite a flick of irritation, Jill Tierce was vaguely relieved. It was upsetting when leopards changed their spots. Superintendent Haggard's were still in place, he wasn't dispensing Christmas cheer but attempting to spread blame; if she reviewed one of his setbacks, she assumed part of the responsibility.

"I'm listening," she said flatly.

To her surprise, Haggard was . . . what? Not hangdog exactly, yet defensive. Obviously shelving a prepared presentation, he said, "Forget so-called perfect crimes— untraceable poisons, trick alibis, some bright spark who's a master of disguise. *Im*perfect crimes are the bastards to deal with. Chap had a brainstorm, lashes out at a total stranger, and runs for his life. Unless he gets collared on the spot, blood still running, we've no chance. Or, say, this respectable housewife is getting messages from Mars, personal relay station in a flying saucer. Eh? Height of the rush hour, she's in a crowd and shoves a child under a bus. Goes on home, like normal. No planning, no sane motive, they don't even try that hard to get away, they just . . . go about their business.

"It gets to me," he admitted needlessly. "Well, this one instance does. Prostitute killed, and what's a streetwalker but somebody in extra danger from crazies? Mitzi Field, twenty-four years old but looked younger. Mitzi was just her working name, mind."

"There's a surprise."

He didn't rise to the sarcasm. "Dorothy Field on the death certificate but we'll stick to Mitzi, that's what she was known as, to the few who did know her.

"She was found in Grand Drive ten days before Christmas three years ago. Dead of repeated blows from something with sharp angles, most likely a brick. I see her getting into some curb crawler's car, and he drove her to where she was attacked. Saw red—wanted what she wouldn't provide, she tried ripping him off, plenty of possible reasons—snatched the nearest weapon, bashed her as she turned to run, kept bashing." The theory was delivered with pointed lack of emotion, Superintendent Haggard back in full control.

"Drove her there . . . the car was seen?" Jill held up a hand. "Sorry, not thinking straight." Mount Wolfe was one of the city's best quarters, Grand Drive its best address.

"Exactly," said Haggard. "Mitzi had started living rough, so she looked tatty. She'd had a mattress in a squat, that old factory on Victoria Quay, but the council demolished it the week before her death. The docks were her beat. She was wearing those big boots, like the movie—"

"*Pretty Woman,*" Jill suggested.

"Those're the jokers, long boots and hot-pants and a ratty leather jacket with her chest hanging out—in December! The boots were borrowed from another girl, too tight, had to be sliced off her feet. Walking two miles from the docks to where she was found would have crippled her. And okay, it was dark, but a feller and a blatantly obvious hooker didn't foot it all the way up the Mount and along to the end of Grand Drive without being noticed. Which they were not, house-to-house checks established that."

Taking another, rationed sip of champagne—the pub sold it by the glass, else Haggard might not have stood for the drink of her choice, she suspected—Inspector Tierce frowned doubtfully.

"Grand Drive's the last place a working girl would pick for business. It's a private road, and they're very territorial round there—sleeping policeman bumps every fifty yards to stop cars using it for a shortcut, and if a non-resident parks in the road, somebody rings us within minutes, wanting him shifted . . ."

"Stresses that the punter was a stranger here," Haggard argued. "Businessman on an overnight, or he tired of motorway driving, detoured into town for a meal and a change of scene. Mitzi wasn't a local, either. Londoner originally, family split up after she was sexually abused. Went on the game after absconding from a council home when she was fifteen. Summer before her death she

worked the transport cafes, Reading, Bath, Bristol, drifted
far as here and stayed.

"For my money, the punter spotted her at the docks.
Then they drove around. She had no crib, did the business
in cars or alleys. Maybe this punter was scared of getting
mugged if they stuck around the docks. Driving at random, they spot a quiet-looking street, plenty of deep
shadow at the far end where the trees are. Must have
seemed safe enough, and so it was—for him. Nobody saw
them arrive or him leaving. Some pet lover daft enough to
walk the dog in a hailstorm found Mitzi's body that night,
but she could have lain there till morning otherwise.

"All known curb crawlers were interviewed and
cleared. Ditto the Dodgy List." Superintendent Haggard
referred to the extensive register of sex offenders whose
misdeeds ranged from assaults to stealing underwear off
washing lines. "Copybook imperfect crime: guy blew a
gasket and got the hell out. Ensuring the perfect result for
him."

"Thanks for hyping me up," Inspector Tierce responded
dryly. She'd been right, ambitious Haggard wanted to distance himself from defeat. Cutting corners to achieve it;
in theory, if not always in practice, the assistant chief de-
creed what files she studied. Unless she made a stand, final disposition of the Dorothy "Mitzi" Field case would
rest with her rather than the superintendent.

"I haven't finished." But he stayed silent for a moment
before seeming to digress. "Know the old wives' tale
about a murderer having to return to the scene of the
crime? Laughable! Only I've got a screwy notion that su-
perstitions have a basis in fact. Anyway, a man has been
hanging about in Grand Drive recently. Sitting in his car
like he's waiting for somebody . . . right where the kid's
body lay. He's a local, which blows my passing stranger
stuff out of the water—still, I'm not proud, I am happy to
take any loose end offered."

But that's the point, Jill parried mentally, keeping a
poker face, you're not taking it. And a helpful colleague
giving loose ends a little tug just might end up under the
pile of rocks they release.

"This fellow," Superintendent Haggard continued doggedly, "has been haunting Grand Drive. Uniformed branch looked into it after several complaints from residents. They're a bit exclusive up there, not to mention paranoid about burglars, scared the bloke was casing their houses. What jumped out at me was one old girl being pretty certain the same chap, leastways somebody in an identical car, did the same thing at Christmastime last year. She was adamant that he was there for an hour or more every day for a week."

He treated her to a phony's smile. "Got to be interesting. Because whatever this man is, he's no burglar. A pest and a pain in the arse, but no record and a steady job, good references. Uniforms didn't have to trace him, they just waited, and sure enough, he rolled up and parked at the end of Grand Drive. Nowhere near his house, incidentally, and well off the route to it. He gave them a cock-and-bull yarn about birdwatching. They pressed him, and he mouthed off about police harassment, started teaching them the law."

The smile turned into a sneer. "The man is Noel Sarum, you'll have heard of him. Yes, *the* Noel Sarum. Spokesman for the Wessex chapter of Fight for Your Rights, does that disgraceful column in the local paper, born troublemaker. Very useful cover if he happens to have a down on hookers and let it get the better of him three years ago."

Inspector Tierce set her flute of champagne aside. "You forgot your oven gloves. Ought to have them on, handing me a hot potato."

Lance Haggard spoke a laugh. "You can deal with it. Routine review of the Field case, search for possible witnesses overlooked in the original trawl. Sarum can't object to an approach on those terms—he's always banging on about being ready to do his civic duty without knuckling under to mindless bullying."

"You tell him that, then. It was your case."

"Ah." Superintendent Haggard took a long pull at his draught Guiness. "It wasn't, you see. I've kept myself *au fait,* but . . . no, it's not down to me."

Shifting restively, he went off on another tangent. "My daughter . . . Beth was nearly eighteen back then, but her mental age is nearer six or seven. Lovely girl, couldn't ask for a nicer, but never mind the current jargon, simpleminded. You knew about that," he accused edgily.

Jill hadn't, but she nodded and waited.

"Beth used to go to special school, homecraft and so forth. . . . She may have to look after herself when me and the wife have snuffed it. I couldn't give Beth a lift every day. No problem, bus stop outside our house. Nell sees the girl aboard, three stops later, out she gets. But one night a water main burst, and the bus went a different way. Beth was set down two streets from us. It confused her.

"Nell phoned me, frantic, when the girl was an hour overdue. I pulled rank, had the area cars searching. What we hadn't imagined was Beth getting on *another* bus, she thought they all went to our house. This one's terminus was the docks, and the driver made her get out. She was crying but he didn't want to know.

"Of course I shot home, and damned if a taxi didn't pull up behind me, with Nell and a young woman who'd found her: Mitzi Field. I recognized her from court, she was a regular. Cut a long story short, Beth was wandering the docks, running away if any male asked why she was crying; we'd drilled that into her, never talk to strange men. Mitzi twigged she needed help, looked us up in the phonebook, and flagged down a cab."

Haggard fiddled with his empty glass. "Nell made her come in for some grub and a cup of tea. God forgive me, grateful or no, I was pleased to see the back of her, the girl was dirty under the paint and dead cheap. Nell, my wife, isn't practical except round the house. Church on Sunday, says her prayers every night. She wanted to help Mitzi, give her a fresh start, once our girl was in bed and I'd explained what Mitzi was. I told Nell to forget it, the best help to her sort is leaving them alone. She'd still sleep rough and be on the game with a thousand quid in her purse.

"Easy to say when you don't want hassle—and how

would it have looked, me taking a common prostitute, a dockside brass, under my wing? A month later she got herself killed."

He put a hand atop Jill Tierce's. "Comes back to me every Christmas, how we owed that girl and . . . we didn't let her down but . . . you follow? It was Len Poole's inquiry, I can't involve myself. You can. Christmas, and I'm asking for a present. Something isn't kosher about Noel Mr. Crusader Bloody Sarum; give him a spin, and help ease my blasted conscience."

Taking his hand back, he blustered, "Any of that personal stuff leaks out, I'll skin you alive." But it was appeal rather than threat. Oh yes, Jill reflected, coppers were human all right—even devoutly ambitious ones.

Noel Sarum lived in one of the Monopoly-board houses of a new estate, Larkspur Crest. For no good reason Inspector Tierce had expected a student-type flat festooned in Death to Tories banners, fragrant with pot fumes and dirty socks.

Like most police officers, she was aware of Sarum. His know-your-rights column in the weekly paper kept sniping at law enforcers. Jill had acknowledged that the diatribes were justified in general terms, yet still she felt resentful, attacked while denied another right—of defense. Somehow she'd formed a picture of an acrid character with a straggly beard and John Lennon glasses, spitting venom via his word processor. He was a teacher, too, probably indoctrinating whole generations of copperbaiters. Not that they needed encouragement.

She was taken aback by the man opening the glossy front door of pin-neat Number 30. Fifty, she judged, but relatively unlined, face open under a shock of silver-gray hair. Track suit and trainers reinforced the youthful, vigorous impression. Before she could speak, he beamed and exclaimed, "Why, it's the lame duck!"

Sensitive over her treacherous leg, she bristled, then recognized the face and decoded his remark. It was the Samaritan from that half-marathon in the happy time before she'd been hurt. Talked into running for charity,

she'd not realized that the friendly fellow partnering her
for the final miles was Sarum, scourge of the police.

Jill had been quite taken with him. He'd struck her as a
man appreciating female company for its own sake. If
he'd been ten years younger or she a decade older, she
might have tried making something of it. As things were,
when the event finished he'd wrapped her in a foil blanket
and trotted away to help somebody else.

"You're a police, um, person," he said, returning Inspector Tierce's warrant card. "I wondered what you did
for a living, never thought of *that*. Come on in."

The living room contrived to be homely and pristine,
sealed woodblock floor reflecting carefully tended plants.
"Passes inspection, huh? I lost my wife five years ago, but
I try to maintain her standards. Must have known you
were coming, that's the coffee perking, not my tummy
rumbling. Take a pew, I'll get it—black, white, sugar, no
sugar?"

He was just as he'd been on the charity run, chatting as
if resuming a relationship after minutes instead of years.
Some people did it naturally, and in her experience, the
majority were as uncomplicated as their manner. He made
reasonable coffee, as well ... "What's the problem?
Can't be anything too shattering, but you're a senior
rank."

Disingenuous, Jill thought; he must have a shrewd idea
what brought her.

"You've been seen in Grand Drive for extended periods
over the last two years. Watching, hanging about. Spare
me the stuff about a free country; you put the wind up the
neighborhood, and no wonder. It's no-hawkers-no-lurkers
territory. Storm in a teacup is your comeback, but the
snag is a woman was done to death at your favorite haunt
three years ago."

"Two and two makes me a murder suspect, is that it?"
His tone was even. Sensing that Noel Sarum savored de-
bate, she gained a better understanding of his newspaper
column.

"No, you invited suspicion all on your own," she
replied calmly. "Gave my uniformed colleagues some

guff about wanting to confirm the presence of a rare bird in Grand Drive, a . . . can't read PC Harris's writing, but he told me the name and I remembered it long enough to make a phone call.

"It's your bad luck that a cousin of mine is an ornithologist—the bird you chose hasn't touched England since 1911, and even that sighting was doubted. However, it's something an intelligent amateur might pick to blind the cops with science. According to my expert." And she smiled cheekily.

Noel Sarum's mouth curved up at the corners, too. "Got me." Then his jaw set. "As a matter of fact, that was my *third* Christmas of going to Grand Drive. Breaking no law, causing no nuisance. Which is all you need from me."

"Believe it or not I'd agree if it weren't for Mitzi Field. The dead girl. Worthless girl, some might say, squalid little life, good riddance. But we don't agree, do we. I've got to account for loose ends, and you're flapping about in the wind, Mr. Sarum."

"Noel," he corrected abstractedly. "The kids call me First Noel, this time of year. Every class thinks it's being brilliantly original. . . ." Stubborn streak resurfacing, he grumbled. "After your pals pounced on me, I went to the *Gazaette* office and researched the murder in the back numbers. That winter I was supply-teaching at Peterborough, didn't get back to the city until the week after it happened. The night she was killed, I was chaperoning a Sixth Form dance more than a hundred miles away from Grand Drive."

"Bloody hell," Jill muttered. "What's the matter with you, why not tell the uniforms that?"

Taken aback by her impatience and the subtext of disgust, he shrugged helplessly. "I didn't think of it at the time."

Fair enough, Inspector Tierce granted. People didn't remember their whereabouts a week ago, let alone years later. Though Noel Sarum might be lying. . . .

Guessing the reaction, he brightened. "Hang on, I'm not escaping, just looking in the glory-hole."

She watched him delve in a cupboard under the stairs. Soon he returned, waving a pamphlet. "Here you are, Beacon School newsletter, date at the top of every page."

It was a slim, computer printed magazine. Sarum's finger jabbed at a poorly reproduced photograph in which he was recognizable, arm round the shoulders of a jolly, overweight woman in owl spectacles. " 'First Noel' got the Christmas spirit, Mrs. May got the grope, and the Sixth 'got down' with a vengeance last Thursday night," ran the disrespectful caption.

"Mrs. May's the head teacher, the kids loved that snap," he chuckled. Tuning him out, Jill found the first page of her notebook. Yes, the date was right, Mitzi Field had died at about nine P.M. that faraway Thursday night when Noel Sarum was hugging the head teacher. His tone hardened. "Sorry to disappoint you."

"Oh, drop it," she said crossly. "I liked you on that stupid run, I still like you, though what I'd really like is to shake you till your stupid teeth rattle."

Taken aback, he fiddled with the school magazine.

"You've got a bee in your bonnet about the police, fine. But that's no excuse for wasting two uniformed officers' time, and mine. Heaven knows what it is with you and Grand Drive, I don't care."

She broke off, eyes narrowing. "Hey! I think this was a setup. You have an ironclad alibi, so why not encourage the dim coppers to hassle you? Weeks and weeks of columns to be wrung out of that. Cancel the liking-you bit, you're sick. Feel free to complain about my attitude. I'll be happy to defend it, on the record."

Appalled, Noel Sarum protested. "It's not like that . . . *setup*? It never crossed my mind!" Cracking his knuckles, he glowered at the carpet. "It's strictly personal, can't you people get that through your heads?" After which, perversely (not only coppers are human), he told her the whole story.

Fifteen minutes later, Inspector Tierce said, "Why the heck didn't you press every bell and find her that way? Can't be that many flats in half a dozen houses."

"What would I say when each door opens?" Sarum demanded. "I don't even know if she's married, she was wearing gloves, I couldn't see if she had a wedding ring. Supposing her husband answered, imagine the trouble I could cause."

"I still can't make out how you chatted her up and didn't have the gumption to get her name, even a first name."

Still high-colored from enthusiasm and embarrassment, Sarum sputtered, "I didn't chat her up. It was . . . idyllic, a little miracle. We looked at each other and started talking as if we'd known each other forever. Somehow I couldn't bring myself to ask her name or give mine, it might have broken the spell."

"Yes, you told me," Jill butted in, lips tingling from the strain of keeping a straight line. The copper-bashing demon she had pictured snarling over his columns turned out to be a hopeless, helpless romantic. Noel Sarum, a widower well into middle age, patrolled Grand Drive once a year because he was suffering belated pangs of puppy love.

Having met his ideal woman one Christmas Eve, driven her home, and departed on air, he'd been unable to decide which house in Grand Drive was hers. Similar period and the same architect, and they looked different by daylight.

She could understand why he hadn't confided in a couple of constables patently ready to take him for some kind of weirdo. After all, he was the Know Your Rights fanatic, worried that they'd turn his romantic vigil into a mocking anecdote to belittle him. Inevitably he'd been combative.

It was already dark when Jill Tierce left Larkspur Crest. Fresh snow crunched under the tires. She slowed as her lights picked up a group of children crossing the road, dragging a muffled-up baby on the improvised sledge of a tin tray. At the foot of the hill a Rotary Club float blared canned carols, a squad of executive Santas providing harness-bells sound effects with their collecting tins.

Everything went a little scatty in this season, though nicely so, Inspector Tierce mused. She'd brought no

presents so far, that was scatty, dooming her to Christmas
Eve panic.

Not the least of her scattiness, either. She thought: I
can't believe I'm doing this, but stayed on course towards
Grand Drive.

By six that evening, bad leg nagging savagely—it dis-
approved of stairs, and she had climbed a number of
flights—Jill was showing her warrant card and saying
with the glibness of practice, "This may sound odd, but
bear with me. . . . Two Christmases ago, if you remember
that far back, did you go Christmas Eve shopping at the
Hi-Save in City Center?"

"I expect so." The woman's voice was unexpectedly
deep and hoarse from such a slim body. "I use Hi-Save for
all but deli stuff, it's loads cheaper."

"I mustn't lead you, put ideas in your head, but that
Christmas Eve did you have help with your shopping, like
your bags carried to the car?"

"I don't take the c—oh, him, the knight errant!" She
opened the door wider and stood aside. "Come in, you
look chilled."

Constance—"Connie, please, the other's so prissy"—
French remembered Noel Sarum, all right.

"He picked me up in the checkout line that Christmas
Eve. Well, I picked him up, had he but known." Brown,
almond eyes sparkled wickedly. "It was such a scrum, the
line was endless, all the trolleys were taken so I was lug-
ging three or four of those wretched baskets, and he did
the polite, offered to share the load while we waited.

"Single men who aren't teenagers are so pathetic, aren't
they? And he was kind and clean and cuddly, I really *took*
to him." She'd insisted on making them mugs of hot
chocolate ("with the teeniest spike of brandy to cheer it
up") after Jill Tierce refused a cocktail.

And I could take to a pad like this, Inspector Tierce reflected a shade drowsily. Connie French had two floors of
one of Grand Drive's former mansions. Her living room
was spacious yet cosy, elegant antique pieces to dress it,
costly modern furniture for wallowing.

Ms. French sat a little straighter. "What's this about, dear?"

"I'm glad you asked that." Jill pulled a face. "Officially I'm eliminating a loose end, confirming somebody's reason for . . . never mind, confirming a story. Don't quote me, but I was curious. A witness was terribly impressed by you and . . ."

Connie waited, and Jill said, "It's just that you knocked him for six, he hasn't got over it—and call it the Christmas syndrome, or downright nosiness, but I wondered if you'd felt the same."

"I have thought about him since." Connie smiled weakly, blushing. "A lot, on and off. Look, there is always enough for two when it's a casserole, and a glass of wine can't put you over the limit for driving. Terrible thing to tell a woman, but you look exhausted. Stay for a meal."

They got on famously. A long while later, table cleared, dishwasher loaded, they'd put the world to rights and compared Most Terrible Male Traits (nasal fur, aggressive driving, and pointless untruths topping the painstakingly compiled list).

Inspector Tierce was deciding that she'd better go home by cab and pick her car up tomorrow—should have known she was unable to drink *one* glass of wine—when Connie French became fretful.

"What is it with that chap, Jill? I could tell he fancied me. Oh, not the flared nostrils and ripping the thin silk from my creamy shoulders, he wasn't that sort, but we really hit it off. Greek gods and toy boys are all very well, but what you need is a man who's comfy as old shoes. I've only met two or three, one was my brother and the others were friends' husbands. . . .

"Tell me his name, I'll ring him." Connie reached for the phonebook on the end table at her side.

"I can't do that, I shouldn't be here anyway, certainly not gossiping. Christmas has a lot to answer for." It struck Jill that they were talking animatedly but with a certain precision over trickier words; perhaps the Beaujolais

Villages in easy reach on the coffee table between them was not the first bottle.

"Wouldn't ring him anyway. My late husband, as in divorced, not RIP, said I had no pride but . . . is he gay? My supermarket chap, not the ex."

"Sarum? Certainly not." Frowning at the alliteration as much as the slip, Jill muttered, "I must make tracks."

"Night's young," Connie said on a pleading note. "He drove me home, I nearly asked him up for a drink—but something stopped me. I wanted him to at least introduce himself first, and after all that, he just took himself off."

"You'd stunned him," Jill said.

"Bull," Ms. French countered. But she was thoughtful. "Honest injun?"

"That's the impression I got. The twit's been keeping a vigil out there in the run-up to Christmas, ever since, hoping to pull the fancy-seeing-you-here bit."

Connie went to the bay window. "Typical of my luck, I never saw him."

"He stayed in his car, from up here he'd be an anonymous roof." Joining her, Inspector Tierce asked, "Were you questioned in the house-to-house sweep after Mitzi Field's body was found?"

"I was playing bridge that night, didn't get home till it was all over." Connie hugged herself. "Just as well. I couldn't bear it if I'd been up here watching some silly TV show while . . . ugh!"

"Looks pretty now." Snow crusted high walls and hedges, whiteness and moonlight giving Grand Drive a luminous quality.

"Christmas card," Connie French suggested, making the comment bleak. "I spend hours at this window sometimes, it's like a box seat for the seasonal stuff—carol singers from St. Stephen's in full Dickens costume, crinolines and caped coats and candle-lanterns. Then there are the children returning to the nest, back from boarding school, or a bit older, very proud of The Car and their university scarves.

"My daughter lives in California, she might ring on

Christmas Day, probably will before New Year's. . . . Mummy's an afterthought."

To Jill's dismay, Connie French was crying silently, a single, fat tear sliding down the side of her elegant nose.

Inspector Tierce woke the next morning with the mildest of hangovers, little more than a nasty taste in the mouth, and a flinching sensation at the memory of her hostess.

The provoking thing was that she didn't pity Connie French. The sorrow had been alcohol-based and transitory; minutes afterwards they'd played an old Dory Previn album, whooping approval of the bitchy lyrics. Connie might have been briefly maudlin, but she was too sparky for extensive self-pity.

No, this was not about Connie, but something she had said or done kept niggling and scratching in the subconscious. Every time Jill recollected the profile etched against the window, decorated by a crystal tear—and the image was persistent, like that pop tune you cannot stop humming—an alarm went off.

"Think of something else," Inspector Tierce advised out loud, competing against the hair dryer's breathy roar. Nearly too late to post greetings cards, not that she'd bought them yet. She *had* bought some in good time one year. They were in A Safe Place to this day, waiting to be found.

Oh dear, she was better off thinking about the Mitzi Field case. Very well, Noel Sarum was in the clear. He could have printed that school magazine himself, or altered the date, but only in a Golden Age detective story. He'd been far away, and Connie French had confirmed his reason for haunting Grand Drive at a particular time of year. Further, while everyone was a potential life-taker, Noel Sarum belonged at the safest, last-resort end of the spectrum.

And that revived Superintendent Haggard's imperfect crime. She could picture a man on perhaps his first and last sojourn in the city, stopping at a street woman's signal and unrecognized, very likely unseen, driving away with her. To drive on, soon afterwards, taking care to stay away.

"Hopeless," Jill mumbled and, skipping breakfast, went off to her broom closet, cardboard-flavored coffee, and the case file.

It assured her that everything needful had been done. A fruitless check for witnesses to the crime, an unrewarding search for tire tracks, footprints, any physical evidence apart from Mitzi Field's body. Local and then regional sexual offenders interrogated. Other prostitutes questioned, fellow tenants of her last known address, the demolished squat, traced and interviewed.

Nothing to go on; conscientious Detective-Inspector Poole, exactly the breed of plodder who catches most criminals, had demonstrated that if nothing else. Or had he?

Inspector Tierce stood up awkwardly, massaging scar tissue through her skirt. She hadn't thought the location significant, merely incongruous, when Superintendent Haggard told her of it. Previous reading of the file had left her cold. But now it was different because . . . because of Connie French. Something—*what?*—that she'd said last night.

She'd said so much, that was the snag. Squinting, lips moving silently, Jill talked herself through a lengthy and meandering conversation. Until reaching the point where Connie had lamented an uncaring daughter . . . bingo.

Children coming home for the holidays, of course. That's what families did at Christmas, families and friends of the family. Driven by nostalgia, tradition, the chance to purge year-long offenses during the annual truce, or (if mercenary souls) simply to collect presents, they headed for hearth and home.

She leafed through to a terse section of the dossier, the London end. A few discreet sentences covered Mitzi's life from just before her ninth birthday until she absconded from the council home six years later.

Lots of digging needed. Inspector Tierce felt sorry for Len Poole, and profoundly grateful that she did not have to follow up her idea.

* * *

Inspector Poole, a careworn, resigned character, took one look at the name on the file and groaned, "Haggard's got you at it as well, has he? Wish he'd mind his own business."

"Amen to that, but I'm stuck with it. Len, what was that girl doing on Grand Drive? Haggard thinks she took a client to a road full of snobs and busybodies because she didn't know any better. Or the punter was ignorant and Mitzi Field didn't care. Did you buy that?"

"No opinion—I'd need facts to form one, and the only certainty was that she was killed there." He wasn't being awkward, that was how his mind worked. "Long way to go for a quickie in a motor, right enough. Then again, Vice was chasing street prozzies at the time, she might have wanted to get well away from the redlight area."

"Supposing," said Jill, "she wasn't taken to Grand Drive and killed? Supposing she was *leaving* there, heading back to her beat, when it happened?"

"I'm not quite with you."

"She didn't walk all the way, wasn't dressed for it, therefore she went in a car, that's the conventional wisdom. Doesn't follow. A bus runs from dockland to a stop round the corner from Grand Drive every half hour. She could have taken herself there, right? Visited somebody, left again, and either her attacker was waiting, or he was the one she'd called on, and he chased her out of doors."

"Try reading the file," Inspector Poole urged. "No known sex offenders among the residents, remember. We grilled all Les Girls, whether or not they'd associated with Ms. Field, and none of them had a client in Grand Drive; far as they were aware, that is. Down-market hookers don't keep names and addresses. Her mates were sure Mitzi had never been up there before."

"Yes, but it was Christmas, Len. When we all get sudden urges to see Mum and Dad, look up Auntie Flo, send a card to that nice former neighbor who nursed us through whooping cough. Mitzi Field had a family of sorts, once upon a time."

Digesting the implications, Inspector Poole said,

"Crumbs." He did not go in for bad language. "You do get 'em, the wild hunches. All right, she was Mitzi Field, but her mother remarried, to a man called, don't tell me . . . Edwardes. The stepfather who supposedly seduced the little girl. The mother died in 1984, Edwardes was never charged, lack of evidence, they just took the child away. He'd dropped off the radar screen by 1990, dead or gone abroad, certainly hasn't paid tax or claimed unemployment benefits for a long time. All in the file, dear. I may be slow but I ain't stupid."

"Perish the thought. But that still leaves Auntie Flo and the kindly neighbor."

"Crumbs," he repeated, even more feelingly, "you don't want much. We're talking ten, fifteen years back, and in London." Inspector Poole took possession of the file. "It's a thought, I can't deny it. More's the pity."

On Christmas Eve afternoon, Len Poole rapped jauntily at Jill's office door. "London doesn't get any better. I've had two days up there, and how those lads in the Met stand the life is beyond me. Noise, pollution, bad manners, homeless beggars everywhere. But I did find a helpful social worker, they do exist even if it's an endangered species, and this chap had a good memory.

"Great idea of yours—but I'm afraid James Edwardes, Mitzi's allegedly wicked stepfather, doesn't live at Grand Drive. He works the fairs in the Republic of Ireland, hasn't been in England for years."

Hitching half his skinny rump onto the corner of the desk, Inspector Poole added innocently, "No trace of Auntie Flo. But I'll tell you who did have a Grand Drive address until recently—Anthony Challis."

Since he had to have worked hard and fast and was full of himself over it, Jill Tierce played along. "Challis?"

"He lodged with Mitzi's family in the eighties. Freelance electrician, good earner, about to get married. But then Mitzi Field, only she was little Dorothy then, accused nice Mr. Challis of doing things to her. Her mother called the police, and then Dorothy admitted it wasn't Challis after all, it was her stepfather who kept raping her." Len Poole grimaced distastefully. "Ugly ... my tame social worker said he'd never believed Challis had touched her. What it was, they discovered, Edwardes not only abused her, he practically brainwashed the poor kid, said she'd be struck down if she told on him. When it got too much for her, she accused Tony Challis—ironically enough, because he was kind, would never hurt her. She'd just wanted it out in the open, so the grownups would make it stop. Ruining Challis wasn't on her agenda, if she had such a thing, but that was the effect.

"After Dorothy-Mitzi was taken into council care, her mother threw Edwardes out, and Tony Challis went to other digs. No charges were brought in the end—the child was considered unreliable on account of changing her story. Rumors spread, mud stuck, Challis's fiancée told him to get lost, his regular customers followed suit . . ."

"Ugly," Jill agreed.

"Gets worse. Challis is a Wessex man, he talked a lot about this part of the world when he was lodging with Mitzi's folks. Maybe that's why she stuck around, having drifted here. Anyway, Challis took to drink, hit the gutter before he straightened up. Returned to his native heath, as posh books put it, found work as a janitor for Coastal Properties. They own several apartment houses on Grand Drive and gave him a basement flat in the end one on the left. Too dark and cramped for letting, and it gave them a good excuse to pay him peanuts.

"Mitzi Field wasn't looking for Challis—if she'd had a grain of sense she would have kept well clear—but she found him. Once a month he picked up supplies from a discount hardware store on her beat in dockland. He didn't notice her, which is natural; the last time he'd seen Dorothy, she was a child. But she must have seen him going in and out of the hardware place and pumped somebody there, discovered where he worked."

Len Poole sighed and shook his head. "Just as you said, it was Christmas. Tony Challis is watching TV in his basement one night, and suddenly this shabby little tart is at the side door, saying, I'm Dorothy, Mr. Challis, don't you remember me? Wanted to say sorry, hoped he was doing all right now, she hadn't wanted to make trouble for him. And so on.

"Challis says, and I believe him, he was in a daze while she talked to him. 'Noises, she was making noises,' he told me. She was dead when the actual words came back to him. Mitzi left, and for a minute—the chap's a drinker, mark you—he wondered whether he'd been hallucinating. Then he wished he had been. Challis hadn't hated *Dorothy*; he understood she was a victim who dragged him down with her, no malice involved. But she'd become Mitzi . . . ruining him and still ending up like that, that was past bearing.

"Next moment, it seemed to him, he was standing over her in the street, holding one of those little stone lions: half the big houses along the drive had them on either side of the porch. He had the lion by its head, the square base was allover blood.

"He accepted that he must have killed her, but he didn't feel like a murderer. All he felt was scared witless. He slipped back to his basement, washed the lion, and put it back in place. Then he prayed. Been praying ever since.

"From Met Police records and that social worker, I got the names of five people linked to Field when she was a child. Only one was among the residents of Grand Drive at the time she was killed. No problem finding him, he didn't move far, one of those new council flats near the marina. Soon as I said who I was, Challis goes, 'Thank God, now I can tell somebody.' "

Jill Tierce addressed her folded hands, almost inaudibly. "She wanted to make amends for what happened all those years ago, and he killed her for trying?"

Inspector Poole slid off the desk, his expression mixing wonder and compassion over her naivete. "If you can make sense of the why and wherefore, be sure to tell Challis. He can't sort it out. It's people, Jill . . . she was one of them that gets sentimental at Christmas, never considered she'd be opening a wound. As for him, he wasn't the kind man who'd lodged with her mum. Not any more. She stirred up an embittered semialcoholic, temper overdue to snap."

Len Poole hesitated, cleared his throat. "Nobody's fault, luv, not even his. Though he'll go away for it."

"We got a result, which is all that matters."

"Not what I meant—though there is always that, at the end of the day."

Inspector Tierce's day, apparently over, had a post-script.

She'd wanted to watch the black and white movie of Scrooge for the fifth Christmas Eve in a row but went to bed instead. Her father would be calling "fairly early" to collect her for Christmas lunch, meaning crack of dawn.

The phone woke her. The caller sounded drunk, though on nothing more than girlish high spirits, it emerged.

"We've just got back from midnight Mass, now we can be the first to wish you Merry Christmas."

"Wha'? Who is it?" Jill pulled the alarm clock radio round on the bedside table, sending paperbacks, a bottle of cough mixture, and her pain tablets cascading to the floor. "It's twenty to two!" The voice's identity registered belatedly. "Connie, I'll kill you."

"Don't be like that. I rang him after all, you see. And I'm so *happy*."

"Bully for you. What in the world are you on about?"

"Noel, of course. You let his name slip the other night—"

"Did I, by gum." Fully awake and up on one elbow, Inspector Tierce rolled gummy eyes. "That was very unprofessional."

"Sarum's an unusual surname, only one in the local phonebook, and we talked for hours—" Following squeaks and a rattle, Noel Sarum came on the phone.

"And here I am! Well, I'll be leaving in a minute," he added sheepishly.

Another interlude of cryptic noises and then Connie French trilled, "He's so stuffy, of course he's not leaving at this time of the morning."

She said something aside, answering Noel in the background. "He wants you to know we're engaged and says I'm indiscreet, the idiot. I say, you must come to our wedding, it'll be February or March. You have to, you're the match-maker."

"Let's talk about it next year. I'm pleased you are pleased, Connie. Tell Noel to go easy on the law in future; he owes me. 'Bye."

Lying back in the darkness, a phrase from the Bible popped into her head, a Sunday school fragment clear as if spoken for her benefit: "Out of the strong came forth sweetness." Something about bees using the remains of a savage lion as their hive. Why think of that? Mitzi Field was battered with a stone lion. Nothing sweet there, that was not the connection.

Connie was gorgeously happy, and Noel worshipped her. It couldn't last, euphoria didn't, yet it was a promising prelude to something better. They might fight eventually, but they would not be lonely.

That was what had triggered the parable of bees and a beast of prey. Out of evil, good can come. "Merry Christmas," Jill Tierce whispered to the pillow.

PASS THE PARCEL
by Peter Lovesey

The roads were treacherous on Christmas Day and Andy and Gemma took longer than they expected to drive the twenty-five miles to Stowmarket. While Gemma concentrated on keeping the car from skidding, Andy complained about the party in prospect. "You and I must be crazy doing this. I mean, what are we putting our lives at risk for? Infantile games that your sister insists on playing simply because in her tiny mind that's the only permissible way of celebrating. The food isn't anything special. If Pauline produces those enormous cheese straws with red streaks like varicose veins, I'll throw up. I promise you. All over the chocolate log."

Gemma said, "We're not going for the food."

"The games?"

"The family."

"Your brother Reg, you mean? The insufferable Reg? I can't wait to applaud his latest stunt. What's he planning for this year, would you say? A stripogram? Or a police raid? He's a real bunch of laughs, is Reg."

Gemma negotiated a sharp bend and said, "Will you shut up about Reg? There are others in my family."

"Of course. There's Geoff. He'll be sitting in the most comfortable chair and speaking to nobody."

"Give it a rest, will you?" Gemma said through her teeth.

"I'd like to. They're showing *Apocalypse Now* on BBC2. I'd like to be giving it a rest in front of the telly with a large brandy in my fist."

Andy's grumbling may have been badly timed, but it was not unreasonable. Any fair-minded person would have viewed Christmas with this particular set of in-laws as an infliction. There were four in the current generation of Weavers, all in their thirties now, the sisters Gemma and Pauline and the brothers Reg and Geoff. Pauline, the hostess, eight years Gemma's junior, was divorced. She would have been devastated if the family had spent Christmas anywhere else but in Chestnut Lodge, the mansion she had occupied with her former husband and kept as her share of the settlement. No one risked devastating Pauline. As the youngest, she demanded and received everybody's cooperation.

"I could endure the food if it wasn't for the games," Andy started up again. "Why do we put up with them? Why not something intelligent instead of charades and—God help us—pass the parcel? I know, you're going to tell me it's a tradition in the family, but we don't have to be lumbered with traditions forevermore just because sweet little Pauline likes playing the games she did when she was a kid. She's thirty-one now, for Christ's sake. Does she sleep with a teddy bear?"

When they reached Stowmarket and swung left, Andy decently dipped into his reserve of bonhomie. "They probably dread it as much as we do, poor sods. Let's do our best to be convivial. You did bring the brandy?"

"On the backseat with the presents," said Gemma.

Chestnut Lodge had been built about 1840 for a surgeon. Not much had been done to the exterior since. The stonework wanted cleaning and there were weeds growing through the gravel drive.

Someone had left a parcel the size of a shoebox on the doorstep. Andy picked it up and carried it in with their presents.

"So sorry, darling," Gemma told Pauline. "The roads were like a rink in places. Are we the last?"

"No, Reg isn't here yet."

"Wanting to make the usual grand entrance?"

"Probably."

"You're wearing your pearls. And what a gorgeous dress."

Pauline always wore something in pink or yellow with

layers of net. She was in competition with the fairy on the tree, according to Andy.

She smiled her thanks for the compliment. "Not very practical for the time of year, but I couldn't resist it. Let's take your coats. And Happy Christmas."

"First I'll park these under the tree," said Andy. "The brown paper one isn't from us, by the way. We found it on your doorstep. Doesn't feel heavy enough for booze, more's the pity."

"I do like surprises," said Pauline.

"A secret admirer?" said Gemma.

"At my age?"

"Oh, come on, what does that say for me, pushing forty?"

"You've got your admirer."

Gemma rolled her eyes upwards and said nothing.

"Come and say hello to Geoff." Pauline cupped her hand to her mouth as she added, "Hasn't had any work for three months, he told me."

"Oh, no."

Their accountant brother, short and fat, with half-glasses, greeted Gemma. "Merry Christmas" was likely to be the extent of his conversation for the day unless someone asked him about his garden.

Pauline brought in a tray of tea things.

Andy said, "Not for me, I'll help myself to a brandy, if you don't mind. Want one, Geoff?"

Geoff shook his head.

"Any trouble getting here?"

Geoff gave a shrug.

"Roads okay your way, then?"

Geoff thought about it and gave another shrug.

Pauline said, "It's nearly four. Reg ought to be here. It's not as if he has far to come. Geoff has a longer trip and he was here by three-thirty."

"Knowing Reg of old, he could be planning one of his stunts," said Andy. "Remember the year of the ghost in the bathroom, Pauline?"

"Don't!" she said. "Will I ever forget it? It was so real, and he *knew* I was scared of living here alone."

Between them, they recalled Reg's party tricks in recent years: the time he arrived with his friend masquerading as an African bishop; the year the Queen's voice came out of the cocktail cabinet; and the live turkey in Geoff's car.

"You've got to give him full marks for trying," said Andy. "It would be a dull old Christmas without him."

"I'd rather have it dull," said Pauline.

"Me, too," said Gemma. "I may be his flesh and blood, but I don't share his sense of humor."

"Only because it could be your turn this time," said Andy. "Poor old Geoff got it last year. The sight of that turkey pecking your hand when you opened the door, Geoff, I'll never forget."

Geoff stared back without smiling.

Ten minutes later, Pauline said, "I've had the cocktail sausages warming for over an hour. They'll be burnt to a cinder. And we haven't even opened a single present."

"Want me to phone him, see if he's left?" Andy offered.

"Of course he's left," said Gemma. "He must have."

Pauline started to say, "I hope nothing's—"

Gemma said quickly, "He's all right. He wants to keep us in suspense. We're playing into his hands. I think we should get on with the party without him. Why don't we open some presents?"

"I think we ought to wait for Reg."

"You could open the one we found on the doorstep," Andy suggested to Pauline.

"Unless it *is* something personal," said Gemma.

That induced a change of mind from Pauline. "I've got nothing to hide from any of you."

Andy retrieved the parcel from under the tree, turned it over, and examined the brown paper wrapping. "There's nothing written on it. Maybe it isn't meant for Pauline after all."

"If it was left on her doorstep, it's hers," said Gemma.

Pauline sat in a chair with the parcel deep in the froth of her skirt and picked at the Sellotape. She was too fastidious to tear the paper.

"You want scissors," said Andy.

"I can manage." She eased open the brown paper. "It's gift-wrapped inside."

"Where's the tag?" said Gemma. "Who's it from?"

"There isn't one." Pauline examined the tinsel-tied parcel in its shiny red wrapper.

"Open it, then."

She worked at one edge of the paper with one of her long, lacquered fingernails. "Look, there's more wrapping inside."

"Just like pass the parcel," said Gemma.

Andy gave his wife a murderous look.

The paper yielded to Pauline's gentle probing. Underneath was yet another wrapping, with a design of holly and Christmas roses. She said, "I think you're right. This is meant for a game."

Andy swore under his breath.

"Let's all play, then," said Gemma with an amused glance at her husband's reaction.

"After tea."

"No, now. While we're waiting for Reg. Pull up a chair everyone and sit in a circle. I'll look after the music."

"Just three of us?" said Andy.

Gemma mocked him with a look. "You know how Pauline adores this game."

Andy and Pauline positioned themselves close to where Geoff was already seated, while Gemma selected a CD and placed it on the deck of the music center.

"What is it—'The Teddy Bears' Picnic'?" said Andy.

Pauline was impervious to sarcasm. " 'Destiny,' " she said as the sound of strings filled the room.

"That's an old one."

"Start passing it, then," said Gemma. "I'm not playing this for my amusement."

Pauline handed the parcel to Andy, who held it to his chest. "No cheating," said Pauline.

He passed it to Geoff and the music stopped. Geoff unwrapped a piece of pink paper and revealed a silver layer beneath.

"Tough," said Andy. "Play on, maestro."

As the game resumed, Pauline told her sister, "You're supposed to have your back to us. It isn't fair if you can see who the parcel has reached."

"She likes playing God," said Andy. "Whoops." The music had stopped and the parcel was on his lap. He ripped it open; no finer feelings. "Too bad. Give it another whirl, Gem."

Geoff was the next to remove a layer. He did it in silence as usual.

"More music?" said Gemma.

"You got it," said Andy.

Three more wrappings came off before Pauline got a turn. The parcel was appreciably smaller.

"This could be it," said Andy. "You can see the shape."

"But of what?" said Pauline "It looks like a box to me." She was pink in the face as she peeled back the paper, but it was clear that another burst of music would be necessary.

When Andy received the parcel he held it to his ear and gave it a shake. Nothing rattled.

"Come on, pass it," said Pauline, drumming her shoes on the carpet.

Geoff fumbled and dropped the parcel as the music stopped. Pauline snatched it up.

"Not so fast," said Andy. "Geoff hadn't passed it to you."

But she had already unfolded the tissue paper from around a matchbox, one of the jumbo size capable of holding two hundred and fifty matches.

"One more round, apparently," said Gemma, and she turned up the music again. To sustain the suspense, a longer stretch of "Destiny" was wanted.

"What could it be?" said Pauline.

"Matches," said Andy.

"A silk scarf would be nice," said Pauline.

"Game on," said Pauline.

The matchbox was sent on its way around the three players.

"No looking," Andy reminded his wife. "We're down to the wire now. This has to be impartial."

"Faster," said Pauline.

"She's a goer, your sister," said Andy.

The matchbox fairly raced from lap to lap.

"Do you mind? I didn't know you cared," said Andy when Pauline's impetuous hand clasped his thigh.

Even Geoff was leaning forward, absorbed in the climax of the game. The music stopped just as he was passing the box to Pauline. They both had their hands on it.

"Mine," she said.

Geoff apparently knew better than to thwart his younger sister.

"I suppose it's only justice that you get the prize, as it was left on your doorstep," said Andy. "Let's see what you've got."

Unable to contain her curiosity, Gemma came over to see.

Pauline slid the box half-open, dropped it into her lap, and said in horror, "Oh, I don't believe it!"

"It's a joke, said Gemma. "It must be a joke."

"It isn't," said Pauline in a thin, strained voice. "That's somebody's thumb. Ugh!" She hooked the box off her skirt as if it were alive and dropped it on the coffee table.

Large and pale, the offending digit lay on a bed of cotton wool.

"No it isn't," said Andy. "It's too big for a thumb. It's a big toe."

"A toe?"

"Yes, it's too fleshy for a thumb."

"It must be out of a joke shop," said Gemma. "If Reg is responsible for this, I'll strangle him."

"Typical of his humor," said Andy.

Then Geoff spoke. "I think it's real."

"It *can't* be," said Gemma.

"Open it right out," said Andy.

"I'm not touching it," said Pauline.

Andy lifted the box and opened it, separating the drawer from its casing.

"I can't bear to look," said Pauline. "Keep it away from me."

"It's the real thing," said Andy. "You can see where it was—"

"God in Heaven—we don't wish to see," said Gemma. "Put it somewhere out of sight and give Pauline some of that brandy we brought."

"What a vile trick," said Pauline.

Andy reunited the two sections of the matchbox and placed it on a bookshelf before going to the brandy bottle. "Anybody else want some Dutch courage?"

Geoff gave a nod.

Andy's hand shook as he poured. Everyone was in a state of shock.

"He's gone too far this time," said Gemma. "He's ruined Christmas for all of us. I shall tell him. Are you all right, love?"

Pauline took a gulp of brandy and gave a nod.

"It's ghoulish," said Gemma.

"Sick," said Andy. "You all right, Geoff? You've gone very pale."

"I'm okay," Geoff managed to say.

"Drink some brandy, mate."

Gemma said, "Andy, would you take it right out of the room and get rid of it? It's upsetting us all."

Andy picked the matchbox off the bookshelf and left the room. Gemma collected the discarded sheets of wrapping paper and joined him in the kitchen. "Where would Reg have got such a ghoulish thing?" she whispered.

Andy shrugged. "Who knows? I don't imagine a branch manager at the Midland Bank comes across many severed toes."

"What are we going to do? Pauline's nerves are shattered and Geoff looks ready to faint."

"A fresh cup of tea is supposed to be good for shock. What am I going to do with this?"

"I don't know. Bury it in the garden."

"Pauline is sure to ask where it went."

"Then we'd better take it with us when we go. We can dump it somewhere on the way home."

"Why should we have to deal with it?" said Andy. "I'll give it back to bloody Reg. He can get rid of it."

"If he has the gall to show his face here. Just keep it out of everyone's sight in the meantime."

To satisfy himself that the toe really was of human origin. Andy slid open the matchbox again. This time he noticed a folded piece of paper tucked into one end. "Hey, there's something inside. I think it's a note." After reading the typed message, he handed it to Gemma. "What do you make of that?"

She stared at the paper. "It can't be true. It's got to be a hoax."

They joined Pauline and Geoff in the living room. "We thought you might appreciate some tea," said Gemma.

"You're marvellous," said Pauline. "I should have thought of that."

"Getting over the shock?"

"I think so."

"You too, Geoff?"

Geoff gave a nod.

Andy cleared his throat. "I found this note in the matchbox."

"A note?" said Pauline. "From Reg?"

"Apparently not. It says, 'If you want the rest of your brother—' "

"Oh, no!" said Pauline.

" 'If you want the rest of your brother, bring ten thousand pounds or equivalent to the telephone box at Chilton Leys at five-thirty. Just one of you. If you don't, or if you call the police, you can find the bits all over Suffolk.' "

"Andy, I think she's going to faint."

"I'm all right," said Pauline. "If this is true, that toe . . ."

"But it isn't true," said Andy, spacing the words. "It's Reg having us on, as he does every year."

"Are you sure?"

"He'll turn up presently grinning all over his fat face. The best thing we can do is get on with the party."

There was little enthusiasm for unwrapping presents or eating overcooked sausage, so they turned on the television and watched for a while.

"How could we possibly put our hands on ten thousand

pounds on Christmas Day?" said Pauline during the com-
mercial break.

"That's the giveaway," said Andy. "A professional kid-
napper would know better."

"You've got three hundred in notes in your back
pocket," said Gemma. "You know you have. You said we
needed it over the holiday in case of emergencies."

"Three hundred is peanuts compared to ten grand."

"I've got about a hundred and twenty in my bag," said
Gemma.

Geoff took out his wallet and counted the edges of his
bank notes.

"Doesn't look as if Geoff can chip in much," said
Andy.

Gemma said on a note of reproach, "Andy."

Andy said, "No offence, mate."

Geoff put his wallet away.

"Well, that's it. We couldn't afford to pay the kidnappers if they existed," Andy summed up. "How much do
you have in the house, Pauline?"

"In cash? About two hundred."

"Less than eight hundred between us."

"But I've got a thousand in travellers' cheques for my
holiday in Florida."

"Still a long way short," said Andy.

"Good thing it's only a hoax," said Gemma.

"There are my pearls," said Pauline, fingering them.
"They cost over a thousand. And I have some valuable
rings upstairs."

"If we're talking jewellery, Gemma's ruby necklace is
the real thing," said Andy.

"So is your Rolex watch," Gemma countered. "And the
gold ingot you wear under your shirt."

"I notice you haven't offered your earrings. They cost a
bomb, if I remember right."

"Oh, shut up."

"Where the hell is Chilton Leys anyway?"

"Not far," said Pauline.

"I passed it on my way here," said Geoff.

They were silent for an interval. Then Andy said,

"Well, has anyone spoken to Reg on the phone in the past twenty-four hours?"

"It must be a week since we spoke," said Pauline.

"What time is it?" said Gemma.

"Five past five."

"He would have been here by now," said Pauline. "Or if he had trouble with the car he would have phoned."

"Anyone care for another drink?" asked Andy.

"How many is that you've had already?" said Gemma.

"I want to say something," said Pauline.

"Feel free," said Andy, with the bottle in his hand.

She smoothed her skirt. "I'm not saying you're wrong, but if it wasn't a hoax and Reg really had been kidnapped, we could never forgive ourselves if these people murdered him because we did nothing about it."

"Come off it," said Andy.

"I mean, why are we refusing to respond to the note? Is it because we're afraid of making fools of ourselves? Is that all it is?"

"We don't believe it, that's why," said Gemma.

"You mean you don't want to run the risk of Reg having the last laugh? It's all about self-esteem, isn't it? How typical of our family—all inflated egos. We'd rather run the risk of Reg being murdered than lay ourselves open to ridicule."

"That isn't the point," said Andy. "We're calling his bluff."

"So you say. And if by some freak of circumstances you're mistaken, how will any of us live with it for the rest of our lives? I'm telling you, Andy, I'm frightened. I know what you're thinking. I can see it in your eyes. I'm gullible, a stupid, immature female. Well I don't mind admitting I'm bloody frightened. If none of you wants to take this seriously that's up to you. I do. I'm going to put all the money I have into a bag and take it to that phone box. If nobody comes, what have I lost? Some dignity, that's all. You can laugh at me every Christmas from now on. But I mean it." She stood up.

"Hold on," said Andy. "We've heard what you think. What about the rest of us?"

"It isn't quite the same for you, is it?" said Pauline. "He's my brother."

"He's Gemma's brother, too. And Geoff's."

Andy switched to his wife. "What do *you* want to do about it?"

Gemma hesitated.

"Or Geoff," said Andy. "Do you have an opinion, Geoff?"

Geoff's hand went to his collar as if it had tightened suddenly.

Gemma said, "Pauline is right. Ten to one it's Reg having us on, but we can't take the risk. We've got to do something."

Geoff nodded. He backed his sisters.

Pauline said, "I'm going upstairs to collect my jewellery, such as it is. We pool everything we have, right?"

"Right," said Gemma, unfixing her gold earrings and turning to Andy. "Do you want to be part of this, or not?"

Andy slapped his wad of bank notes on the table. "I don't believe in these kidnappers anyway."

"Let's have your watch, then," said Gemma. "And the ingot."

Geoff took out his wallet and emptied it.

The heap of money and valuables markedly increased when Pauline returned. She'd found some family heirlooms, including their grandmother's diamond-studded choker, worth several thousand alone. With her own pieces and the travellers' cheques, the collection must have come close to the value demanded in the note. She scooped everything into a denim bag with bamboo handles and said, "I'll get my coat."

Gemma told her, "Not you, sweetie. That's a job for one of the men."

Andy said, "Give the bag to me."

"You're not going anywhere," said Gemma. "You're way over the limit with all the brandy you've had. Besides, you don't know the way."

They turned to look at Geoff. He knew the way. He had said so.

"I'll go," he said, rising quite positively from the armchair. He looked a trifle unsteady in the upright position, but he'd been seated a long time. Maybe the brandy hadn't gone to his head. He had certainly drunk less than Andy.

Gemma still felt it necessary to ask, "Will you be all right?"

Geoff nodded. He had spoken. There was no need for more words.

Pauline asked, "Would you like me to come?"

Andy said, "The instruction was clear. If you believe it, Geoff's got to go alone."

In the hall, Pauline helped Geoff on with his padded jacket. "If you see anyone, don't take them on, will you? We just want you and Reg safely back."

Geoff looked incapable of taking anyone on as he shuffled across the gravel to his old Cortina, watched from the door by the others. He placed the bag on the passenger seat and got in.

"Is he sober?" Gemma asked.

"He only had a couple," said Andy.

"He looked just the same when he arrived," said Pauline. "He's had a hard time lately. So many businesses going bust. They don't need accountants."

Gemma said, "If anything happened to him just because Reg is acting the fool, I'd commit murder, I don't mind saying."

They heard the car start up and watched it trundle up the drive.

When the front door closed again, Gemma asked, "What time is it?"

"Twenty past," said Pauline. "He should just about make it."

Andy said, "I don't know why you two are taking this seriously. If I believed for a moment it was a genuine ransom demand I wouldn't have parted with three hundred pounds and a Rolex, I assure you."

"So what would you have done, cleverclogs?" said Gemma.

This wrongfooted Andy. He spread his hands wide as if the answer were too obvious to go into.

"Let's hear it," said Gemma. "Would you have called the police and put my brother's life at risk?"

"Certainly I'd have called them," said Andy, recovering his poise. "They have procedures for this sort of emergency. They'd know how to handle it without putting anyone's life at risk."

"For example?"

"Well, they'd observe the pickup from a distance. Probably they'd attach some tiny bugging device to the goods being handed over. They might coat some of the banknotes with a dye that responds to ultraviolet light."

Gemma turned to Pauline. "I'm wondering if we should call them."

Andy said, "It's too late. The police would have no option but to come down like a ton of bricks. Someone would get hurt."

Pauline said, "Oh God, no. Let's wait and see what happens."

"We won't have long to wait. That's one thing," said Andy. "You don't mind if I switch on the telly, Pauline?"

They sat in silence watching a cartoon film about a snowman.

Before it finished, Pauline went to the window and pulled back the curtain to look along the drive.

"See anything," asked Gemma.

"No."

"How long has he been gone?"

"Twenty-five minutes. Chilton Leys is only ten minutes from here, if that. He ought to be back by now."

"Stop fussing, you two," said Andy. "You give me the creeps."

Just after six, Pauline announced, "A car's coming. I can see the headlights."

"Okay," said Andy from his armchair. "What are we going to do about Reg when he pisses himself laughing and says it was a hoax?"

Pauline ran to the front door and opened it. Gemma was at her side.

"That isn't Geoff's Cortina," said Gemma. "It's a bigger car."

Without appearing to hurry, Andy joined them at the door. "That's Reg's Volvo. Didn't I tell you he was all right?"

The car drew up beside Andy's and Reg got out, smiling. He was alone. "Where's the red carpet, then?" he called out. "Merry Christmas, everyone. Wait a mo. I've got some prezzies in the back." He dipped into his car again.

"You'd think nothing had happened," muttered Gemma.

Laden with presents, Reg strutted towards them. "Who gets to kiss me first, then?" He appeared unfazed, his well-known ebullient self.

Andy remarked. "He's walking normally. We've been suckered."

Gemma said, "You bastard, Reg. Don't come near me, you sadist."

Pauline shouted, "Dickhead."

Reg's face was a study in bewilderment.

Andy said, "Where's Geoff?"

"How would I know?" answered Reg. "Hey, what is this? What am I supposed to have done?"

"Pull the other one, matey," said Andy.

"You've ruined Christmas for all of us," said Pauline, succumbing to tears.

"I wish I knew what you were on about," said Reg. "Shall we go inside and find out?"

"You're not welcome," Pauline whimpered.

"Okay, okay," said Reg. "It's a fair cop and I deserve it after all the stunts I pulled. Who thought of unloading all this on me? Andy, I bet."

Suddenly Gemma said in a hollow voice, "Andy, I don't think he knows what this is about."

"What?"

"I know my own brother. He isn't bluffing. He didn't expect this. Listen, Reg did anyone kidnap you?"

"Kidnap me?"

"We'd better go inside, all of us," said Gemma.

"Kidnap me?" repeated Reg, when they were in Pauline's living room. "I'm gobsmacked."

Pauline said, "Andy found this parcel on my doorstep and—"

"Shut up a minute," said Andy. "You're playing into his hands. Let's hear his story before we tell him what happened here. You've got some answering to do, Reg. For a start, you're a couple of hours late."

Reg frowned. "You haven't been here all afternoon?"

"Of course we have. We were here by four o'clock."

"You didn't get the message, then?"

"What message?"

"I've been had then. Geoff phoned at lunchtime to say that Pauline's heating was off. A problem with the boiler. He said the party had been relocated to his place at five."

Pauline said, "There's nothing wrong with my boiler."

"Shut up and listen," said Gemma.

Reg continued, "I turned up at Geoff's house and there was a note for me attached to the door. Hold on—I should have it here." He felt in his pocket. "Yes, here it is." He handed Gemma an envelope with his name written on it.

She took out the note and read to the others, " 'Caught YOU this year. Now go to Pauline's and see what reception you get,' It's Geoff's handwriting."

"He's a slyboots," said Reg, "but I deserve it. He was pretty annoyed by the turkey episode last year."

"You're not the only victim," said Gemma.

"Were you sent on a wild-goose chase?"

"No. But I think he may have tricked us. He *must* have. He led us to believe you were kidnapped. That's why he went to this trouble to keep you away."

"Crafty old devil."

"He took ten grand off us," said Andy.

"What?"

"He persuaded us to put up a ransom for you."

"Now who are you kidding?"

"It's true," said Gemma. "We put together everything we had, cash, jewellry, family heirlooms, and Geoff went off to deliver it to the kidnappers."

"Strike me pink!"

"And he isn't back yet," said Andy.

Pauline said, "Geoff wouldn't rob his own family."

"Don't count on it," said Reg. "He doesn't give a toss for any of us."

"Geoff?"

"Did you know he's emigrating?"

"No."

"It's true," said Reg. "He's off to Australia any day now. I picked this up on the grapevine through a colleague in the bank. I think the accident made him reconsider his plan, so to speak."

"What accident?"

"There you are, you see. I only heard about that from the same source. Old Geoff was in hospital for over a week at the end of September and the last thing he wanted was a visit from any of us."

"A road accident?"

"No, he did it himself. You know how keen he is on the garden. He's got this turfed area sloping down to the pond. He ran the mower over his foot and severed his big toe."

NEVER TWO WITHOUT THREE;
or, A Christmas Tragedy
by Agatha Christie

"I have a complaint to make," said Sir Henry Clithering.

His eyes twinkled gently as he looked round at the assembled company. Colonel Bantry, his legs stretched out, was frowning at the mantelpiece as though it were a delinquent soldier on parade; his wife was surreptitiously glancing at a catalogue of bulbs which had come by the late post; Dr. Lloyd was gazing with frank admiration at Jane Helier, and that beautiful young actress herself was thoughtfully regarding her pink polished nails. Only the elderly spinster lady, Miss Marple, was sitting bolt upright, and her faded blue eyes met Sir Henry's with an answering twinkle.

"A complaint?" she murmured.

"A very serious complaint. We are a company of six, three representatives of each sex, and I protest on behalf of down-trodden males. We have had three stories told thus far—and told by the three men! I protest that the ladies have not done their fair share."

"Oh!" said Mrs. Bantry with indignation. "I'm sure we have. We've listened with the most intelligent appreciation. We've displayed the true womanly attitude."

"It's an excellent excuse," said Sir Henry, "but it won't do. And there's a very good precedent in the Arabian Nights! So, forward, Scheherazade!"

"Meaning me?" said Mrs. Bantry. "But I don't know anything to tell. I've never been surrounded by blood or mystery."

"I don't absolutely insist on blood," said Sir Henry. "But I'm sure one of you three ladies has got a pet mystery. Come now, Miss Marple—'The Curious Coincidence of the Charwoman' or 'The Mystery of the Mothers' Meeting.' "

Miss Marple shook her head.

"Nothing that would interest you, Sir Henry. We have our little mysteries, of course—there was that gill of pickled shrimps that disappeared so incomprehensibly; but that wouldn't interest you because it all turned out to be so trivial, though throwing a considerable light on human nature."

"You have taught me to dote on human nature," said Sir Henry solemnly.

"What about you, Miss Helier?" asked Colonel Bantry. "You must have had some interesting experiences."

"Yes, indeed," said Dr. Lloyd.

"Me?" said Jane. "You mean—you want me to tell you something that happened to me?"

"Or to one of your friends," amended Sir Henry.

"Oh!" said Jane vaguely, "I don't think anything has ever happened to me—I mean not that kind of thing. Flowers, of course, and queer messages—but that's just men, isn't it? I don't think"—she paused and appeared lost in thought.

"I see we shall have to have that epic of the shrimps," said Sir Henry. "Now then, Miss Marple."

"You're so fond of your joke, Sir Henry. The shrimps are only nonsense; but now I come to think of it, I *do* remember one incident—at least not exactly an incident, something very much more serious—a tragedy. And I was, in a way, mixed up in it; and for what I did, I have never had any regrets—no, no regrets at all. But it didn't happen in St. Mary Mead."

"That disappoints me," said Sir Henry. "But I will endeavor to bear up. I knew we should not rely on you in vain."

He settled himself in the attitude of a listener. Miss Marple grew slightly pink.

"I hope I shall be able to tell it properly," she said anxiously. "I fear I am very inclined to become *rambling*. One wanders from the point—altogether without knowing that one is doing so. And it is so hard to remember each

fact in its proper order. You must all bear with me if I tell
my story badly. It happened a very long time ago now. As
I say, it was not connected with St. Mary Mead. As a matter of fact, it had to do with a Hydro—"

"Do you mean a seaplane?" asked Jane with wide eyes.

"You wouldn't know, dear," said Mrs. Bantry, and
explained.

Her husband added his quota. "Beastly places—
absolutely beastly! Got to get up early and drink filthy-
tasting water. Lot of old women sitting about. Ill-natured
tittle-tattle. God, when I think—"

"Now, Arthur," said Mrs. Bantry placidly. "You know
it did you all the good in the world."

"Lot of old women always sitting round talking scandal," grunted Colonel Bantry.

"That, I am afraid, is true," said Miss Marple. "I myself—"

"My dear Miss Marple," cried the colonel, horrified. "I
didn't mean—"

With pink cheeks and a little gesture of the hand, Miss
Marple stopped him.

"But is is *true*, Colonel Bantry. Only I should just like
to say this. Let me recollect my thoughts. Yes. Talking
scandal, as you say—well, it *is* done a good deal. And
people are very down on it—especially young people. My
nephew, who writes books—and very clever ones, I believe—has said some most *scathing* things about taking
people's characters away without any kind of proof—and
how wicked it is, and all that.

"But what I say is that none of these young people ever
stop to *think*. They really don't examine the facts. Surely
the whole crux of the matter is this: *How often is tittle-
tattle*—as you call it—*true*! And I think if, as I say, they
really examined the facts they would find that it was true
nine times out of ten! That's really just what makes
people so annoyed about it."

"The inspired guess," said Sir Henry.

"No, not that, not that at all! It's really a matter of practice and experience. An Egyptologist, so I've heard, if
you show him one of those curious little beetles, can tell

you by the look and the feel of the thing what date B.C. it is, or if it's a Birmingham imitation. And he can't always give a definite rule for doing so. He just *knows*. His life has been spent handling such things.

"And that's what I'm trying to say—very badly, I know. What my nephew calls 'superfluous women' have a lot of time on their hands, and their chief interest is usually *people*. And so, you see, they get to be what one might call *experts*.

"Now young people nowadays—they talk very freely about things that weren't mentioned in my young days, but on the other hand their minds are terribly innocent. They believe in everyone and everything. And if one tries to warn them, ever so gently, they say that one has a Victorian mind—and that, they say, is like a *sink*."

"After all," said Sir Henry, "what is wrong with a *sink*?"

"Exactly," said Miss Marple eagerly. "It's the most necessary thing in any house—but, of course, not romantic. Now I must confess that I have my *feelings,* like everyone else, and I have sometimes been cruelly hurt by unthinking remarks. I know gentlemen are not interested in domestic matters, but I must just mention my maid Ethel—a very good-looking girl and obliging in every way.

"Now I realized as soon as I saw her that she was the same type as Annie Webb and poor Mrs. Bruitt's girl. If the opportunity arose *mine and thine* would mean nothing to her. So I let her go at the end of the month and I gave her a written reference saying she was honest and sober, but privately I warned old Mrs. Edwards against taking her; and my nephew, Raymond, was exceedingly angry and said he had never heard of anything so wicked—yes, *wicked*.

"Well, she went to Lady Ashton, whom I felt no obligation to warn—and what happened? All the lace cut off her underclothes and two diamond brooches taken—and the girl departed in the middle of the night and never heard of since!"

Miss Marple paused, drew a long breath, and then went on.

"You'll be saying this has nothing to do with what went on at Keston Spa Hydro—but it has in a way. It explains why I felt no doubt in my mind the first moment I saw the Sanderses together that he meant to do away with her."

"Eh?" said Sir Henry, leaning forward.

Miss Marple turned a placid face to him.

"As I say, Sir Henry, I felt no doubt in my own mind. Mr. Sanders was a big, good-looking, florid-faced man, very hearty in his manner and popular with all. And nobody could have been pleasanter to his wife than he was. But I *knew*! He meant to make away with her."

"My dear Miss Marple—"

"Yes, I know. That's what my nephew Raymond West, would say. He'd tell me I hadn't a shadow of proof. But I remember Walter Hones, who kept The Green Man. Walking home with his wife one night she fell into the river—and *he* collected the insurance money! And one or two other people that are walking about scot-free to this day—one indeed in our own class of life. Went to Switzerland for a summer holiday climbing with his wife. I warned her not to go—the poor dear didn't get angry with me as she might have done—she only laughed. It seemed to her funny that a queer old thing like me should say such things about her Harry. Well, there was an accident—and Harry is married to another woman now. But what could I *do*? I *knew*, but there was no proof."

"Oh, Miss Marple," cried Mrs. Bantry. "You don't really mean—"

"My dear, these things are very common—very common indeed. And gentlemen are especially tempted, being so much the stronger. So easy if a thing looks like an accident. As I say, I knew at once with the Sanderses. It was on a tram. It was full inside and I had had to go on top. We all three got up to get off and Mr. Sanders lost his balance and fell right against his wife, sending her headfirst down the stairs. Fortunately the conductor was a very strong young man and caught her."

"But surely that must have been an accident."

"Of course it was an accident—nothing could have looked more accidental. But Mr. Sanders had been in the Merchant Service, so he told me, and a man who can keep his balance on a nasty tilting boat doesn't lose it on top of a tram if an old woman like me doesn't. Don't tell *me*!"

"At any rate we can take it that you made up your mind, Miss Marple," said Sir Henry. "Made it up then and there."

The old lady nodded. "I was sure enough, and another incident in crossing the street not long afterwards made me surer still. Now I ask you, what could I do, Sir Henry? Here was a nice contented happy little married woman shortly going to be murdered."

"My dear lady, you take my breath away."

"That's because, like most people nowadays, you won't face facts. You prefer to think such a thing couldn't be. But it was so, and I knew it. But one is so sadly handicapped! I couldn't, for instance, go to the police. And to warn the young woman would, I could see, be useless. She was devoted to the man. I just made it my business to find out as much as I could about them.

"One has a lot of opportunities, doing one's needlework round the fire. Mrs. Sanders—Gladys, her name was—was only too willing to talk. It seems they had not been married very long. Her husband had some property that was coming to him, but for the moment they were very badly off. In fact, they were living on her little income. One has heard that tale before. She bemoaned the fact that she could not touch the capital. It seems that somebody had had some sense somewhere!

"But the money was hers to will away—I found that out. And she and her husband had made wills in favor of each other directly after their marriage. Very touching. Of course, when Jack's affairs came right— That was the burden all day long, and in the meantime they were very hard up indeed—actually had a room on the top floor, all among the servants—and so dangerous in case of fire, though, as it happened, there was a fire escape just outside their window. I inquired carefully if there was a balcony—dangerous things, balconies. One push, you know!

"I made her promise not to go out on the balcony—I said I'd had a dream. That impressed her—one can do a lot with superstition sometimes. She was a fair girl, rather washed-out complexion, and an untidy roll of hair on her neck. Very credulous. She repeated what I had said to her husband and I noticed him looking at me in a curious way once or twice. *He* wasn't credulous, and he knew I'd been on that tram.

"But I was very worried—terribly worried—because I couldn't see how to circumvent him. I could prevent anything happening at the Hydro, just by saying a few words to show him I suspected. But that only meant his putting off his plan till later. No, I began to believe that the only policy was a bold one—somehow or other to lay a trap for him. If I could induce him to attempt her life in a way of my own choosing—well, then he would be unmasked, and she would be forced to face the truth however much of a shock it was to her."

"You take my breath away," said Dr. Lloyd. "What conceivable plan could you adopt?"

"I'd have found one—never fear," said Miss Marple. "But the man was too clever for me. He didn't wait. He thought I might suspect, so he struck before I could be sure. He knew I would suspect an accident. So he made it murder."

A little gasp went round the circle. Miss Marple nodded and set her lips grimly together.

"I'm afraid I've put that rather abruptly. I must try and tell you exactly what occurred. I've always felt very bitterly about it—it seems to me that I ought, somehow, to have prevented it. But doubtless Providence knew best. I did what I could at all events.

"There was what I can only describe as a curiously eerie feeling in the air. There seemed to be something weighing on us all—a feeling of misfortune. To begin with, there was George, the hall porter. Had been there for years and knew everybody. Bronchitis and pneumonia, and passed away on the fourth day. Terribly sad. A real blow to everybody. And four days before Christmas too.

And then one of the housemaids—such a nice girl—a septic finger, actually died in twenty-four hours.

"I was in the drawing-room with Miss Trollope and old Mrs. Carpenter, and Mrs. Carpenter was being positively ghoulish—relishing it all, you know.

" 'Mark my words,' she said. '*This isn't the end.* You know the saying? *Never two without three.* I've proved it true time and again. There'll be another death. Not a doubt of it. And we shan't have long to wait. *Never two without three.*'

"As she said the last words, nodding her head and clicking her knitting needles, I just chanced to look up and there was Mr. Sanders standing in the doorway. Just for a minute he was off guard and I saw the look in his face as plain as plain. I shall believe till my dying day that it was Mrs. Carpenter's ghoulish words that put the whole thing into his head. I saw his mind working.

"He came forward into the room smiling in his genial way.

" 'Any Christmas shopping I can do for you ladies?' he asked. 'I'm going down to Keston presently.'

"He stayed a minute or two, laughing and talking, and then went out. I tell you I was troubled, and I said straight away, 'Where's Mrs. Sanders?'

"Mrs. Trollope said she'd gone out to some friends of hers, the Mortimers, to play bridge, and that eased my mind for the moment. But I was still very worried and just on half-past five, I remember. Now I'm very anxious to put clearly what happened next. I was still in the lounge at a quarter to seven when Mr. Sanders came in. There were two gentlemen with him and all three of them were inclined to be a little on the lively side. Mr. Sanders left his two friends and came right over to where I was sitting with Miss Trollope. He explained that he wanted our advice about a Christmas present he was giving his wife. It was an evening bag.

" 'And you see, ladies,' he said. 'I'm only a rough sailorman. What do I know about such things? I've had three sent to me on approval and I want an expert opinion on them.'

"We said, of course, that we would be delighted to help him, and he asked if we'd mind coming upstairs, as his wife might come in any minute if he brought the things down. So we went up with him. I shall never forget what happened next—I can feel my little fingers tingling now.

"Mr. Sanders opened the door of the bedroom and switched on the light. I don't know which of us saw it first . . .

"Mrs. Sanders was lying on the floor, face downwards —dead.

"I got to her first. I knelt down and took her hand and felt for the pulse, but it was useless—the arm itself was cold and stiff. Just by her head was a stocking filled with sand—the weapon she had been struck down with.

"Miss Trollope, silly creature, was moaning and moaning by the door and holding her head. Sanders gave a great cry of 'My wife, my wife,' and rushed to her. I stopped him touching her. You see, I was sure at the moment that he had done it, and there might have been something that he wanted to take away or hide.

" 'Nothing must be touched,' I said. 'Pull yourself together, Mr. Sanders. Miss Trollope, please go down and fetch the manager.'

"I stayed there, kneeling by the body. I wasn't going to leave Sanders alone with it. And yet I was forced to admit that if the man was acting, he was acting marvelously. He looked dazed and bewildered and scared out of his wits.

"The manager was with us in no time. He made a quick inspection of the room, then turned us all out and locked the door, the key of which he took. Then he went off and telephoned to the police. It seemed a positive age before they came—we learned afterwards that the line was out of order. The manager had to send a messenger to the police station, and the Hydro is right out of the town, up on the edge of the moor; and Mrs. Carpenter tried us all very severely. She was so pleased at her prophecy of 'Never two without three' coming true so quickly.

"Sanders, I learned later, wandered out into the grounds, clutching his head and groaning and displaying every sign of grief.

"However, the police came at last. They went upstairs with the manager and Mr. Sanders. Later they sent for me and I went up. The Inspector was there, sitting at a table writing. He was an intelligent-looking man and I liked him.

" 'Miss Marple?' he said.

" 'Yes.'

" 'I understand, madam, that you were present when the body of the deceased was found?'

"I said I was and I described exactly what had occurred. I think it was a relief to the poor man to find someone who could answer his questions coherently, having previously had to deal with Sanders and Emily Trollope, who, I gather, was completely demoralized—she would be, the silly creature! I remember my dear mother teaching me that a gentlewoman should always be able to control herself in public, however much she may give way in private."

"An admirable maxim," said Sir Henry gravely.

"When I had finished, the Inspector said, 'Thank you, madam. Now I'm afraid I must ask you just to look at the body once more. Is that exactly the position in which it was lying when you entered the room? It hasn't been moved in any way?"

"I explained that I had prevented Mr. Sanders from doing so, and the Inspector nodded approval.

" 'The gentleman seems terribly upset,' he remarked.

" 'He seems so—yes,' I replied.

"I don't think I put any special emphasis on the 'seems,' but the Inspector looked at me rather keenly.

" 'So we can take it that the body is exactly as it was when found?' he said.

" 'Except for the hat, yes,' I replied.

"The Inspector looked up sharply.

" 'What do you mean—the hat?'

"I explained that the hat had been on poor Gladys' head, whereas now it was lying beside her. I thought, of course, that the police had done this. The Inspector, however, denied it emphatically. Nothing had, as yet, been moved or touched.

"He stood looking down at that poor prone figure with a puzzled frown. Gladys was dressed in her outdoor clothes—a big dark-red tweed coat with a gray fur collar. The hat, a cheap affair of red felt, lay just by her head.

"The Inspector stood for some minutes in silence, frowning to himself. Then an idea struck him.

" 'Can you, by any chance, remember, madam, whether there were earrings in the ears, or whether the deceased habitually wore earrings?'

"Now fortunately I am in the habit of observing closely. I remembered that there had been a glint of pearls just below the hat brim, though I had paid no particular notice to it at the time. I was able to answer his first question in the affirmative.

" 'Then that settles it. The lady's jewel case was rifled —not that she had anything much of value, I understand—and the rings were taken from her fingers. The murderer must have forgotten the earrings and come back for them after the murder was discovered. A cool customer! Or perhaps'—He stared round the room and said slowly, 'He may have been concealed here in this room all the time.'

"But I negatived that idea. I myself, I explained, had looked under the bed. And the manager had opened the doors of the wardrobe. There was nowhere else where a man could hide. It is true the hat cupboard was locked in the middle of the wardrobe, but as that was only a shallow affair no one could have been concealed there.

"The Inspector nodded his head slowly while I explained all this.

" 'I'll take your word for it, madam,' he said. 'In that case, as I said before, he must have come back. A very cool customer.'

" 'But the manager locked the door and took the key!'

" 'That's nothing. The balcony and the fire escape— that's the way the thief came. Why, as likely as not, you actually disturbed him at work. He slips out of the window, and when you've all gone, back he comes and goes on with his business.'

" 'You are sure,' I said, 'that there *was* a thief?'

"He said dryly, 'Well, it looks it, doesn't it?'

"But something in his tone satisfied me. I felt that he wouldn't take Mr. Sanders in the role of the bereaved widower too seriously.

" 'You see, I admit it frankly, I was absolutely under the opinion of what I believe our neighbors, the French, call the *idée fixe*. I knew that man, Sanders, intended his wife to die. What I didn't allow for was that strange and fantastic thing, coincidence.

"My views about Mr. Sanders were—I was sure of it— absolutely right and *true*. The man was a scoundrel. But although his hypocritical assumptions of grief didn't deceive me for a minute, I do remember feeling at the time that his *surprise* and *bewilderment* were marvelously well done. They seemed absolutely *natural*—if you know what I mean.

"I must admit that after my conversation with the Inspector, a curious feeling of doubt crept over me. Because if Sanders had done this dreadful thing, I couldn't imagine any conceivable reason why he should creep back by means of the fire escape and take the earrings from his wife's ears. It wouldn't have been a *sensible* thing to do, and Sanders was such a very sensible man—that's just why I always felt he was so dangerous."

Miss Marple looked round at her audience.

"You see, perhaps, what I am coming to? It is, so often, the unexpected that happens in this world. I was so *sure*, and that, I think, was what blinded me. The result came as a shock to me. *For it was proved, beyond any possible doubt, that Mr. Sanders could not possibly have killed his wife.*"

A surprised gasp came from Mrs. Bantry. Miss Marple turned to her.

"I know, my dear, that isn't what you expected when I began this story. It wasn't what I expected. But facts are facts, and if one is proved to be wrong, one must just be humble about it and start again. That Mr. Sanders was a murderer at heart I knew—and nothing ever occurred to upset that firm conviction of mine.

"And now, I expect, you would like to hear the actual

facts themselves. Mrs. Sanders, as you know, spent the afternoon playing bridge with some friends, the Mortimers. She left them at about a quarter past six. From her friends' house to the Hydro was about a quarter of an hour's walk—less if one hurried. She must have come in, then, about six thirty.

"No one saw her come in, so she must have entered by the side door and hurried straight up to her room. There she changed—the fawn coat and skirt she wore to the bridge party were hanging up in the cupboard—and was evidently preparing to go out again, when the blow fell. Quite possibly, they say, she never even knew who struck her. The sandbag, I understand, is a very efficient weapon. That looks as though the attackers were concealed in the room, possibly in one of the big wardrobe cupboards—the one she didn't open.

"Now as to the movements of Mr. Sanders. He went out, as I have said, at about five thirty—or a little after. He did some shopping at a couple of shops and at about six o'clock he entered the Grand Spa Hotel where he encountered two friends—the same with whom he returned to the Hydro later. They played billiards and, I gather, had a good many whiskies and sodas together. These two men—Hitchock and Spender, their names were—were actually with him the whole time from six o'clock onwards. They walked back to the Hydro with him and he only left them to come across to me and Miss Trollope. That, as I told you, was about a quarter to seven—at which time his wife must have been already dead.

"I must tell you that I myself talked to these two friends of his. I did not like them. They were neither pleasant nor gentlemanly men, but I was quite certain of one thing—they were speaking the absolute truth when they said that Sanders had been in their company the whole time.

"There was just one other little point that came up. It seems that while bridge was going on, Mrs. Sanders was called to the telephone. A Mr. Littleworth wanted to speak to her. She seemed both excited and pleased about something—and incidentally made one or two bad mistakes at cards. She left rather earlier than they had expected her to do.

"Mr. Sanders was asked whether he knew the name of Littleworth as being one of his wife's friends, but he declared he had never heard of anyone of that name. And to me that seems borne out by his wife's attitude—she too did not seem to know the name of Littleworth. Nevertheless she came back from the telephone smiling and blushing, so it looks as though whoever it was did not give his real name, and that in itself has a suspicious aspect, does it not?

"Anyway, that is the problem that was left. The burglar story, which seems unlikely—or the alternative theory that Mrs. Sanders was preparing to go out and meet somebody. Did that somebody come to her room by means of the fire escape? Was there a quarrel? Or did he attack treacherously?"

Miss Marple stopped.

"Well?" said Sir Henry. "What is the answer?"

"I wondered if any of you could guess."

"I'm never good at guessing," said Mrs. Bantry. "It seems a pity that Sanders had such a wonderful alibi; but if it satisfied you it must have been all right."

Jane Helier moved her beautiful head and asked a question.

"Why," she said, "was the hat cupboard locked?"

"How very clever of you, my dear," said Miss Marple, beaming. "That's just what I wondered myself, though the explanation was quite simple. In it were a pair of embroidered slippers and some pocket handkerchiefs that the poor girl was embroidering for her husband for Christmas. That's why she locked the cupboard. The key was found in her handbag."

"Oh!" said Jane. "Then it isn't very interesting after all."

"Oh, but it is," said Miss Marple. "It's just the one really interesting thing—the thing that made all the murderer's plans go wrong."

Everyone stared at the old lady.

"I didn't see it myself for two days," said Miss Marple.

"I puzzled and puzzled—and then suddenly there it was, all clear. I went to the Inspector and asked him to try something and he did."

"What did you ask him to try?"

"I asked him to fit that hat on the poor girl's head— and of course he couldn't. It wouldn't go on. *It wasn't her hat, you see."*

Mrs. Bantry stared.

"But it was on her head to begin with?"

"Not on *her* head—"

Miss Marple stopped a moment to let her words sink in, and then went on.

"We took it for granted that it was poor Gladys' body there; but we never looked at the face. She was face downwards, remember, and the hat hid everything."

"But she *was* killed?"

"Yes, later. At the moment that we were telephoning to the police, Gladys Sanders was alive and well."

"You mean it was someone pretending to be her? But surely when you touched her—"

"It was a dead body, right enough," said Miss Marple gravely.

"But, dash it all," said Colonel Bantry, "you can't get hold of dead bodies right and left. What did they do with the—the first corpse afterwards?"

"He put it back," said Miss Marple. "It was a wicked idea—but a very clever one. It was our talk in the drawing-room that put it into his head. The body of poor Mary, the housemaid—why not use it? Remember, the Sanders' room was up in the servants' quarters. Mary's room was two doors off. The undertakers wouldn't come till after dark—he counted on that. He carried the body along the balcony—it was dark at five—dressed it in one of his wife's dresses and her big red coat. *And then he found the hat cupboard locked!* There was only one thing to be done—he fetched one of the poor girl's own hats. No one would notice. He put the sandbag down beside her. Then he went off to establish his alibi.

"He telephoned to his wife—calling himself Mr. Little-worth. I don't know what he said to her—she was a credulous girl, as I've already said. But he got her to leave the bridge party early and not to go back to the Hydro, and arranged with her to meet him in the grounds of the Hydro near the fire escape at seven o'clock. He probably told her he had some surprise for her.

"He returns to the Hydro with his friends and arranges that Miss Trollope and I shall discover the crime with him. He even pretends to turn the body over—and I stop him! Then the police are sent for, and he staggers out into the grounds.

"Nobody asked him for an alibi *after* the crime. He meets his wife, takes her up the fire escape, they enter their room. Perhaps he has already told her some story about the body. She stoops over it, he picks up his sand-bag and strikes . . . Oh, dear! it makes me sick to think of, even now! Then quickly he strips off her coat and skirt, hangs them up, and dresses her in the clothes from the other body.

"But the hat won't go on.

"Mary's head is shingled. Gladys Sanders, as I said, had a great bun of hair. He is forced to leave the hat beside the body and hope no one will notice. Then he carries poor Mary's body back to her own room."

"It seems incredible," said Dr. Lloyd. "The risks he took. The police might have arrived too soon."

"You remember the line was out of order," said Miss Marple. "That was a piece of *his* work. He couldn't afford to have the police on the spot too soon. When they did come, they spent some time in the manager's office before going up to the bedroom. That was the weakest point—the chance that someone might notice the difference between a body that had been dead two hours and one that had been dead just over half an hour; but he counted on the fact that the people who first discovered the crime would have no expert knowledge of criminal matters."

Dr. Lloyd nodded.

"The crime would be supposed to have been committed about a quarter to seven or thereabouts, I suppose," he said. "It was actually committed at seven or a few minutes after.

When the police surgeon examined the body it would be about half-past seven at earliest. He couldn't possibly tell."

"I am the person who should have known," said Miss Marple. "I felt the poor girl's hand and it was icy cold. Yet a short time later the Inspector spoke as though the murder must have been committed just before we arrived—and I saw nothing!"

"I think you saw a good deal, Miss Marple," said Sir Henry. "The case was before my time. I don't even remember hearing of it. What happened?"

"Sanders was hanged," said Miss Marple crisply. "And a good job too. I have never regretted my part in bringing that man to justice. I've no patience with modern humanitarian scruples about capital punishment."

Her stern face softened.

"But I have often reproached myself bitterly with failing to save the life of that poor girl. But who would have listened to an old woman jumping to conclusions? Well, well—who knows? Perhaps it was better for her to die while life was still happy than it would have been for her to live on, unhappy and disillusioned, in a world that would have seemed suddenly horrible. She loved that scoundrel and trusted him. She never found him out."

"Well, then," said Jane Helier, "she was all right. Quite all right. I wish—" She stopped.

Miss Marple looked at the famous, the beautiful, the successful Jane Helier and nodded her head gently.

"I see, my dear," she said very gently. "I see."

THE GHOST OF CHRISTMAS PAST
by Robert Richardson

It snowed heavily on Christmas Eve, 1889, the year of my marriage. When we rose on Christmas morning, London was muffled in white, familiar landmarks unidentifiable as presents wrapped in thick paper, stillness and silence the more pronounced in thoroughfares that normally clattered with the ceaseless activity of the city. We entertained no company, and, after exchanging gifts, enjoyed of our first Christmas luncheon together. As we finished, Mary's kindly mind turned to one she knew was alone that day.

"I still regret Mr. Holmes would not join us," she said. "I find it depressing to think of him on his own in those gloomy rooms."

"He will be perfectly content," I replied. "He will read his books, smoke, and play the violin. His only irritation will be the inertia of a day when even criminals may observe goodwill to men."

"So you have told me," she replied. "But will he eat?"

"He will certainly not starve."

"Nonetheless, I insist that you take him some cold goose and mince pies," she said. "I shall ask cook to prepare them immediately."

"Go to Baker Street in this weather?" I protested. "There can be no cabs operating."

"It is now a fine, sunny day," she replied. "The snow is not so deep that you cannot walk half a mile."

I protested no further. Her consideration was Christian and sincere and it would have been churlish to refuse my role in fulfilling it. Holmes would be indifferent to whether I visited or not, and a walk after such an abundant meal was not a displeasing prospect.

The snow, while deep, was not impassable and there were others abroad with whom I exchanged seasonal greetings as I trudged my way. I turned out of Marylebone Road into Baker Street, where I followed another's footprints before they crossed to the other side. I knew that Mrs. Hudson was visiting relatives and, on knocking, expected to have to wait some moments until Holmes descended. In fact, I heard him hurry down the stairs, and he opened the front door with alacrity.

"You, Watson?" he said in evident surprise. "I was expecting . . ." He stepped out and looked up and down the street. "Have you seen anybody?"

"Not in Baker Street. Are you expecting a visitor?"

"Yes. She will approach from that direction"—he pointed to the north—"once she has decided. . . ." Abruptly, he became aware of his lack of greeting. "Watson, I treat you without ceremony. Come in, my dear fellow. What brings you?"

"My wife's insistence." I held up the canvas bag I was carrying. "She is concerned lest you go hungry on Christmas Day."

He laughed as he ushered me inside. "Your wife is too kind, Watson—as are you for coming. A very Merry Christmas. We will drink to the festive day."

I followed him to the familiar rooms and he poured tots of whisky for each of us as I removed my greatcoat.

"Who is your expected visitor?" I inquired.

"A young woman of good sense and comfortable means who lives within a mile of here. She is in the greatest distress, but is tormented by uncertainty. She is spending time on her own while she considers how best to present her problem to me."

"What is her name?"

"I don't know," he replied as he handed me the glass. "I didn't see her."

"You didn't see her? Then how can you know?"

He appeared amused. "You have lunched—or perhaps

wined—too well, Watson. The explanation is clearly visible in Baker Street."

"I told you I saw nobody."

"But as you walked up from Marylebone Road, did you not observe footprints preceding you?"

"Yes, but they crossed to the other side and I took no further notice."

"You should have done. They were very informative." He moved to the window and beckoned me to join him. "About half an hour ago, I came to stand here and noticed those footprints directly opposite, crossing to this door. Unaware of anyone having knocked, I went outside to investigate.

"The footprints begin out of Marylebone Road on the correct side for this address. However, outside the first house where the number is visible, she realised and crossed to the other side. She stood opposite for a few minutes—there are clear indications of her stamping her feet to keep them warm—then summoned up courage to approach. She paused on the step and at one point lifted the knocker—the snow that had settled on it was disturbed. She then withdrew and continued up the street."

"Very well," I agreed. "I cannot dispute the pattern of movement. But how is it a woman, and the other details?"

"The prints were made by new boots sold by Thomson and Weekes. Such footwear is not cheap and is bought by sensible young women who place more importance on quality than fashion. She would not venture out to see me in such weather on Christmas Day unless there was a serious reason, and I would suggest that a mile is the farthest she could walk in such conditions."

"And she is now thinking the matter over?"

"Of course. At the end of Baker Street towards which she has walked lies Regent's Park, an ideal spot to be alone for meditation."

"But will she return?"

"I hope so. She is clearly in urgent need of help, but I can only give it if she overcomes her reservations. . . . Ah." He stepped back from the window, drawing me with him. "This must be she, and her face reveals she has made her resolution. Admit her when she knocks. The presence of a respectable professional man may help to ease her misgivings."

As he spoke, the knocker was struck with some timidity. "Quickly, Watson, or she may flee again!"

I hurried downstairs, mentally composing myself; so nervous a caller needed to be greeted with calm. She was some twenty-three years of age, dressed in an ankle-length tweed coat, the boots Holmes had identified, a smart but practical bonnet, and sensible, fur-lined leather mittens. Her striking grey eyes were troubled as she saw me.

"Mr. Holmes?" she inquired hesitantly.

"No, I am his colleague, Dr. John Watson," I said. "However, if you will step inside, he is at home."

She shook her head as though regretting what she had managed to accomplish. "I have no appointment and Mr. Holmes is not expecting me."

"He is," I replied. "And is anxious to meet you." I stepped forward and took her arm. "You are in great distress and have come to the best man in England for assistance."

Clearly bewildered, but responding to my assurance, she allowed me to lead her inside and up the stairs. Holmes had prepared a third whisky, smaller than those he had poured for us.

"You must be very cold after walking in the park," he said as she entered. "This will warm you. It has been diluted with water."

"In the park? How can you . . . ?" Despite her agitated state, she smiled slightly. "But of course, you are Sherlock Holmes."

"You have not come here to pay me compliments," my friend replied. "I suggest you first sit by the fire and compose yourself."

"Thank you." She took the offered chair, removing her bonnet to reveal long fine hair the colour of wheat coiled into a bun. For a few minutes, we waited in silence until Holmes spoke again.

"You clearly have some familiarity with my methods,

so we will accept that from the evidence in the snow of your earlier visit I know this is a matter of urgency. When you are ready, please tell me what it is as briefly as you are able. We might begin with your name."

Our visitor had obviously calmed herself, for she proceeded without further delay. "My name is Anne Fortescue and I am the only daughter of the Reverend Alfred Fortescue, vicar of St. Andrew's Church in St. John's Wood. Do you know it?"

"A baroque building in the style of St. Martin-in-the-Fields," Holmes commented. "I have frequently passed it, but never had occasion to enter. Pray continue."

"It has a small but well-populated parish," Miss Fortescue went on. "My father received the living more than fifteen years ago, after a short curacy in East London, and has always been highly regarded by his flock. Apart from our cook and maid, we live alone, my mother having died when I was less than a year old."

She placed the glass, its contents unfinished, on a table beside her before she continued. "Our lives are, and always have been, unremarkable, and I can think of nothing in the past that could be of any relevance to what occurred last night."

"When your father would have been occupied with his clerical duties."

"Indeed, and it was at the last—the Watchnight service—that something utterly inexplicable happened."

"Not inexplicable," Holmes corrected. "Extraordinary, perhaps. To you, frightening. But, like all things in this mortal world, it can be explained. That is my business. The details, if you please, and my compliments on the conciseness of your narrative."

"Thank you. . . . The service began at eleven-thirty and was to be a series of lessons and carols with my father conducting the choir. There were some fifty people in the congregation, the numbers being reduced by the weather. The service proceeded without incident until the fifth lesson, which my father was to read. He climbed the steps to the pulpit—I was in the pew directly in front of him, but paying no particular attention—but instead of speaking he looked straight ahead."

Miss Fortescue paused, as though the moment she was describing was so vivid in her mind that it still shook her. She raised her face to Holmes with a look of remembered terror.

"He said nothing! There was just a long silence. To relate it sounds prosaic, but it was totally unnatural. I feared he was taken suddenly ill and rose to go to him. Then he shouted 'No! No! No!' Three times it rang through the church. Then he almost fell back down the pulpit steps and ran—he is not a young man, Mr. Holmes, but he ran—towards the vestry. We were all so startled that for a moment we just stared in disbelief, then I ran myself, followed by others sitting near me.

"The outer door of the vestry leading into the churchyard was open, and as I reached it I saw him racing away through the falling snow. I cried after him and pursued him out and along the road until I lost him in the darkness. No one has seen him since."

Holmes looked at his watch. "And this was nearly fifteen hours ago. Have you consulted the police?"

"One of our local officers was in the congregation and raised the alarm, but in the darkness of a winter's night a man may vanish in London without difficulty. They are searching even now, but I can give them no help as to where he might have fled or what has driven him there. They counsel patience, but remaining in the vicarage unable to do anything was intolerable! Like so many, Mr. Holmes, I have heard of you, but never thought that one day I might come to you myself."

"You were right to do so now," Holmes told her. "But why did you hesitate when you first arrived?"

"As I walked here, it seemed to me so bizarre an occurrence—with no suggestion of a crime—that I feared you would resent being disturbed on such a matter on such a day. When I first reached your door, my misgivings overcame me. I nearly returned home without seeing you."

"You were right to change your mind," Holmes told her. "As you say, there is no apparent criminality, but the confounding may also concern me, especially when it causes the innocent such distress. At this stage, I have only one question. You mentioned that your father is not a young man. How old is he?"

Miss Fortescue seemed puzzled. "He will be sixty-eight in February."

"Yet he was appointed vicar of St. Andrew's some fifteen years ago, after what you describe as a brief curacy. He must have taken holy orders late in life. What was his profession previously?"

"He was a doctor, Mr. Holmes. A general practitioner."

"And where did he practise?"

"In Liverpool . . . is there any relevance in this?"

"I cannot imagine so," Holmes said dismissively. "The point merely intrigued me. However, we can accomplish nothing here. Watson, you will want to return home, but we are for St. John's Wood."

"I have no commitments," I said. "If this lady has no objection, I should like to accompany you."

"As you wish," Holmes said. "But we leave immediately. The afternoon light will quickly fade. Miss Fortescue, will you be so kind as to wait in the hall downstairs while I attire myself?"

"Of course. I am very grateful to you, Mr. Holmes."

He nodded his thanks, and as our visitor left the room moved swiftly to where he kept his collection of newspaper clippings. They covered, I knew, many years and included narratives of the most recondite events that had caught his attention; on more than one occasion their contents had provided some invaluable fragment of information. He picked up the first volume and turned its pages before pausing for a moment. Then he closed the book and glanced at me.

"Has it ever struck you, Watson, how our existence is constantly governed by chance?"

"What do you mean?"

"You and I first met at a haphazard point when our lives touched. Years of unrelated movements brought our paths together at that moment. Today is an occasion when such a random pattern has the additional spark of the incredible, what we call a coincidence."

"Then you knew of this matter even before Miss Fortescue arrived?"

"Only in part. Her name immediately struck me. Having ascertained part of her father's history, I am convinced her visit is connected with something that happened more than twenty years ago. I investigated it once, but could not resolve it to my satisfaction. Now, because an obscure curate was offered a living relatively near this house, his daughter has brought it to my attention again."

"And what was the original occurrence?"

"There is no time to explain now," he replied. "We must not keep Miss Fortescue waiting. Do not reveal that I know anything and I will afford you the details when we have the opportunity. Fate has delivered what may prove to be an ominous Christmas present, Watson. That young woman downstairs has sought my help out of a natural and sincere love for her father. I trust she will not live to regret her decision to come to me."

Public-spirited citizens having made efforts to clear the pavements outside their homes, our journey was accomplished more speedily than would otherwise have been the case. St. Andrew's stood back from the road, surrounded by its churchyard, with the vicarage behind, from which Miss Fortescue collected the key while we waited in the portico beneath the Ionic columns of soot-smeared white Portland stone. Inside, it was a handsome square building with a gallery supported by iron pillars round three sides of the nave, the section facing the altar bearing the organ, and rows of box pews. At the chancel steps, Holmes looked back down the flagstones of the central aisle, covered in a deep-blue runner.

"How tall is your father, Miss Fortescue?"

"How tall? I really cannot understand how . . ."

"People are often puzzled when they see my methods in action," he interrupted. "Be so good as to indulge my questions. There is always a purpose to them."

"As you wish. . . . About Dr. Watson's height."

"Very well. Now, your father's exact movements from the moment the service began. I presume he entered from the vestry, which is where?"

"Over there, to your left. He walked to the chancel steps, bowed to the altar, then crossed to the choir stalls to conduct them for the first carol."

"For which the congregation rose? Thank you. And then?"

"He sat on a chair by the choir as the lessons were read and . . ."

"And remained in that position, except for leading the choir in further carols, until he entered the pulpit to read the fifth lesson," Holmes concluded. "That is perfectly clear. Let us first see if the vestry affords any clues."

The room contained a high cupboard in which the choir's surplices were stored, a desk and chair, and a large padlocked chest for the safekeeping of church plate. Holmes opened the outer door and looked across the gravestones for a moment, then remarked on a pair of rubber overshoes just inside the threshold.

"They are my father's," Miss Fortescue explained. "He wore them as he walked from the vicarage."

"And clearly fled without them," Holmes commented. "Watson, will you wait here with Miss Fortescue for a moment, then enter the church and imitate her father's movements. . . . Incidentally, I noticed a pool of water near the altar. Take care you don't slip."

After he left us, I assured Miss Fortescue that Holmes would not request such a pantomime without good reason before I followed his instructions. There was no sign of him as we reentered the church, but I heard his voice call me from some part of the building.

"First to the choir stalls, then enter the pulpit."

I did as he bade me, finally climbing the nine steps that curved round the oak pulpit and standing before the Bible, set on the outspread wings of a carved eagle. I gazed across the ranks of dark deal pews and saw Holmes sitting in one of them towards the back.

"Oh, there you are," I remarked.

"Yes, Watson . . . where you could not see me until

now." He rose and unfastened the brass catch securing the gate at the end of the pew and strode down the aisle. "During the first part of the service, Miss Fortescue, your father would only have been able to see part of his congregation. Even when they rose to sing, his attention would have been directed to the choir. Only when he entered the pulpit and instinctively raised his eyes would everyone have been visible."

"But whom did he see?" she asked.

"That we must discover. You said there were some fifty people in the congregation. Were there any strangers?"

"Not to my knowledge, but latecomers may have arrived after I took my place."

"Is it the habit of this church to greet worshipers at the door?"

"Yes. My father's curate, David Sinclair, does it."

"Then we must talk to him. Where may he be found?"

"In the curate's cottage in the adjacent road. It is but a short distance."

The "cottage" was imaginatively named, being in fact the end house of a short terrace. Miss Fortescue knocked, and the door was speedily opened by an upright, black-haired young man in clerical garb. His face transmuted into instant relief and his dark eyes lit with affection and concern as he saw our companion.

"Anne!" he cried. "Where have you been? I spent an hour at the vicarage waiting for you to return."

"I have been to seek help, David," she replied. "This is Mr. Sherlock Holmes and his companion, Dr. Watson. Mr. Holmes wishes to talk to you."

"Of course. Gentlemen, this way please."

As we stepped inside, Sinclair placed his hand on Miss Fortescue's arm with such natural familiarity that it was clear their relationship was deeper than that of a young man showing courtesy to his vicar's daughter. In the front room, he set her on a comfortable chair before turning to Holmes.

"Clearly you are aware of what has occurred, sir," he said. "I do not know how I can assist, but if there is anything in my power I shall do it."

"I wish to ascertain if anyone unknown to you attended the Watchnight service. I assume you recognized most of the congregation."

"Yes. Except for a young man and woman who arrived just before the service began."

"Did you speak to them?"

"Hardly at all. With the service about to commence, I wished to take my own seat. I welcomed them and handed them each a service sheet."

"Where did they sit?"

"In a vacant pew near the back. I noticed because I followed them as I went to my place at the front."

"Did you see them again?"

"No. As you may imagine, there was great confusion after the incident with Mr. Fortescue. I was too shocked by what had happened even to remember the strangers. It is only now that you have recalled them to my mind. Are they of importance?"

"Almost certainly," Holmes replied. "They appear to have been the only unusual feature present during the service. A connection between them and the vicar's behaviour seems irrefutable."

Sinclair turned to Miss Fortescue with a look of anguish. "But I did not realise! Forgive me for not paying attention to them! Had I done so, perhaps . . ."

"No blame attaches to you," Holmes interrupted. "Many churches are attended by strangers at Christmastime. You were not to know that this man and woman were anything other than seasonal visitors to the parish."

"But now they have disappeared!"

"They are not likely to have travelled far in this weather. It may be possible to locate them."

"My concern is locating my father," Miss Fortescue said.

"We share your anxiety," Holmes said. "And it is possible that the police's activities may have yielded results. If so, they will seek you at the vicarage. Mr. Sinclair may escort you home and leave you in the care of the household staff. We will return to the church."

The possibility, however faint, of the best of news

awaiting her at home roused Miss Fortescue to action and
we left the curate's house. We separated in the churchyard, with Sinclair assuring us that he would find us if the
vicar had returned or the police had information. The late-
December light was dying as we passed between the
gravestones amid attendant elms and yews, and fresh
flakes of snow drifted about us.

"An explanation first, Watson," Holmes said after we
had lit several gas mantles in the nave. "I told you earlier
that this matter contains echoes of an old story."

We sat in one of the pews, the mantles throwing light
and shadow about us as he related his narrative.

"Alfred Fortescue was the son of a distinguished Scot-
tish surgeon. By the 1860s, he was established as a general practitioner in Liverpool. The neighbourhood was
one of well-to-do merchants and the practice an advanta-
geous one, but he also held a weekly surgery in the dockside area of the city, asking of his patients no more than
they could afford, which in many cases was nothing. In
1866 he married Emily Dawson, the daughter of a ship-
owner and a woman of volatile temperament who lacked
neither ambition nor pride. His comfortable private income was insufficient to satisfy her. She complained
about the time he spent attending impoverished patients
when he could have been attracting high fees from others;
she grumbled at what she saw as the paucity of her
wardrobe; she resented the modesty of their lifestyle. In
short, she became a scold.

"Fortescue refused to abandon the underprivileged, and
the couple quarrelled frequently. The arrival of a daughter—the young woman we have met today—might have
reconciled their differences, but in fact had the opposite
effect. The wife irrationally complained that if her child
was to be raised as a ragamuffin, she would have nothing
to do with her, and from the time of the birth Fortescue
was obliged to employ a nurse. He appointed a woman
called Jane Smith, whose arrival aggravated the mother's
behaviour to the extent that she became unbalanced in her
mind.

"Tragedy struck when the child was six months old.

Emily Fortescue had started to wander the house at night, now weeping, now laughing. When they heard her, the staff or Fortescue himself would return her to her room and she would be given a sedative. On Christmas Eve of 1867 the household was awoken by screaming followed by the sound of breaking glass coming from the nursery. Hastening to the room, they found a terrible scene. Jane Smith, whose bedroom was adjacent, was clutching the baby, and Fortescue was standing by the shattered sash window, staring at the terrace below where his wife lay dead from a broken neck.

"The doctor appeared too shaken to speak, but Smith was totally calm. She handed the infant to the cook and asked the butler to summon the police. When they arrived, she confessed to responsibility for Emily Fortescue's death. She said she had heard sounds from the nursery and on entering had seen a figure standing near the cradle. Afraid for the safety of her charge and not recognising the intruder in the darkness, she had run across the room and pushed her violently away. The woman had staggered backwards through the window. Moments later, Fortescue had burst in, followed by the staff. It was a story she never altered, and she was subsequently imprisoned for manslaughter. After her trial, Fortescue left Liverpool with his daughter and was never heard of again.

"The matter attracted scant attention in the London papers, but the provincial press reported it in detail and an acquaintance of mine in Liverpool sent me the cuttings as he felt they would be of interest."

"In what way?" I inquired. "It was a tragedy, but no mystery is apparent."

"It was to my perceptive correspondent," Holmes replied. "He pointed out that Jane Smith had been one of the doctor's dockside patients, the very class of person his wife had so resented. Fortescue's behaviour marked him as a sympathetic man, so why did he employ someone likely to cause his wife such offence? The question intrigued me also, but other cases drove it from my mind.

"Some ten years later, however, I was engaged on an

inquiry in Lancashire and I made a detour to Merseyside before leaving the county. The practice was in the hands of a newcomer, but many people remembered Fortescue, including his former butler, whom I was able to trace. He said that on the night of Mrs. Fortescue's death he had been awoken by raised voices, although he could not be certain from which part of the house they came.

"He rose and left his room, which was on the floor above the nursery. At the foot of the stairs, he heard the scream and the breaking glass and at that moment could see the door to the nursery at the far end of the corridor. He hurried to the room and could recollect no sign of Fortescue until he entered the nursery himself. In other words, Watson, the doctor was in the room at the moment his wife went through the window, a completely different account to that given by Smith."

"Did he give evidence at Smith's trial?" I asked.

"Yes, but made no mention of what he told me. He said that Smith was so adamant in her version of events—a version that condemned her—that he felt he could have been mistaken in the confusion. But even so many years later, he wondered if he had really been in error.

"I used my influence with Scotland Yard to secure an interview with Smith in Holloway Prison. She greeted me courteously, but expressed surprise at my interest. Her story remained unchanged. I put to her an alternative narrative but, rightly suspecting that I had no firm evidence, she denied it. When I left, she asked that I should not approach her again, a request I have honoured."

Holmes stared thoughtfully at the pulpit at the far end of the church. "So is the truth now within my grasp?"

"What was the alternative story you put to Smith?"

"A bow at a venture, Watson, and fatally lacking a reason. It seemed clearly possible that—" He broke off as the creak of the west door opening behind us sounded through the silent church. As we turned in our seats, Sinclair and Miss Fortescue entered, accompanied by a young man, his hat held respectfully in his hands.

"Mr. Holmes," Sinclair said. "This is one of the strangers who attended the Watchnight service. The lady is his wife. He came to the vicarage to inquire about Mr. Fortes-cue."

"Indeed?" said Holmes, as we both rose and joined them. "And where is your wife?"

"She is unable to come, sir," the man replied. "But she was concerned and I said I would make inquiries. I'm told he has not returned."

"No, but your interest does you credit," Holmes said as his keen eyes examined the stranger in the light of the gas mantle.

"What is a newly married, left-handed ledger clerk from Manchester doing in St. John's Wood?" he inquired.

"Do you know me, sir?" the man demanded in amaze-ment.

"No, but your accent is unmistakable, the new ring on your wedding finger visible, and it is the elbow of the right sleeve of your jacket that has required repair. That is the one you must lean on your desk while writing with the opposite hand. What is your name?"

"Michael Chester. My wife and I are visiting relatives of hers in London for Christmas."

"And what brought you to St. Andrew's last night?"

"We wished to attend Watchnight service and this was the nearest church."

"And you've never been here before?"

"This is the first time either of us has visited London."

"Do you have any connection with Liverpool?" Holmes asked him.

"My wife's grandmother was born there."

"And your own family?"

"I was raised in an orphanage in the city of Chester, from which I was given my name. I know nothing of my parents."

"For one so disadvantaged, you appear to have ad-vanced yourself."

"I had a benefactor, the wife of a councillor who sup-ported the orphanage. When I showed skill in letters and numbers, she arranged additional education for me and later helped me secure a position with my present em-ployer."

"Most commendable," Holmes commented. "I'm obliged
to you for answering my questions. Your attendance last
night appears clearly irrelevant to what has happened.
Thank your wife for her concern. When Mr. Fortescue returns we will let you know. Where are you staying?"

Chester gave an address nearby and turned to go.

"One final question," Holmes added. "When were you
born?"

"Eighteen sixty-two," he replied. "Why do you wish to
know?"

"It's of no consequence. We will contact you when
there is news."

Chester closed the west door behind him and Holmes
stared at it for a moment until Miss Fortescue spoke.

"You indicated to that young man that my father will
return. Are you certain?"

"As I know where he is, yes."

She cried and grasped the lapels of his greatcoat. "In
pity's name, take me to him!"

"You have my assurance he is safe." He unclasped her
trembling fingers. "I must insist that for the moment you
leave this in my hands. You and your father will soon be
reunited. In the meantime, return to the rectory and await
my arrival. Mr. Sinclair will accompany you."

"You are a cruel man, Mr. Holmes!" she protested.

"That is how it may appear," he agreed. "But you must
trust me."

"Come, Anne," said Sinclair. "I am certain we can have
faith in Mr. Holmes."

With reluctant obedience, she allowed the curate to lead
her out through the west door again. I observed a look of
misgiving on Holmes's face as he watched them depart,
then he stood for several minutes absorbed in thought.

"Paths again, Watson," he said finally. "After many
strange turnings, those that crossed once may cross again.
I now know what Fortescue saw when he mounted that
pulpit."

"What was it?"

"He saw himself on the night of his wife's death. And
now he must face a terrible truth."

* * *

After Sinclair had led the distressed Anne Fortescue away, Holmes was silent for a long time and I was not moved to question him. In the sombre light of the nave, his face appeared grave with concern as much as occupied by thought.

"The unravelling of this will cause pain, Watson," he said finally. "But unravelled it must be, even after so long. I am sure I must have the answer, and you will be privy to it. But anything you learn must be treated with the confidence of the confessional."

"Of course," I agreed. "But where is Fortescue, and why did you refuse to take his daughter to him?"

"Because she must never know the story," he replied. "And, he should be allowed to reappear when he chooses. As to where he is, it was nearly midnight when he fled. Had he gone to the home of one of his parishioners, they would in charity have advised his daughter. A hotel would have been suspicious of the appearance of an elderly vicar arriving in some distress and without luggage and alerted the police. Similarly had he collapsed and been taken to a hospital dead or alive. No public transport is running, so he has not left the area.

"It is obvious that he can only have returned to this church after everyone had left. He entered through the vestry and prayed. When I asked you to imitate his movements during the service, I drew your attention to the pool of water near the altar, the result of snow melting from his shoes."

"But why has he still not revealed himself?"

"He is greatly troubled in his mind and . . ." Holmes stopped abruptly as we heard the sudden clang of a bell, muffled inside the building but clearly audible in the silence. The note was followed by another, than a third, fainter this time. Holmes whirled on his heel, features alert and apprehensive.

"In God's name!" he cried. "Where is the ringing chamber?"

"I'm not certain," I replied. "But I know a similar

church which has an entrance by the organ. If we tried the stairs from the lobby . . ."

But Holmes was gone, racing like a man possessed. I hurried after him up the stairs I had suggested. We emerged on the gallery by the organ, next to which was an iron spiral staircase.

"This way!" Holmes cried, and leapt up the steps with the speed of a cat. By the time I reached the door at the top, he was already in the chamber. Suspended from one of the bell ropes was a figure in a long gold and silver chasuble; Holmes had grasped his legs and was lifting the body as best he could to reduce the deadly pressure on the neck.

"The chair, Watson!" he shouted. "Get him down! Quickly!"

I snatched up the chair, then stood on it and began to tug at the simple noose into which the rope had been tied, but the crude knot had tightened. Instinctively, I fumbled in my pocket for the sturdy army knife I invariably carried out of old habit, snapped open the blade, and cut the rope.

"I have him!" Holmes cried, and let the vicar's body slide through his arms until he could lift it like a child's and carry him to a wooden bench alongside the wall. I felt for a pulse; the beat beneath the skin of the wrist was as faint and irregular as the flutter of a butterfly's wing and the flesh around his thin lips was livid blue.

"He is not long for this world," I said. "He is bitterly cold, and now this. . . ."

"Then may Heaven forgive me for such folly!" Holmes exclaimed. "I had assumed he would have found warmth as well as shelter."

He undid the knot and gently lifted the rope clear, then removed his coat and wrapped it around the vicar. Fortescue's grey eyes opened and his lips moved as he croaked an attempt at speech.

"Rest yourself," Holmes told him. "You may talk later."

"He has very little time left in which to speak," I said. "Perhaps it will be better if he does so while he can."

"Yes," Fortescue whispered. "Mr. Holmes, you must be my confessor."

"I can grant no absolution."

"Then your understanding will be the best I can hope for. How much do you know, sir?"

"Much, but there are gaps in my knowledge. Can you answer my questions?" Fortescue nodded. "How much did you hear of our conversation in the church?"

"Not all, but enough. When I heard voices, I crept into the organ loft, still lacking the courage to return. You must know that until I heard what you said this had been no more than an insane nightmare. When you said I had to face a terrible truth, I knew what it must be."

"But I am still uncertain of parts of that truth," Holmes told him. "Where did you meet Jane Smith?"

Fortescue's face darkened, but he looked Holmes straight in the eyes. "On the Liverpool dockside. She was standing alone beneath a riverside lamp. I knew what she was because I was seeking one. A young man is taught to temper his desires, but it is not always possible. After that first encounter, I visited her regularly, during which time I began to have affection for her, although our relationship could never be more than what it was. Then she left Liverpool without explanation and I neither saw nor heard of her again for some two years.

"She returned as a patient at my dockside surgery shortly after I had married. I was dismayed that she still followed the same sordid profession, but she pointed out she had no choice. While intelligent, she was poor, ill-educated, and without advantages. Her only skill, she said, was that of tending to young children; as the eldest daughter of a large family, she had been obliged to undertake the care of younger brothers and sisters.

"When my wife refused to accept Anne, I realised I could offer Jane respectable employment. You must believe me when I tell you there was no impropriety while she was under my roof."

"But her appointment offended your wife," Holmes remarked.

"I paid no regard to that. Emily had proved a bad wife

and would be a worse mother; she would have resented whomsoever I had engaged. Jane was excellent at her duties, attentive and gentle to my daughter. That was all that mattered to me."

"And the night your wife died," Holmes said. "Tell me if the theory Jane Smith rejected when I put it to her was correct. Your wife had become dangerously unbalanced. That night she entered the nursery and in some manner threatened her child. Awakened by the disturbance, you went into the room and saw what was happening. Having ensured your daughter's safety, you attempted to calm your wife, but she was too agitated. In the struggle, she fell through the window to her death."

Fortescue shook his head. "You are too charitable, Mr. Holmes. I deliberately forced my wife through that window. She had threatened to kill our child and would try again. Before the police arrived, Jane spoke to me. She said the truth would leave Anne parentless and insisted she must take the blame. If I supported her story that Emily's death was a tragedy caused by her protecting Anne, there was a chance she would not hang. To save myself, I placed her life in peril. Although she escaped the executioner, I have never been able to escape my conscience. I entered the church as a form of penance."

Holmes looked at me. "You understand now why I said certain things must never be revealed, especially to Miss Fortescue."

"Indeed," I said, then turned to the vicar. "But why did you attempt to take your life?"

"Mr. Holmes knows that," he replied.

"Yes," my friend agreed. "Had I realised you were listening, there were things I would not have said. It was very stupid of me."

"It does not matter now. I . . ." The vicar's breath caught painfully in his throat and I felt for the pulse again, then shook my head at Holmes's inquiring and anxious glance.

"You must . . ." Fortescue's voice was fading, "protect her as you have promised, Mr. Holmes. I lied for the wrong reasons, but you must do so for the right ones.

Condemn me only in your secret heart and let God . . ."
He was gone, and Holmes looked at him with a great sadness.

"There were three principals in this tragedy, Watson," he said. "A wealthy doctor, a proud woman, and a common prostitute. And the meanest of them was the noblest."

"She is to be admired for taking the blame," I admitted. "And one hardly expects self-sacrifice from a woman of the streets."

"You display the prejudices of our age, Watson. Can't you see the full extent of her sacrifice?"

"I acknowledge she sacrificed her freedom and . . ."

"Damn it, man!" Holmes cried. "She did infinitely more than that. She sacrificed her child!"

"What do you mean? I don't understand."

"You rarely do!" Holmes cried in a great passion and whirled away. He stood for several moments with his back to me before speaking again. "Forgive me, Watson. Your long loyalty deserves better, but this is a wretched business. Michael Chester is Jane Smith's son. The son who has grown to manhood while his mother has been incarcerated for a crime she did not commit. And when I saw the greyness in his eyes that is echoed in those of Anne Fortescue, I knew who his father must be."

"You mean . . . ?"

"Yes. The vicar of St. Andrew's, whose flock would condemn Jane Smith as shameful. He didn't know because she never told him. But last night, the anniversary of a tragedy he can never have forgotten, he looked across the pews of this church and saw a face so like his own as a younger man that he fled in terror. Then he overheard my conversation with Michael Chester and began to guess the truth; he knew it when Chester told me when he had been born—the period during which Jane Smith was away from Liverpool. At that moment he recognised how much she had sacrificed, and a lifetime of remorse became too much to bear."

"And what will you tell Miss Fortescue—and Michael Chester?"

"Michael Chester and his wife need know nothing, least of all that their chance attendance at this church led to his father's death. We shall tell them that the vicar perished in the cold and his actions are inexplicable. They will leave London none the wiser and continue with their lives. As for Miss Fortescue . . . it's possible an inquest might not detect that a rope had been about her father's neck?"

I stooped and pulled the high embroidered collar of the chasuble away from the flesh; there were faint marks, but the thick material had protected him and he had hanged for but a few moments.

"Unless a doctor was looking for them, they would probably be overlooked," I said.

"Then better some think I have failed than the truth be known," Holmes said. "Help me bear him into the church-yard, where it may be supposed that he died from the cold."

Darkness had fallen and there was little danger of our being seen as we carried our burden. We laid him between two rows of gravestones, then hastened to the vicarage and said we had found him. Miss Fortescue was too distraught to pay attention when Holmes expressed regret at being mistaken in all his reasonings, and we left her in the care of Sinclair and her staff. On leaving the vicarage we visited the house where Michael Chester and his wife were staying; they were dismayed and saddened at what we told them and we left them in happy ignorance.

"There is one final matter," Holmes said as we returned to Baker Street. "I shall write to Jane Smith and request that she will see me again. She is the only person who can answer what questions are left."

I accompanied Holmes for the encounter at Holloway. Jane Smith bore the marks of long imprisonment, but retained the looks of a striking woman. When the wardress who escorted her to us had left, she reached into the pocket of her prison gown and produced Holmes's letter.

"Is my son a good man, Mr. Holmes?" she asked.

"That was my impression. And with a kind-hearted wife."

"I am pleased. When you visited me some years ago, I refused to answer your questions but I am prepared to do so now."

Holmes nodded his appreciation. "Why did you protect Alfred Fortescue?"

"For the same reason any woman would protect a man, whatever he had done. Because I loved him." She saw the expression on my face and smiled. "Yes, Dr. Watson. Such feelings are not expected among women of my profession, but they are possible. After we first met, he was kind and considerate, and had our situation been different we might have married. But we both knew that was impossible.

"It was through me that he learnt of the deprivations my sort of people suffer and it was because of what I told him that he opened his charitable surgery. Our relationship continued—for true affection, doctor—until I knew I was with child. I could have demanded that he support me, but knew that if the truth ever emerged he would be ruined. I left Liverpool, bore my son, and placed him in an orphanage as I was unable to raise him myself. When I returned to the city, Alfred had married and later employed me.

"His wife was intolerable, and on the night of her death entered the nursery and threatened to kill her own daughter. When Alfred murdered her, I immediately knew what I had to do. He protested, but he was always a man I could persuade." She looked down at the letter again. "You say you have protected Anne from the truth of this, for which I am grateful. She was not in my care for long, but I loved her."

"I understand from the governor that you will be released soon," Holmes said. "I could assist you to trace your son."

Jane Smith shook her head. "I abandoned him, Mr. Holmes. I have no right to reappear in his life after so long."

"What will you do?"

She smiled at both of us grimly. "I shall return to the

streets, Mr. Holmes. Apart from the few months I was Anne Fortescue's nurse, that is all society holds me worthy of."

"I cannot allow that," Holmes protested. "Dr. Watson and I have influential friends who would assist you."

"Many of your friends, sir, are the sort of men who will have only one interest in me," she replied. "I know a side of their respectable lives of which you gentlemen are ignorant."

"Nonetheless, you must approach me on your release."

"Thank you, but I doubt that I shall." She rose from the wooden chair on which she had been sitting. "I must now return to my cell."

Holmes had stood up with her. "I deem it an honour to have met you, Miss Smith," he said.

She bowed her head in acknowledgement and was led away.

"You cannot add this case to your chronicles, Watson," Holmes remarked. "Fortescue's crime must remain unpublished for his daughter's sake—and of course your polite readers would be grossly offended at being asked to admire one they are taught to despise. But it is a pity that so remarkable a woman should be forgotten."

As I write, I am an old man and our society is much changed since the case of The Ghost of Christmas Past, now for the worse, now for the better. Later in this twentieth century, Holmes's admiration may be accepted and shared. Anne Fortescue married David Sinclair, who became an archdeacon; she recently died an honoured and beloved woman in the diocese. Jane Smith was beaten to death in an alleyway in Cheapside, and Holmes counted it one of his greatest regrets that he was never able to identify her murderer. At his expense, she was buried in a Sussex churchyard. He and I were the only mourners.